PRAISE FOR

"Humorous, romantic and sus ... paced and impossible to put down. . . . The final romantic cliff-hanger will leave you thirsty for the next book in this 'jewel' of a series."

—*Justine* magazine

"The characters in Kerstin Gier's stellar story come fully to life, and veteran translator Anthea Bell (who translated Cornelia Funke's Inkheart books) preserves the book's abundant humor. . . . There's something here for everyone." —*Shelf Awareness*

"As she narrates this fast-paced puzzler, Gwen convincingly conveys the bewilderment, fear and excitement of a teen rooted in the present but catapulted from her schoolgirl routine into the past."

—*Kirkus Reviews*

"This first installment of a trilogy will soon find a new crop of fans in the United States. It's a fun, engaging read that will be an easy sell for teens wanting to time travel with a delightful narrator."

—*School Library Journal*

"The first in a trilogy, *Ruby Red* offers romance, adventure, small details of various eras, and the complications that families can bring. It will mostly appeal to teenage girls who have a preference for reading romance." —*VOYA*

". . . Gier's characters and plotting are first-rate, creating an adventure that should leave readers eager for the rest of the trilogy."

—*Publishers Weekly*

"A smart, entertaining read . . . Gwen, an outsider in her own family, is the perfect spunky, skeptical heroine."

—*Bulletin of the Center for Children's Books*

KERSTIN GIER

RUBY RED

Translated from the German
by Anthea Bell

SCHOLASTIC INC.

Originally published in Germany by Arena Verlag GmbH
under the title *Rubinrot: Liebe geht durch alle Zeiten*

ISBN 978-0-545-52469-8

12 11 10 9 8 7 6 5 4 3 2 1 12 13 14 15 16 17/0

Printed in the U.S.A. 40

First Scholastic printing, October 2012

For Elk, Dolphin, and Owl,
who kept me company while I was writing,
and for a little red double-decker bus
that made me happy at just
the right moment

PROLOGUE

Hyde Park, London
8 April 1912

AS SHE FELL to her knees and burst into tears, he looked all around the park. Just as he'd expected, it was empty at this early hour. Jogging wouldn't be fashionable for a long time yet, and it was too cold for the beggars who slept on park benches with nothing but newspaper over them.

He carefully wrapped the chronograph in its cloth and slipped it into his backpack.

She was huddled beside one of the trees on the north bank of the Serpentine, on a carpet of faded crocuses.

Her shoulders were shaking, and her sobs sounded like the desperate cries of an injured animal. He could hardly bear it. But he knew from experience that it was better to leave her alone. So he sat down beside her in the dew-covered grass, gazed at the smooth surface of the water, and waited.

"Have tissues been invented yet?" she finally sniffed, turning her tearstained face to him.

"No idea," he said. "But I can offer you a monogrammed hanky—dead right for this period."

"G.M. Did you pinch it from Grace?"

"She gave it to me, don't worry. You can blow your nose on it all you like, Princess."

She smiled wryly as she handed him the handkerchief. "Now it's ruined. Sorry about that."

"Oh, never mind!" he said. "Just so long as you've stopped crying."

Tears shot straight back into her eyes. "We shouldn't have abandoned her. She needs us! We've no idea if our bluff will work . . . and no chance of ever finding out now."

"We'd have been even less use to her dead."

"If we could only have hidden away with her somewhere far off, under other names, until she was old enough to—"

He interrupted her, shaking his head firmly. "They'd have found us anywhere we went; we've discussed that a thousand times already. We didn't abandon her. We did the only right thing: we made it possible for her to live in safety. At least for the next sixteen years."

For a moment she said nothing. Somewhere in the distance a horse whinnied, and voices drifted over from West Carriage Drive, although it was nearly dark now.

"I know you're right," she said at last. "It just hurts so much to know we'll never see her again." She gently rubbed her red-rimmed eyes. "At least we're not going to be bored. Sooner or later they'll track us down, even here, and set the Guardians on us. He's not about to give up either the chronograph or his plans, not without a fight."

He smiled, seeing the light of adventure come back into her eyes. "Maybe we'll outwit him after all. Either that, or in the end the other device won't work. Then he'll be finished."

"Right. But if it does work, we're the only ones who can stop him."

"That's just why we've done the right thing." He stood up and brushed the earth off his jeans. "Come on! This damn grass is wet, and you're supposed to be taking things easy."

She let him pull her to her feet and kiss her. "What are we going to do now? Look for a place to hide the chronograph?" she asked, looking undecidedly at the bridge separating Hyde Park from Kensington Gardens.

"Yes, but first let's raid the Guardians' deposits and stock up with cash. Then we could take the train to Southampton. The *Titanic* leaves on Wednesday. For her maiden voyage."

She laughed. "So that's your idea of taking things easy! But right, I'm with you!"

He was so glad she could laugh again that he kissed her once more. "I was really thinking. . . . You know that out at sea a ship's captain can marry people, don't you, Princess?"

"You want to marry me? On board the *Titanic*? Are you out of your mind?"

"It would be so romantic."

"Except the bit with the iceberg." She laid her head on his chest and buried her face in his jacket. "I love you so much," she murmured.

"Will you be my wife?"

"Yes," she said, her face still buried against his chest. "But only if we leave the ship in Queenstown, Ireland, at the latest."

"Ready for the next adventure, Princess?"

"Ready when you are," she said softly.

Uncontrolled time travel usually announces itself a few minutes in advance, but sometimes hours or even days ahead. The symptoms are sensations of vertigo in the head, stomach, and/or legs. Many gene carriers also speak of a headache similar to migraine.

The first journey back in time—also known as the initiation journey—takes place between the sixteenth and seventeenth years of the gene carrier's life.

FROM *THE CHRONICLES OF THE GUARDIANS,*
VOLUME 2: *GENERAL LAWS OF TIME TRAVEL*

ONE

I FIRST FELT IT in the school canteen on Monday morning. For a moment it was like being on a roller coaster when you're racing down from the very top. It lasted only two seconds, but that was long enough for me to dump a plateful of mashed potatoes and gravy all over my school uniform. I managed to catch the plate just in time, as my knife and fork clattered to the floor.

"This stuff tastes like it's been scraped off the floor anyway," said my friend Lesley while I mopped up the damage as well as I could. Of course everyone was looking at me. "You can have mine too, if you fancy spreading some more on your blouse."

"No thanks." As it happens, the blouse of the St. Lennox High School uniform was pretty much the color of mashed potatoes anyway, but you still couldn't miss seeing the remaining globs of my lunch. I buttoned up my dark blue blazer over it.

"There goes Gwenny, playing with her food again!" said Cynthia Dale. "Don't you sit next to me, you mucky pup."

"As if I'd ever sit next to you of my own free will, Cyn." It's a fact, I'm afraid, that I did quite often have little accidents with school lunches. Only last week my pudding had hopped out of its dish and landed a few feet away, right in a Year Seven boy's spaghetti carbonara. The week before that I'd knocked my cranberry juice over, and everyone at our table was splashed. They looked as if they had measles. And I really couldn't count the number of times the stupid tie that's part of our school uniform had been drenched in sauce, juice, or milk.

Only I'd never felt dizzy at the same time before.

But I was probably just imagining it. There'd been too much talk at home recently about dizzy feelings.

Not mine, though: my cousin Charlotte's dizzy spells. Charlotte, beautiful and immaculate as ever, was sitting right there next to Cynthia, gracefully scooping mashed potatoes into her delicate mouth.

The entire family was on tenterhooks, waiting for Charlotte to have a dizzy fit. On most days, my grandmother, Lady Arista, asked Charlotte how she was feeling every ten minutes. My aunt Glenda, Charlotte's mother, filled the ten-minute gap by asking the same thing in between Lady Arista's interrogations.

And whenever Charlotte said that she didn't feel dizzy, Lady Arista's lips tightened and Aunt Glenda sighed. Or sometimes the other way around.

The rest of us—my mum, my sister Caroline, my brother Nick, and Great-aunt Maddy—rolled our eyes. Of course it was exciting to have someone with a time-travel gene in the family, but as the days went by, the excitement kind of wore off. Sometimes we felt that all the fuss being made over Charlotte was just too much.

Charlotte herself usually hid her feelings behind a mysterious Mona Lisa smile. In her place, I wouldn't have known whether to be excited or worried if dizzy feelings failed to show up. Well, to be honest, I'd probably have been pleased. I was more the timid sort. I liked peace and quiet.

"Something will happen sooner or later," Lady Arista said every day. "And we must be ready."

Sure enough, something did happen after lunch, in Mr. Whitman's history class. I'd left the canteen feeling hungry. I'd found a black hair in my dessert—apple crumble with custard—and I couldn't be sure if it was one of my own hairs or a lunch lady's. Anyway, I didn't fancy the crumble after that.

Mr. Whitman gave us back the history test we'd taken last week. "You obviously prepared well for it. Especially Charlotte. An A-plus for you, Charlotte."

Charlotte stroked a strand of her glossy red hair back from her face and said, "Oh, my!" as if the result came as a surprise to her. Even though she always had top marks in everything.

But Lesley and I were pleased with our own grades this time, too. We each had an A-minus, although our "preparation" had consisted of eating crisps and ice cream while we watched Cate Blanchett in *Elizabeth* and then *Elizabeth: The Golden Age* on DVD. We did pay attention in history class, though, which I'm afraid couldn't be said for all our other courses.

Mr. Whitman's classes were so intriguing that you couldn't help listening. Mr. Whitman himself was also very interesting. Most of the girls were secretly—or not so secretly—in love with him. So was our geography teacher, Mrs. Counter. She went bright red whenever Mr. Whitman passed her. And he *was* terribly good-looking. All the girls thought so, except Lesley. She thought Mr. Whitman looked like a cartoon squirrel.

"Whenever he looks at me with those big brown eyes, I feel like giving him a nut," she said. She even started calling the squirrels running around in the park Mr. Whitmans. The silly thing is that somehow it was infectious, and now, whenever a squirrel scuttled past me, I always said, "Oh, look at that cute, fat little Mr. Whitman!"

I'm sure it was the squirrel business that made Lesley and me the only girls in the class who weren't crazy about Mr. Whitman. I kept trying to fall in love with him (if only because the boys in our class were all somehow totally childish), but it was no good. The squirrel comparison had lodged itself in my mind and wouldn't go away. I mean, how can you feel romantic about a squirrel?

Cynthia had started the rumor that when he was studying, Mr. Whitman had worked as a male model on the side. By way of evidence, she'd cut an ad out of a glossy magazine, with a picture showing a man not unlike Mr. Whitman lathering himself with shower gel.

Apart from Cynthia, however, no one thought Mr. Whitman was the man in the shower-gel ad. The model had a dimple in his chin, and Mr. Whitman didn't.

The boys in our class didn't think Mr. Whitman was so great. Gordon Gelderman, in particular, couldn't stand him. Because before Mr. Whitman came to teach in our school, all the girls in our class were in love with Gordon. Including me, I have to admit, but I was only eleven at the time and Gordon was still quite cute. Now, at sixteen, he was just stupid. And his voice had been in a permanent state of breaking for the last two years. Unfortunately, the mixture of squealing and growling still didn't keep him from spewing nonsense all the time.

He got very upset about getting an F on the history test. "That's discrimination, Mr. Whitman. I deserve a B at least. You can't give me bad marks just because I'm a boy."

Mr. Whitman took Gordon's test back from him, turned a page, and read out, "Elizabeth I was so ugly that she couldn't get a husband. So everyone called her the Ugly Virgin."

The class giggled.

"Well? I'm right, aren't I?" Gordon defended himself. "I mean, look at her pop-eyes and her thin lips and that weird hairstyle."

We'd gone to study the pictures of the Tudors in the National Portrait Gallery, and in those paintings, sure enough, Queen Elizabeth I didn't look much like Cate

Blanchett. But first, maybe people in those days thought thin lips and big noses were the last word in chic, and second, her clothes were really wonderful. Third, no, Elizabeth I didn't have a husband, but she had a lot of affairs, among them one with Sir . . . oh, what was his name? Anyway, Clive Owen played him in the second film with Cate Blanchett.

"She was known as the Virgin Queen," Mr. Whitman told Gordon, "because . . ." He paused and looked anxiously at Charlotte. "Are you feeling all right, Charlotte? Do you have a headache?"

Everyone looked at Charlotte, who had her head in her hands. "I feel . . . I just feel dizzy," she said, looking at me. "Everything's going round and round."

I took a deep breath. So here we go, I thought. Lady Arista and Aunt Glenda would be over the moon.

"Wow, cool," whispered Lesley. "Is she going to turn all transparent now?" Although Lady Arista had repeatedly told us that under no circumstances were we ever to tell any outsider what was special about our family, I'd decided to ignore the ban when it came to Lesley. After all, she was my very best friend, and best friends don't have secrets from each other.

Since I'd known Charlotte (which in fact was all my life), she'd always seemed somewhat helpless. But I knew what to do. Goodness knows Aunt Glenda had told me often enough.

"I'll take Charlotte home," I told Mr. Whitman, as I stood up. "If that's okay."

Mr. Whitman's gaze was fixed on Charlotte. "I think that's a good idea, Gwyneth," he said. "I hope you feel better soon, Charlotte."

"Thanks," said Charlotte. On the way to the door, she swayed slightly. "Coming, Gwenny?"

I grabbed her arm. For the first time I felt quite important to Charlotte. It was a nice feeling to be needed for a change.

"Don't forget to phone and tell me all about it," Lesley whispered as we passed her.

Feeling slightly better outside the classroom, Charlotte wanted to fetch some things from her locker, but I held her firmly by the sleeve. "Not now, Charlotte! We have to get home as fast as possible. Lady Arista says—"

"It's gone again," said Charlotte.

"So? It could come back any moment." Charlotte let me steer her the other way. "Where did I put that chalk?" As we walked on, I searched my jacket pocket. "Oh, good, here it is. And my mobile. Shall I call home? Are you scared? Silly question, sorry. I'm so excited."

"It's okay. No, I'm not scared."

I glanced sideways at her to check whether she was telling the truth. She had that snooty little Mona Lisa smile on her face. You could never tell what she was hiding behind it.

"Well, *shall* I call home?"

"What use would that be?" Charlotte replied.

"I just figured—"

"You can leave the thinking to me, don't worry," said Charlotte.

We went down the stone steps to the place where James always sat. He rose to his feet when he saw us, but I just smiled at him. The trouble with James was that no one else could see or hear him—only me.

James was a ghost. Which is why I avoided talking to him when other people were around, except for Lesley. She'd never doubted James's existence for a second. Lesley believed everything I said, and that was one of the reasons she was my best friend. She was only sorry she couldn't see and hear James herself.

But I was glad of it, because when James first set eyes on Lesley, he said, "Good heavens above, the poor child has more freckles than there are stars in the sky! If she doesn't start using a good bleaching lotion at once, she'll never catch herself a husband!"

Whereas the first thing Lesley said when I introduced them to each other was "Ask him if he ever buried treasure anywhere."

Unfortunately James was not the treasure-burying type, and he was rather insulted that Lesley thought he might be. He was easily insulted.

"Is he transparent?" Lesley had asked at that first meeting. "Or kind of black and white?"

James looked just like anyone I'd ever met. Except for his clothes, of course.

"Can you walk through him?"

"I don't know. I've never tried."

"Then try now," Lesley suggested.

James was not about to let me try that.

"What does she mean, a ghost? The Honorable James Augustus Peregrine Pympoole-Bothame, heir to the fourteenth Earl of Hardsdale, is taking no insults from young girls!"

Like so many ghosts, he refused to accept that he wasn't alive anymore. Try as he might, he couldn't remember dying. James and I had met five years ago, on my first day at St. Lennox High School, but to James it seemed only a few days ago that he was sitting in his club playing cards with friends and talking about horses, beauty spots, and wigs. (He wore both a beauty spot and a wig, but they looked better on him than you might think.) He completely ignored the fact that I'd grown several inches since we first met, had acquired breasts, and braces on my teeth, and had shed the braces again. He dismisssed the fact that his father's grand town house had become a school with running water, electric light, and central heating. The only thing he did seem to notice from time to time was the ever-decreasing length of our school uniform skirts. Obviously girls' legs and ankles hadn't often been on show in his time.

"It's not very civil of a lady to walk past a highborn gentleman without a word, Miss Gwyneth," he called after me now. He was deeply offended that I'd brushed past him.

"Sorry. We're in a hurry," I said.

"If I can help you in any way, I am, of course, entirely at your service," James said, adjusting the lace on his cuffs.

"I don't think so, but thanks anyway. We just have to

get home, fast." As if James could possibly have helped in any way! He couldn't even open a door. "Charlotte isn't feeling well," I explained.

"I'm very sorry to hear it," said James, who had a soft spot for Charlotte. Unlike "that ill-mannered girl with the freckles," as he called Lesley, he thought my cousin was "delightful, a vision of beguiling charm." Now he offered more of his flowery flattery. "Pray give her my best wishes. And tell her she looks as enchanting as ever. A little pale, but as captivating as a fairy."

"I'll tell her," I said, rolling my eyes.

"If you don't stop talking to your imaginary friend," snapped Charlotte, "you'll end up in the nuthouse."

Okay, then I *wouldn't* tell her. She was conceited enough as it was.

"James isn't imaginary, just invisible. There's a great difference."

"If you say so," replied Charlotte. She and Aunt Glenda thought I just made up James and the other ghosts for attention. Now I was sorry I'd ever told Charlotte about them. As a small child, though, I couldn't manage to keep my mouth shut about gargoyles coming to life—scrambling down the fronts of buildings before my very eyes and twisting their Gothic faces for me to see. The gargoyles were funny, but there were also some dark, grim-looking ghosts, and I was afraid of those. It took me a couple of years to realize that ghosts can't hurt you. All they can really do to people is scare them.

Not James, of course. He was not frightening in the least.

"Lesley thinks it may be a good thing that James died young. With a name like Pympoole-Bothame, how would he ever have found a wife?" I said, after making sure James was out of hearing distance. "I mean, who'd marry a man with a name that sounds like Pimple-Bottom?"

Charlotte rolled her eyes.

"He's not bad-looking," I went on. "And he's filthy rich too—if he's telling the truth about his family. It's just his habit of raising a perfumed lace hanky to his nose that doesn't exactly make me swoon."

"What a shame there's no one but you to admire him," said Charlotte.

I thought so myself.

"And how stupid of you to talk about how weird you are outside the family," added Charlotte.

That was another of Charlotte's typical digs. It was meant to hurt me, and as a matter of fact, it did.

"I'm not weird!"

"Of course you are!"

"You're a fine one to talk, *gene carrier*!"

"Well, I don't go blabbing on about it all over the place," said Charlotte. "You're like Great-aunt Mad Maddy. She even tells the postman about her visions."

"You're a jerk."

"And you're naive."

Still quarreling, we walked through the front hall,

past the janitor's glazed cubicle, and out into the school yard. The wind was picking up, and the ominous sky held the promise of rain. I wished we had grabbed our coats from our lockers.

"Sorry I said that about you being like Great-aunt Maddy," said Charlotte, suddenly sounding remorseful. "I'm excited, but I am a bit nervous as well."

I was surprised. Charlotte never apologized.

"I know," I replied almost too quickly. I wanted her to know that I appreciated her apology. But in reality, I couldn't have been further from understanding how she felt. I'd have been scared out of my wits. In her shoes, I'd have been about as excited as if I were going to the dentist. "Anyway, I like Great-aunt Maddy," I added. That was true. Great-aunt Maddy might be a bit talkative and inclined to say everything four times over, but I liked that a lot better than the mysterious way the others carried on. And Great-aunt Maddy was always very generous when it came to handing out sherbet lemons.

But of course Charlotte didn't like sweets.

We crossed the road and hurried on along the pavement.

"Don't keep glancing at me sideways like that," said Charlotte. "You'll notice if I disappear, don't worry. Then you'll have to make your silly chalk mark on the pavement and hurry on home. But it's not going to happen. Not today."

"How can you know? And don't you wonder where you'll end up? I mean, *when* you'll end up?"

"Yes, of course I do," said Charlotte.

"Let's hope it's not in the middle of the Great Fire of 1664."

"The Great Fire of London was in 1666," said Charlotte. "That's easy to remember. And at the time this part of the city wasn't built up yet, so there'd have been hardly anything to burn here."

Did I say that Charlotte was also known as Spoilsport and Miss Know-it-all?

But I wasn't dropping the subject. It may have been mean of me, but I wanted to wipe the silly smile off her face, if only for a couple of seconds. "These school uniforms would probably burn like tinder," I said casually.

"I'd know what to do" was all Charlotte said, still smiling.

I hated myself for admiring how cool she was right now. To me, the idea of suddenly landing in the past was totally terrifying.

The past would have been awful, no matter what period you landed in. There was always some horrible thing lurking there—war, smallpox, the plague. If you said the wrong thing, you could be burnt as a witch. Plus, everyone had fleas, and you had to use chamber pots, which were tipped out of upstairs windows in the morning—even if someone was walking along the street below.

But Charlotte had been carefully prepared to find her way around in the past from the time she should have been rocking dolls in her elegant arms. She'd never had time to play or make friends, go shopping, go to the cinema, or date boys. Instead she'd been taught dancing, fencing, and riding, foreign languages, and history. And since last year she'd been going out every Wednesday afternoon with Lady Arista and Aunt Glenda, and they didn't come home until late in the evening. They called it an introduction to the mysteries. But no one—especially not Charlotte—would say what kind of mysteries.

Her first sentence when she learnt to talk had probably been "It's a secret." Closely followed by "That's none of your business."

Lesley always said our family must have more secrets than MI5 and MI6 put together. She was probably right.

Normally we took the bus home from school. The number 8 stopped in Berkeley Square, and it wasn't far from there to our house. Today we went the four stops on foot, as Aunt Glenda had told us we should when Charlotte had a dizzy spell. I kept my bit of chalk at the ready the whole time, but Charlotte never disappeared.

As we went up the steps to our front door, I was somewhat disappointed, because this was where my part in the ordeal came to an end. Now my grandmother would take over, and I would once again be exiled from the world of mysteries.

I tugged at Charlotte's sleeve. "Look! The man in black is there again."

"So?" Charlotte didn't even look around. The man was standing in the entrance of number 18, opposite. As usual, he wore a black trench coat and a hat pulled right down over his face. I'd taken him for a ghost until I realized that Nick, Caroline, and Lesley could see him too.

He'd been keeping watch on our house almost around the clock for months. Or maybe there were several men who looked exactly the same taking turns. We argued about whether the man was a burglar casing the joint, a private detective, or a wicked magician. That last one was my sister's theory, and she firmly believed in it. Caroline was nine and loved stories about wicked magicians and good fairies. My brother, Nick, was twelve and thought stories about magicians and fairies were silly, so he figured the man must be a burglar. Lesley and I backed the private detective.

If we tried to cross the road for a closer look at the man, he would either disappear into the building behind him or slip into a black Bentley, which was always parked by the curb, and drive away.

"It's a magic car," Caroline claimed. "It turns into a raven when no one's looking. And the magician turns into a tiny little man and rides through the air on the raven's back."

Nick had made a note of the Bentley's license plate, just in case. "Although they're sure to paint the car after the burglary and fit a new license plate," he said.

The grown-ups acted as if they saw nothing suspicious about being watched day and night by a man wearing a hat and dressed entirely in black.

Nor did Charlotte. "What's biting you lot about the poor man? He's just standing there to smoke a cigarette, that's all."

"Oh, really?" I was more likely to believe the story about the enchanted raven.

It had started raining. We reached home not a moment too soon.

"Do you at least feel dizzy again?" I asked as we waited for the door to be opened. We didn't have our own front-door keys.

"Just leave me alone," said Charlotte. "It will happen when the time comes."

Mr. Bernard opened the door for us. Lesley said Mr. Bernard was our butler and the ultimate proof that we were almost as rich as the Queen or Madonna. But I didn't know exactly who or what Mr. Bernard really was. To Mum, he was "Grandmother's lackey," but Lady Arista called him "an old family friend." To Caroline and Nick and me, he was simply Lady Arista's rather weird manservant.

At the sight of us, his eyebrows shot up.

"Hello, Mr. Bernard," I said. "Nasty weather."

"Very nasty." With his hooked nose and brown eyes behind his round, gold-rimmed glasses, Mr. Bernard always reminded me of an owl. "You really ought to wear your coats when you leave the house on a day like this."

"Er . . . yes, we ought to," I said.

"Where's Lady Arista?" asked Charlotte. She was never particularly polite to Mr. Bernard. Perhaps because, unlike the rest of us, she hadn't felt any awe of him when she was a child. Although, and this really was awe-inspiring, he seemed able to materialize out of nowhere right behind you in any part of the house, moving as quietly as a cat.

Nothing got past Mr. Bernard, and he always seemed to be on the alert for something.

Mr. Bernard had been with us since before I was born, and Mum said he had been there when *she* was still a little girl. That made Mr. Bernard almost as old as Lady Arista, even if he didn't look it. He had his own rooms on the second floor, with a separate corridor in which we children were forbidden even to set foot.

My brother, Nick, said Mr. Bernard had built-in trapdoors and elaborate alarm systems up there, so that he could watch out for unwelcome visitors, but Nick couldn't prove it. None of us had ever dared to venture into the out-of-bounds area.

"Mr. Bernard needs his privacy," Lady Arista often said.

"How right," said Mum. "I think we could all of us do with some of that." But she said it so quietly that Lady Arista didn't hear her.

"Your grandmother is in the music room," Mr. Bernard informed Charlotte.

"Thank you." Charlotte left us in the hall and went upstairs. The music room was on the first floor, and no one knew why it was called that. There wasn't even a piano in it.

The music room was Lady Arista's and Great-aunt Maddy's favorite place. It smelled of faded violet perfume and the stale smoke of Lady Arista's cigarillos. The stuffy room wasn't aired nearly often enough, and staying in it for too long made you feel drowsy.

Mr. Bernard closed the front door. I took one more quick look past him at the other side of the street. The man with the hat was still there. Was I wrong, or was he just raising his hand almost as if he were waving to someone? Mr. Bernard, maybe, or even me?

The door closed, and I couldn't follow that train of thought any longer because my stomach suddenly flipped again, as if I were on a roller coaster. Everything blurred before my eyes. My knees gave way, and I had to lean against the wall to keep from falling down.

But as quickly as it had come on, the feeling was gone.

My heart was thumping like crazy. There must be something wrong with me. Without being on an actual carnival ride, you couldn't possibly feel dizzy this often without something being terribly wrong.

Unless . . . oh, nonsense! I was probably just growing too fast. Or I had . . . I had a brain tumor? Or maybe, I thought, brushing that nasty notion aside, it was only that I was hungry.

Yes, that must be it. I hadn't eaten anything since breakfast. My lunch had landed on my blouse. I breathed a sigh of relief.

Only then did I notice Mr. Bernard's owlish eyes looking attentively at me.

"Whoops," he said, a little too late.

I felt myself blushing. "I'll . . . I'll go and do my homework," I muttered.

Mr. Bernard just nodded casually. But as I climbed the stairs, I could feel his eyes on my back.

Back from Durham, where I visited Lord Montrose's younger daughter, Grace Shepherd, whose daughter was unexpectedly born the day before yesterday. We are all delighted to record the birth of

Gwyneth Sophie Elizabeth Shepherd
5 lbs 8 oz., 20 in.

Mother and child both doing well.

Heartfelt congratulations to our Grand Master on the birth of his fifth grandchild.

FROM *THE ANNALS OF THE GUARDIANS*
10 OCTOBER 1994
REPORT: THOMAS GEORGE, INNER CIRCLE

TWO

LESLEY SAID OUR HOUSE was posh as a palace because it was so big and full of paintings, wooden paneling, and antique furniture. She suspected that there was a secret passage behind every wall and at least one hidden compartment in every cupboard. When we were younger, we went on journeys of exploration through the house whenever Lesley came to visit. We were strictly forbidden to snoop around, which made it even more exciting. We worked out increasingly crafty strategies for not getting caught. In the course of time we really did find some secret compartments, and even a secret door. It was in the stairwell behind an oil painting of a fierce-looking fat, bearded man who was sitting, with his sword drawn, atop a great white horse.

According to Great-aunt Maddy, the fierce man was my great-great-great-great-great-uncle Hugh sitting on his bay mare, Fat Annie. The door behind the picture hid only a few steps that led down to a rather unimpressive bathroom, but the fact that it was a secret passage made it exciting—well, to Lesley and me anyway.

"You're just so lucky to live here!" Lesley always said.

Personally, I thought Lesley was the lucky one. She lived with her mother and father and a shaggy dog called Bertie in a comfortable house with a cozy garden in North Kensington. There were no secrets there, no mysterious servants, and no relatives to get on your nerves all the time.

We used to live in a house like that ourselves: my mum, my dad, Nick, Caroline, and me. A little house in Durham, in the north of England. But then my dad died. Caroline was just six months old when Mum decided to move us all to London. Probably because she felt lonely. And maybe she was short of money as well.

Mum had grown up in this house herself, along with her sister, Glenda, and her brother, Harry. Uncle Harry was the only one who didn't live in London now. He lived in Gloucestershire, with his wife.

At first the house had looked like a palace to me too. But when you have to share a palace with a big, annoying family, it doesn't seem quite so big after a while. Even though there were a lot of unnecessary rooms that didn't get used, like the ballroom on the first floor stretching the entire breadth of the house.

The ballroom would have been a great place for roller-skating, only we weren't allowed to. It was lovely, with its tall windows, its stucco ceiling, and all those chandeliers, but there's never been a ball there, or not in my lifetime, not even a big party.

The only things that did happen in the ballroom were Charlotte's dancing and fencing lessons. The musicians' gallery, which you reached by climbing up steps from the front hall, was also totally useless, except maybe for Caroline and her friends, who used the dark corner under the stairs when they were playing hide-and-seek.

My mum, my brother and sister, and I lived on the third floor, just under the roof, where a lot of the walls were slanted, but there were two little balconies. We each had a cozy little room of our own. Charlotte was envious of our big bathroom, because the second-floor bathroom had no windows at all, but ours had two. Another reason I liked our floor was that Mum, Nick, Caroline, and I had it all to ourselves, which was often a blessing in that madhouse.

The only disadvantage was that we were miles away from the kitchen, I noted as I gloomily climbed the stairs. I should have grabbed myself an apple to bring up. I'd have to make do with butter cookies from the stock Mum kept in reserve on our floor.

I was so afraid the dizzy feeling would come back that I stuffed eleven cookies into my mouth, one after another. Then I took off my shoes and my jacket, sat down on the sewing room sofa, and stretched out flat on my back.

It had been such a strange day. I mean, even stranger than usual.

It was only two o'clock. At least another two and a

half hours before I could call Lesley and tell her all about it. My brother and sister wouldn't be home from school until four, and Mum worked until five. Normally I loved being alone on our floor of the house. I could take a bath in peace without anyone knocking on the door, desperate to go to the loo. I could turn up the music and sing along at the top of my voice without anyone laughing. And I could watch what I liked on TV without anyone whining, "But it's going to be *Sponge Bob* in a minute."

But I didn't feel like doing any of that today. I didn't even feel like taking a little nap. Far from it. The sofa, which was usually a sanctuary, felt like a wobbly raft on a torrential river. I was afraid I might be washed away on it the moment I closed my eyes.

Trying to turn my mind to something else, I stood up and began tidying the sewing room a bit. It was kind of our own, unofficial living room, because luckily neither the aunts nor my grandmother ever came up to the third floor. There wasn't a sewing machine here either, but there was a narrow flight of steps leading up to the roof. These were originally meant for a chimney sweep, but now it was Lesley and I who used them. The roof was one of our favorite places.

Of course it was a little risky, because there was no balustrade, just a decorative knee-high galvanized iron border along the ledge, but you didn't actually *have* to practice long jump up there, or dance all the way to the edge of the drop. The key to the door was kept in a rose-patterned sugar bowl. No one in my family knew that *I* knew its hiding place, or you can bet all hell would have broken loose. That was why I always made sure no one saw me sneaking up to the roof. You could sunbathe there, or simply hide away if you wanted to be left in peace. Which, like I said, I often did want, only not just this minute.

I folded our blankets neatly, swept cookie crumbs off the sofa, plumped up the cushions, and put a set of chessmen scattered about the place back into their box. I even watered the azalea standing in a pot on the bureau in the corner and wiped down the coffee table with a damp cloth. Then I looked around the now spotlessly tidy room, wondering what to do next. Just ten minutes had passed, and I wanted company even more than before.

Was Charlotte having a dizzy spell again down in the music room? What actually happened if you traveled from the first floor of a house in twenty-first century Mayfair to the Mayfair of, let's say, the fifteenth century, when there weren't any houses here yet, or only very few? Did you arrive in midair and drop to the ground from a height of twenty feet or so? Maybe landing on top of an anthill? Poor Charlotte. But I supposed they could be teaching her to fly in her secret instruction in the mysteries, so maybe she wouldn't end up with ants in her pants.

Speaking of mysteries, I suddenly thought of something to take my mind off it all. I went into Mum's room and looked down at the street. Yes, the man in black was still down there outside number 18. I could see his legs and part of his trench coat. The distance three floors down had never seemed so great. I tried working out how far it was from here to the ground.

Could you actually survive a fall from so far up? Well, maybe, if you were lucky and landed in the middle of a marsh. Apparently all London had once been marshland, or that's what Mrs. Counter, our geography teacher, said. A marsh was okay—at least you'd have a soft landing. But only to drown horribly in mud.

I swallowed. I didn't like the turn my own thoughts were taking.

I really, really didn't want to be on my own any longer, so I decided to pay a visit to my family down in the music room, even if I risked being sent straight out again because there were top-secret discussions going on.

WHEN I WENT IN, Great-aunt Maddy was sitting in her favorite armchair by the window, and Charlotte was standing near the other window with her hands flat on the Louis Quatorze desk, although we weren't supposed to touch its colorfully lacquered and gilded surface with any part of the body at all. (How anything as hideous as that desk could be as valuable as Lady Arista always said I didn't know. It didn't even have any secret drawers. Lesley and I had checked that out years ago.) Charlotte had gotten changed, and instead of her school uniform, she was wearing a dress that looked like a cross between a nightie, a dressing gown, and a nun's habit.

"I'm still here," she said. "As you can see."

"Well . . . well, that's nice," I said, trying not to stare at her dress with a noticeable expression of horror.

"This is intolerable," said Aunt Glenda, who was pacing up and down between the windows. Like Charlotte, she was tall and slender and had bright red, curly hair. My mum had the same curly hair, and my grandmother's hair had once been red too. Caroline and Nick had inherited the red hair as well, leaving me as the only one with dark, straight hair like my father's.

I used to long for red hair, but Lesley had convinced me that my black hair was a striking contrast to my blue eyes and fair skin. Lesley also managed to persuade me that the little crescent-shaped birthmark on my temple—the one Aunt Glenda always called my "funny little banana"—was intriguingly mysterious and chic. These days I thought I looked quite pretty, especially now that I no longer had braces, which had put my front teeth back where they ought to be and stopped me looking like a rabbit. Although of course I wasn't nearly such a "delightful vision of beguiling charm" as Charlotte, which was how James would have put it. Ha, ha. I wished he could see her in that shapeless sack of a dress.

"Gwyneth, my angel, would you like a sherbet lemon?" Great-aunt Maddy patted the stool next to her chair. "Sit down here and take my mind off all this a bit. Glenda is getting on my nerves, pacing up and down like that."

"You have no idea of a mother's feelings, Maddy," said Aunt Glenda.

"No, I don't suppose I do," sighed Great-aunt Maddy.

Maddy was a plump little person with cheerful, blue, child-like eyes and hair dyed golden blond. There was often a forgotten roller left in it.

"Where's Lady Arista?" I asked, taking a sherbet lemon.

"Next door on the phone," said Great-aunt Maddy. "But she's speaking softly, so I'm afraid you can't make out a word of it. By the way, those were the last sherbet lemons. You wouldn't by any chance have time to pop around to Selfridges and get some more, would you?"

"Of course I'll go," I said.

Charlotte shifted her weight from one leg to the other, and Aunt Glenda instantly spun around.

"Charlotte?"

"No, it's nothing," said Charlotte.

Aunt Glenda's lips tightened.

"Shouldn't you be waiting on the ground floor?" I asked Charlotte. "Then you wouldn't have so far to fall."

"Shouldn't you just shut up when you've no idea what this is all about?" Charlotte snapped back.

"Really, the last thing Charlotte can do with right now is silly remarks," said Aunt Glenda.

I was already beginning to regret coming downstairs.

"On the first occasion the gene carrier never travels back farther than a hundred and fifty years," explained Great-aunt Maddy kindly. "This house was finished in 1781, so Charlotte is perfectly safe here in the music room. At worst she might scare a couple of ladies playing the harpsichord."

"You bet she would, in that dress," I said, so quietly that only my great-aunt could hear me. She giggled.

The door swung open and Lady Arista came in. As usual, she looked as if she'd swallowed a ramrod. Or several. One for each arm, one for each leg, and one holding it all together in the middle. Her white hair was combed severely back from her face and pinned into a bun at the back of her neck, like a ballet teacher. The strict sort you wouldn't want to tangle with. "There's a driver on his way. The de Villiers family are expecting us at the Temple. Then Charlotte can be read into the chronograph the moment she returns."

I didn't understand a word of this.

"But suppose it doesn't happen today after all?" asked Charlotte.

"Charlotte, darling, you've felt dizzy three times already," said Aunt Glenda.

"It *will* happen sooner or later," said Lady Arista. "Come along, the driver will be here any minute now."

Aunt Glenda took Charlotte's arm, and together with Lady Arista, they left the room. As the door closed behind them, Great-aunt Maddy and I looked at each other.

"Some people might think a person was invisible, don't you agree?" said Great-aunt Maddy. "At least a good-bye or hello now and then would be nice. Or something really clever, like *Dear Maddy, did you by any chance have one of those visions of yours that might help us?*"

"And did you?"

"No," said Great-aunt Maddy. "Thank God, I didn't.

I'm always ravenously hungry after those visions, and I need to lose weight as it is." She patted her middle.

"Who are these de Villiers people?" I asked.

"A bunch of arrogant show-offs, if you ask me," said Great-aunt Maddy. "All of them lawyers and bankers. They own the de Villiers private bank in the city. That's where we have our accounts."

That didn't sound particularly mystical.

"So what do they have to do with Charlotte?"

"Well, let's say they have problems like ours."

"Meaning what?" Did they have to live under the same roof as a tyrannical grandmother, a frightful aunt, and a cousin who thought herself something special?

"The time-travel gene," said Great-aunt Maddy. "It's passed down through the male line in the de Villiers family."

"You mean they have a Charlotte as well?"

"The male counterpart. His name's Gideon, as far as I know."

"And he's waiting to feel dizzy too?"

"He's already over that part of it. He's two years older than Charlotte."

"So he's been time traveling for the last two years?"

"That's what I assume."

I tried to reconcile this new information with the little I already knew. But since Great-aunt Maddy was being so talkative today I allowed myself only a couple of seconds for that. "And what's a chroni . . . a chrono-thingummy?"

"Chronograph." Great-aunt Maddy rolled her round blue eyes. "It's a kind of apparatus that can be used to send the gene carriers—only them, no one else!—back to a specific time. It's something to do with blood."

"A *time machine*?" Fueled by blood? Good heavens!

Great-aunt Maddy shrugged. "I've no idea how the thing works. You're forgetting, I know only what I've overheard, same as you, sitting here acting as if butter wouldn't melt in my mouth. It's all a deadly secret."

"Yup. And very complicated," I said. "How do they know Charlotte has the gene, anyway? I mean, why her and not . . . well, let's say *you*?"

"I can't have it, thank goodness," she said. "We Montroses were always a funny lot, but the gene came into our family through your grandmother. Because my brother just had to go and marry her." Aunt Maddy grinned. She was my late grandfather Lucas's sister. Never having been married herself, she'd moved in to keep house for him when they were quite young. "The first time I heard about this gene was after Lucas's wedding. The last gene carrier in Charlotte's hereditary line was a lady called Margaret Tilney, and she in her turn was the grandmother of your grandmother Arista."

"So Charlotte inherited the gene from this Margaret?"

"Well, in between Lucy inherited it. Poor girl."

"Lucy? What Lucy?"

"Your cousin Lucy. Harry's eldest daughter."

"Oh, *that* Lucy," My uncle Harry, the one in Gloucestershire, was a good deal older than Glenda and my mum. His three children had grown up ages ago. David, the youngest, was a twenty-eight-year-old British Airways pilot. Which unfortunately didn't mean we got a discount on flights. And Janet, the middle one, had children of her own, pains in the neck, both of them, Poppy and Daisy by name. I'd never met Lucy, the eldest. I didn't know much about her either. The Montroses never said a thing about Lucy. She was kind of the black sheep of the family. She'd run away from home at the age of seventeen, and nothing had been heard of her since.

"Lucy's a gene carrier too?"

"Oh, yes," said Great-aunt Maddy. "All hell broke loose here when she disappeared. Your grandmother practically had a heart attack. It was the most shocking scandal." She shook her head so vigorously that her golden curls got all tangled up.

"I can just imagine it." I thought of what would happen if Charlotte simply packed her cases and made for the wide blue yonder.

"No, you can't. You don't know the circumstances in which she disappeared, and it was all to do with that young man—Gwyneth! Take your finger out of your mouth this minute! That's a disgusting habit."

"Sorry." I really hadn't noticed myself beginning to bite my fingernails. "It's just there's so much going on—so much I don't understand."

"Same here," Great-aunt Maddy assured me. "And I've been listening to all this stuff since I was fifteen. What's more, I have what you might call a natural talent for mystery. All the Montroses love secrets. They always have. That's the only reason my poor brother married your grandmother in the first place, if you ask me. It can't have been her alluring charms, anyway, because she didn't have any." She reached into the box of sherbet lemons, and sighed when her fingers met empty air. "Oh, dear, I'm afraid I must be addicted to these things."

"I'll run to Selfridges and get you some more," I offered.

"You're my darling child, you always will be. Give me a kiss and put your coat on, it's raining. And never bite your nails again, all right?"

My coat was still in my locker at school, so I borrowed Mum's raincoat and pulled the hood over my head as I stepped out of the front door. The man in the entrance of number 18 was just lighting himself a cigarette. On a sudden impulse I waved to him as I ran down the steps.

He didn't wave back, of course.

"Weirdo," I muttered as I hurried off toward Oxford Street. It was raining cats and dogs, and I wished I'd put on my wellies. The flowers on my favorite magnolia tree on the corner were drooping in a melancholy way. Before I reached it, I'd already splashed through three puddles. Just as I was trying to steer my way around a fourth, I was swept suddenly off my soggy feet. My stomach flip-flopped, and before my eyes the street blurred into a gray river.

Ex hoc momento pendet aeternitas.
(Eternity hangs from this moment.)

Inscription on a sundial
in the Middle Temple, London

THREE

WHEN I COULD SEE properly again, I noticed a car was coming around the corner—a real old-timer—and I was kneeling on the pavement shaking with fear.

Something was wrong with this street. It didn't look the same as usual. Everything had changed so suddenly.

The rain had stopped, but an icy wind was blowing, and it was much darker than a moment ago, almost night. The magnolia tree had no flowers or leaves. I wasn't even sure whether it was still a magnolia at all.

The spikes of the fence around it were gilded at the tips. I could have sworn they'd been black when I'd seen it not a moment before.

Another vintage car came chugging around the corner. A strange vehicle with tall wheels and shiny spokes. I looked along the pavement—the puddles were nowhere to be seen. Nor were the traffic signs. The paving was bumpy and out of shape, and even the street lamps looked different. Their flickering yellowish light hardly reached the entrance to the next building.

Deep down inside me, a nasty idea stirred, but I wasn't about to entertain it seriously yet.

I forced myself to breathe deeply. Then I looked around again, more thoroughly this time.

Okay, strictly speaking, there wasn't that much difference. Most of the buildings really looked the same as usual. But still—the teashop where Mum bought the delicious Duchy Originals made by the Prince of Wales had disappeared, and I'd never set eyes on the colossal columned building on the corner.

A man wearing a hat and a dark coat looked at me with a touch of curiosity as he passed, but he didn't try talking to me, or even helping me to stand up. Finally, I did it myself and brushed the dirt off my knees.

The nasty thought that had occurred to me was slowly but surely becoming a ghastly certainty.

Who did I think I was kidding?

I hadn't run into a vintage car rally, and the magnolia hadn't suddenly lost all its leaves. And although I'd have given anything to see Nicole Kidman suddenly come around the corner, this was not, unfortunately, the set of a film from a Henry James novel.

I knew exactly what had happened. I simply knew. And I also knew that there must be some mistake.

I'd landed in another time.

Not Charlotte. Me. Someone or other had gotten the whole thing wrong.

My teeth immediately began chattering. Not just from nerves but with cold as well. There was a bitter chill in the air.

I'd know what to do. Charlotte's words were still echoing in my ears.

Of course Charlotte would have known what to do. But no one had told me.

So I stood there shivering, teeth chattering, at the corner of my own street while people gaped at me. Not that there were many of them out and about. A young woman in an ankle-length coat with a basket over her arm passed me, and behind her came a man in a hat with his collar turned up.

"Excuse me," I said. "Can you by any chance tell me what year this is?"

The woman acted as if she hadn't heard me and walked faster.

The man shook his head. "What impertinence!" he growled.

I sighed. Although the information wouldn't really have helped me much anyway. Basically it didn't make much difference whether this was 1899 or 1923.

At least I knew where I was. I lived less than a hundred yards away. The obvious thing was just to go inside my house.

I had to do something, after all.

The street seemed calm and peaceful in the twilight as I slowly walked back, looking all around me. What was different, what hadn't changed? The buildings looked very like those of my own time, even on closer examination. I did have the feeling that I'd not seen certain details before, but perhaps it was just that so far I hadn't noticed them. Automatically I glanced at number 18, but the entrance to it was empty—no man in black anywhere in sight.

I stopped.

Our house looked just as it did in my own time. The windows on the ground floor and the first floor were brightly lit, and there was a light on in Mum's room up at the top of the house as well. I felt really homesick as I looked up. Icicles hung from the dormer windows.

I'd know what to do.

So what would Charlotte do? It would soon be dark, and it was already bitterly cold. Where would Charlotte go to keep from freezing? Home?

I stared up at the windows. Maybe my grandfather was still alive in there. Maybe he'd even recognize me? After all, he used to let me ride on his knees when I was little. . . . Oh, don't be so stupid, I thought.

Even if he were alive now, he could hardly recognize me when he hadn't met me yet.

The cold was creeping in under Mum's raincoat. Okay, I'd just ring the bell and ask for shelter for the night.

The only question was how to go about it.

"Hello, my name is Gwyneth, and I'm Lord Lucas Montrose's granddaughter, but he may not have been born yet."

I couldn't expect anyone to believe that. I'd probably find myself in a psychiatric hospital much sooner than I liked. And psychiatric hospitals were probably dismal places at this period. Once inside, you might never get out again.

On the other hand, I had few alternatives. It wouldn't be long before it was pitch-dark, and I had to spend the night somewhere without freezing to death. Or being spotted by Jack the Ripper. Why couldn't I remember when Jack the Ripper had prowled the streets of London? And where? Surely not the elegant surroundings of Mayfair, I hoped.

If I did manage to speak to one of my ancestors, I might be able to convince him that I knew more about the family and the house than any normal stranger could. Who but me, for instance, could say straight off that the name of Great-great-great-great-great-uncle Hugh's horse was Fat Annie?

A gust of wind made me shiver. It was so cold. I wouldn't have been surprised if snow soon swirled down on top of me.

"Hello, I'm Gwyneth, and I come from the future. I can prove it—take a look at this zipper. I bet those haven't been invented yet, right? Or jumbo jets or TV sets or refrigerators . . ."

Well, it was worth a try. Taking a deep breath, I went up to the front door.

The steps seemed, in an odd way, both familiar and strange. Automatically I felt for the bell-push, but there wasn't one. Obviously electric bells hadn't been invented yet. Unfortunately, however, that still gave me no hint about the exact date. I didn't even know when they'd found out how to use electricity. Before or after steamships? Had we learnt that in school? If so, I couldn't remember it now.

I found a handle hanging from a chain, like the one that flushed the old-fashioned toilet in Lesley's house. I pulled it, hard, and heard a bell ring behind the door.

Oh, my God.

One of the domestic staff would probably open the door. What could I say to make him or her take me to a member of the family? Maybe Great-great-great-great-great-uncle Hugh was still alive? Or already alive. Alive, anyway. I'd simply ask for him. Or Fat Annie.

Footsteps were coming closer, and I plucked up all my courage, but I never saw who opened the door, because once again the strange feeling swept me off my feet, flung me through time and space, and spat me out on the other side.

I found myself back on the doormat outside our house again, jumped up, and looked around. Everything seemed the same as when I'd left just a little while ago to go and buy Great-aunt Maddy's sherbet lemons. The buildings, the parked cars, even the rain.

The man in black at the entrance of number 18 was staring across the road at me.

"And you're not the only one to be surprised," I muttered.

How long had I been gone? Had the man in black seen me disappear at the corner of the street and then appear again on our doormat? If so, I bet he couldn't believe his eyes. It served him right.

I rang the bell frantically. Mr. Bernard opened the door.

"In a hurry, are we?" he asked.

"Maybe not you, but I am!"

Mr. Bernard raised his eyebrows.

"'Scuse me, I forgot something important." I made my way past him and ran upstairs two steps at a time.

Great-aunt Maddy looked up in surprise when I raced through the door. "I thought you'd already left, my love."

Out of breath, I stared at the clock on the wall. It was now exactly twenty minutes since I had left the room.

"I'm glad you're here, though. There's something I forgot to tell you. They have the same sherbet lemons at Selfridges but sugar-free, and the packaging looks just the same. But don't buy the sugar-free sherbet lemons, whatever you do, because those give me . . . well, diarrhea."

"Aunt Maddy, why is everyone so sure that Charlotte has the gene?"

"Because . . . oh, ask me something simpler, can't you?" Great-aunt Maddy was looking rather confused.

"Have they tested her blood? Couldn't someone else have the same gene too?" My breathing was slowly calming down.

"Oh, Charlotte is definitely a gene carrier."

"Because it's been found in her DNA?"

"My little angel, you're asking the wrong person. I was always useless at biology—in fact, I don't even know what DNA is. I was no good at maths either. Anything about numbers and formulas goes straight in one ear and out the other. I can only tell you that Charlotte came into the world on the very day calculated for her hundreds of years ago."

"So your date of birth decides whether you have this gene or not?" I bit my lower lip. Charlotte had been born on the seventh of October, and I'd been born on the eighth. We were only a single day apart.

"More like the other way around," said Great-aunt Maddy. "The gene decides the time of the carrier's birth. They've worked it all out."

"Well, suppose they made a mistake?"

One day's difference! It was that simple. Someone had mixed the dates up. It wasn't Charlotte who had this wretched gene, it was me. Or maybe we both had it. Or else . . . I sat down on the stool.

Great-aunt Maddy shook her head. "They didn't make a mistake, my little angel. If there's one thing these people are really good at, you can bet it's arithmetic."

Who were "these people," anyway?

"Anyone can make a mistake now and then," I said.

Great-aunt Maddy laughed. "Not Sir Isaac Newton, I'm afraid."

"*Newton* worked out the date of Charlotte's birth?"

"My dear child, I understand your curiosity. When I was your age, I was just the same. But for one thing, it's sometimes better not to know all the answers, and for another, I really, really would like my sherbet lemons."

"None of this makes any sense," I said.

"That's only how it looks." Great-aunt Maddy patted my hand. "Even if you're no wiser now than you were before, this conversation must stay private. If your grandmother finds out all I've told you, she'll be furious. And when she's furious, she's even worse than usual."

"I won't say anything, Aunt Maddy. And I'll go and get your sherbet lemons right now."

"You're a good child."

"Just one more question. How long after gene carriers have first traveled in time do they do it again?"

Great-aunt Maddy sighed.

"Please!" I said.

"I don't think there are any rules," said Great-aunt Maddy. "Every gene carrier is probably different. But none of them can fix the times for themselves. If the travel is uncontrolled, it can happen every day, sometimes several times a day. That's why the chronograph is so important. With its help, as I understand, Charlotte won't be flung around helplessly in time. She can be sent to times that aren't very dangerous, where nothing can harm her. So don't worry about your cousin."

To be honest, I was much more worried about myself.

"Then when a gene carrier is in the past, how long has she been gone in the present?" I asked breathlessly. "And the second time a traveler goes back in time, could it be all the way to the dinosaurs, when there was nothing but swamps around here?"

My great-aunt cut me short. "That's enough, Gwyneth. I've no more idea than you have!"

I got to my feet. "Thanks for answering my questions, anyway," I said. "You've been a great help."

"I don't think so. I have a dreadfully guilty conscience. I really shouldn't be satisfying your curiosity, particularly since I'm not supposed to know about any of it myself. In the old days, when I used to ask my brother—that's your dear grandfather—about all these secrets, he always told me the same thing. The less you know, he said, the better for your health. Now, are you going to get me my sherbet lemons? And *not* the sugar-free kind, remember!"

Great-aunt Maddy waved as I left.

How could secrets be bad for anyone's health? And how much had my grandfather known about it all?

"SIR ISAAC NEWTON?" repeated Lesley, baffled. "Wasn't that the force of gravity guy?"

"That's him, all right. But he also calculated the date of Charlotte's birth." I was standing in front of the yogurts in Selfridges Food Hall, holding my mobile to one ear with my right hand and covering the other ear with my left hand. "Only the crazy thing is that no one will believe he made a mistake. Who'd expect Newton to get his sums wrong? But he must have been wrong, Lesley. I was born one day after Charlotte, and *I* traveled back in time. Not her."

"That's more than mysterious. Oh, this stupid thing

is taking forever to start up. Come *on*, will you?" Lesley shouted at her computer.

"Lesley, it was so—so weird! I almost spoke to one of my ancestors! Maybe that fat man on the painting in front of the secret door, Great-great-great-great-great-uncle Hugh, for instance. Well, if it was in his time and not some other period. They could have had me sent off to a loony bin."

"I hate to think what could have happened to you," said Lesley. "I still can't get my mind around this! So much fuss made of Charlotte all these years, and now this happens! Look, you have to tell your mum right away. You'd better go straight back home. It could happen again any moment!"

"Scary, right?"

"Very. Okay, I'm online now. First off I'll Google Newton. And you just go home! Any idea how long Selfridges has been there in Oxford Street? Could have been a deep pit in the old days, and you'd fall twelve yards down!"

"My grandmother will freak right out when she hears about this," I said.

"Yes, and then there's poor Charlotte . . . well, just think, all these years she's had to give up everything, and now she gets nothing in return. Ah, here we are. Newton. Born 1643 in Woolsthorpe—where on earth is that?—died 1727 in London. Blah blah blah. Nothing about time travel here, just stuff about infinitesimal calculus—never heard of it, how about you? Transcendence of all spirals. . . .

Quadratics, optics, sky mechanics, blah blah—ah, here we are, here's the law of gravity. . . . Tell you what, that bit about transcendental spirals sounds kind of closest to time travel, don't you think?"

"To be honest, no," I said.

A couple standing next to me were discussing the yogurt variety they were going to buy at the tops of their voices.

"Are you by any chance still in Selfridges?" shouted Lesley, who had obviously overheard the yogurt orders. "Go home!"

"On my way," I said, waving the yellow paper bag containing Great-aunt Maddy's sherbet lemons in the direction of the exit. "But, Lesley, I *can't* tell them this at home. They'll think I'm crazy."

Lesley spluttered down the phone. "Gwen! Any other family might well send you to the loony bin, but not yours! They're always talking about time-travel genes and chronometers and instruction in mysteries."

"It's a chronograph," I corrected her. "The thing runs on blood! Is that gross or what?"

"Chro—no—graph! Okay, I've Googled it."

I made my way through the crowds in Oxford Street to the next traffic lights. "Aunt Glenda will say I'm just making it all up to look important and steal the show from Charlotte."

"So? When you next travel back in time, at the very latest, she's going to notice that there's been a mistake."

"And suppose I never travel back again? Suppose it was just the once?"

"You don't believe that yourself, do you? Okay, here we are, a chronograph seems to be a perfectly normal wristwatch. You can get them by the ton on eBay, ten pounds and upward. Oh, damn . . . wait, I'll Google Isaac Newton plus chronograph plus time travel *plus* blood."

"Well?"

"Nothing that helps us. At least I don't think so." Lesley sighed. "I wish we'd looked all this up earlier. The first thing I'm going to do is find some books about it. Anything I can dig up on time travel. Where did I put that stupid library card? Where are you now?"

"Crossing Oxford Street, then turning down Duke Street." Suddenly I had to giggle. "Why? Are you planning to come here and draw a chalk circle just in case our connection suddenly breaks? But now I'm wondering what good the silly chalk circle was supposed to do Charlotte."

"Maybe they'd have sent that other time traveler after her—what was his name again?"

"Gideon de Villiers."

"Cool name! I'll Google it. Gideon de Villiers. How do you spell it?"

"How should I know? Back to the chalk circle—where would they have sent this Gideon guy? I mean, what period? Charlotte could have been anywhere. In any minute, any hour, any year, any century. Nope, the chalk circle makes no sense."

Lesley screeched down my ear so loud that I almost dropped my mobile. "*Gideon de Villiers*. Got him!"

"Really?"

"Yep. It says here, 'The polo team of the Vincent School, Greenwich, has won the All England Schools Polo Championship again this year. Celebrating with the cup, from left to right, headmaster William Henderson, team manager John Carpenter, team captain Gideon de Villiers . . .' and so on and so forth. Wow, so he's the captain too. Only it's such a tiny picture you can't make out where the horses leave off and the team members begin. Where are you now, Gwen?"

"Still in Duke Street. That figures: school in Greenwich, polo, yeah, that must be him. And does it say he sometimes disappears? Maybe straight off his horse?"

"Oh, I've just noticed, this report is three years old. He must have left the school by now. Are you feeling dizzy again?"

"Not so far."

"Where are you now?"

"Oh, Lesley, still in Duke Street. I'm walking as fast as I can."

"Okay, we'll stay on the phone until you get to your front door, and the moment you're home, you have to talk to your mum."

I looked at my watch. "She won't be back from work yet."

"Then wait until she is, but you really must talk to her,

okay? She'll know what to do to keep you out of harm's way. Are you still there? Did you hear what I said?"

"Yes, I'm here, and yes, I did. Lesley?"

"Hm?"

"I'm so glad I have you. You're the best friend in the world."

"You're not so bad as a friend yourself," said Lesley. "I mean, you'll soon be able to bring me back cool stuff from the past. What other friend can do that? And next time we have a history test, you can research the whole thing on the spot."

"I don't know what I'd do if I didn't have you." Listening to myself, I realized how pathetic I sounded—but what the hell, I was feeling pretty pathetic right now.

"*Can* time travelers bring stuff back from the past?" asked Lesley.

"No idea. Not the faintest. I'll try it next time. I'm in Grosvenor Square now."

"Nearly home, then," said Lesley, relieved. "Apart from the polo business, Google hasn't found anything about any Gideon de Villiers. But there's a whole lot about the de Villiers private bank and the de Villiers legal chambers in the Temple."

"That must be them."

"Any dizzy feelings?"

"No, but thanks for asking all the same."

Lesley cleared her throat. "I know you're scared of it, but all this is kind of cool. I mean, it's a real adventure, Gwen! And you're right in the middle of it."

Oh, yes, I was certainly right in the middle of it.

Just my luck.

LESLEY WAS RIGHT. There was no reason to think that Mum wouldn't believe me. She had always listened to my "ghost stories" as seriously as they deserved. I'd always been able to go to her with anything, so why should this time be any different?

When we were still living in Durham, I'd been followed about for months on end by the ghost of a demon who was supposed to be haunting the cathedral roof in the form of a stone gargoyle. His name was Asrael, and he looked like a cross between a human, a cat, and an eagle. When he realized that I could see him, he'd been so pleased to be able to talk to someone at last that he followed me everywhere, even wanting to sleep in my bed at night. After I got over my first fright—like all gargoyles, he had a rather scary face—we slowly became friends. Sadly, Asrael hadn't been able to move from Durham to London with me, and I still missed him. The few gargoyle demons I'd seen here were not very nice creatures. So far I hadn't met one who was as sweet as Asrael.

If Mum had believed me about Asrael, then she'd probably believe me about the time-travel gene as well. I waited for a good moment to talk to her. But somehow the right moment never seemed to come. As soon as she was home from work, she had to discuss something with Caroline, who had put down her name to look after her class's terrarium in the summer, particularly the class mascot, a chameleon called Mr. Bean. The summer break was still months away, but it seemed that the discussion couldn't wait.

"You can't look after Mr. Bean, Caroline! You know perfectly well that your grandmother won't have pets in the house," said Mum. "And Aunt Glenda is allergic."

"But Mr. Bean doesn't have any fur," said Caroline. "And he'll be in his terrarium all the time. He won't be in anyone's way."

"He'll be in your grandmother's way."

"Then my grandmother is just silly!"

"Caroline, we can't keep him this summer. No one here knows the first thing about chameleons. Suppose we did something wrong, and Mr. Bean got sick and died?"

"He wouldn't. And I do know how to look after him. Please, Mummy! If I don't bring him home, then Tess will have him again, and she's always saying that she's Mr. Bean's favorite in the class."

"Caroline, I said no!"

Quarter of an hour later, they were still arguing, even when Mum went into the bathroom and closed the door behind her. Caroline stood outside the door and said, "Lady Arista wouldn't need to know. We could smuggle the terrarium into the house while she wasn't here. And she never goes into my room."

"Can't a person get any peace around here, at least when she's in the loo?" Mum called back.

"No," said Caroline. She could be a terrible pain. She didn't stop going on about it until Mum promised that she personally would plead with Lady Arista to let Mr. Bean spend the summer with us.

I spent the time that Caroline and Mum were wasting on their argument getting chewing gum out of Nick's hair.

We were sitting in the sewing room. He had about half a pound of the stuff sticking to his head and couldn't remember how it got there.

"You must have some idea!" I said. "I'm going to have to cut some of these strands of hair off."

"Doesn't matter," said Nick. "You can cut it all off. Lady Arista said I looked like a girl the other day."

"Lady Arista thinks everyone with hair longer than stubble looks like a girl. It would be a real shame to cut your lovely curls so short."

"They'll grow back. Cut it all off, okay?"

"Not with nail scissors. You'll have to go to the barber's."

"Oh, go on, you can do it," said Nick confidently. Obviously he'd completely forgotten that I'd already cut his hair with a pair of nail scissors once, and he'd looked like a freshly hatched vulture chick. I'd been seven at the time, and he was four. I'd needed his curls to make myself a wig. But it hadn't worked, and I got a scolding and a day's house arrest.

"Don't you dare," said Mum, who had come back into the room. She took the scissors away from me for safety's sake. "If it has to be done, it'll be done by a barber. Tomorrow. We must go down to supper now."

Nick groaned.

"Don't worry. Lady Arista is out today!" I grinned at him. "No one will scold you for the chewing gum. Or the dirty mark on your sweatshirt."

"What dirty mark?" Nick looked down at himself. "Oh, darn. That must be pomegranate juice."

"Like I said, you won't get in trouble."

"But it isn't even Wednesday," said Nick.

"Well, they're not here today either."

"Cool."

When Lady Arista, Charlotte, and Aunt Glenda were there, dinner was tense and uncomfortable. Lady Arista criticized people's table manners, mostly Caroline's and Nick's (but sometimes Great-aunt Maddy's as well); Aunt Glenda was always pestering me about my marks at school so she could compare them with Charlotte's. Then Charlotte would smile like Mona Lisa and say, "None of your business," if anyone asked her anything.

All things considered, we could have done without these cozy get-togethers, but our grandmother insisted on having all of us there.

The only way you could get out of family dinner was if you had a note from the doctor or a noticeably infectious disease like the plague. Mrs. Brompton, who was the housekeeper during the week, cooked all our meals. (Unfortunately, at weekends either Aunt Glenda or Mum did the cooking, which was usually so gross, Nick and I could barely force it down—and we never got to order out.)

But on Wednesday evenings, when Lady Arista, Aunt Glenda, and Charlotte were away, busy with their mysteries, supper was much more relaxed. And we all thought it was great that today felt like a Wednesday evening, although it was only Monday. Not that we slurped our food, smacked our lips, and belched, but we did venture to interrupt each other, put our elbows on the table, and discuss subjects that Lady Arista would have thought unsuitable.

Chameleons, for instance.

"Do you like chameleons, Aunt Maddy? Wouldn't you like to have one someday? A really tame one?"

"Well, er, now that you mention it, I realize I've always wanted a chameleon," said Great-aunt Maddy, heaping rosemary-seasoned potatoes on her plate. "Yes, definitely."

Caroline beamed. "Maybe your wish will come true someday soon."

"Did Lady Arista and Glenda leave any message?" asked Mum.

"Your mother called this afternoon to say they wouldn't be home for supper," said Great-aunt Maddy. "I said how sorry we'd all be not to see them. I hope that was all right."

"You bet." Nick giggled.

"And Charlotte? Has she . . . ?" asked Mum.

"I don't think so. Not yet." Great-aunt Maddy shrugged. "But they're expecting it any moment now. The poor girl keeps feeling dizzy, and now she has a migraine as well."

"Oh, dear, I do feel sorry for her," said Mum. She put her fork down and stared absentmindedly at the dark paneling of the dining room, which looked as if someone had confused the walls with the floor and covered them with wooden parquet.

"Suppose Charlotte doesn't travel back in time *at all*?" I asked.

"It will happen sooner or later," said Nick, imitating our grandmother's confident tones.

Everyone laughed except for Mum and me.

"But suppose it doesn't? Suppose they've made a mistake, and Charlotte doesn't have this gene after all?" I persisted.

This time Nick imitated Aunt Glenda's voice. "Even when she was a baby, anyone could see that Charlotte was born to higher things. She can't be compared with ordinary people."

Once again everyone laughed. Except for Mum. "What makes you think that, Gwyneth?"

"I was only . . ." I hesitated.

"I told you why there can't possibly be any mistake, dear," said Great-aunt Maddy.

"Yes, because Sir Isaac Newton was a genius, and a genius can't get his sums wrong," I said. "I know. But why did Newton work out Charlotte's date of birth in the first place?"

"Aunt Maddy!" Mum looked reproachfully at Great-aunt Maddy.

Great-aunt Maddy tut-tutted. "Oh, dear, she went on and on at me, asking questions. What was I to do? She's just like you when you were little, Grace. And apart from that, she promised to keep quiet as a mouse about it."

"Only to Grandmother," I said. "Did Isaac Newton invent that chronograph thing as well?"

"You little telltale," said Great-aunt Maddy. "I'm not saying any more."

"What chronograph thing?" asked Nick.

"It's a time machine for sending Charlotte back into the past," I explained. "And it uses Charlotte's blood for fuel."

"Gross!" said Nick, and Caroline screeched, "Yuck, blood!"

"Can you travel into the future with the chronograph as well?" asked Nick.

Mum groaned. "Now look what you've done, Aunt Maddy."

"They're your children, Grace," said Great-aunt Maddy, smiling. "It's only natural for them to want to know what's going on."

"Yes." Mum looked at us one by one. "But you must never ask your grandmother such questions. Do you understand?"

"Although she's probably the only one who knows the answers," I said.

"But she wouldn't give them to you."

"And how much do you know about it all, Mum?"

"More than I like." Mum was smiling as she said that, but I thought it was a sad smile. "And no, you *can't* travel into the future, Nick, for the simple reason that the future hasn't happened yet."

"Huh?" said Nick. "What sort of sense does that make?"

There was a knock, and Mr. Bernard came in with the telephone. Lesley would probably have freaked out if she'd seen the phone lying on a silver platter. Sometimes Mr. Bernard overdid the butler thing a bit.

"A telephone call for Miss Grace," he said.

Mum picked up the phone, and Mr. Bernard turned around to leave the dining room. He didn't eat dinner with us unless Lady Arista invited him to, which was about twice a year. Nick and I suspected that he ordered out for Italian or Chinese meals and enjoyed them in the comfort of his own room.

"Yes? Oh, Mother, it's you."

Great-aunt Maddy's eyes twinkled. "Your grandmother can read thoughts!" she whispered. "She guesses we're discussing forbidden subjects here. Who's going to clear these plates away? We must make room for Mrs. Brompton's apple cake."

"And the vanilla custard!" I'd eaten a huge mound of rosemary potatoes with glazed carrots and pork medallions, but I wasn't full yet. All the excitement had made me extra hungry. I stood up and began clearing the dirty dishes into the dumbwaiter.

"If Charlotte goes back in time far enough, could she bring me back a baby dinosaur?" asked Caroline.

Great-aunt Maddy shook her head. "Animals and humans without the gene can't move through time. And no one can travel that far back anyway."

"Oh," said Caroline, looking rather disappointed.

"Just as well, if you ask me," I said. "Imagine what it

would be like if time travelers were always bringing back dinosaurs and saber-toothed tigers—or Attila the Hun or Adolf Hitler."

Mum had finished talking on the phone. "They're staying the night there," she said. "To be on the safe side."

"Staying the night where?" asked Nick.

Mum didn't answer. "Aunt Maddy?" she said. "Are you all right?"

Twelve pillars the castle of time will bear.
Twelve creatures rule land and sea.
The eagle is ready to soar in the air,
Five's the foundation and also the key.
In the Circle of Twelve, Number Twelve becomes Two.
The hawk hatches seventh, yet Three is the clue.

From the secret writings of Count Saint-Germain

FOUR

GREAT-AUNT MADDY looked curiously rigid. She sat staring into space, her hands clutching the arms of the chair. All the color had drained from her face.

"Aunt Maddy? Oh, Mum, has she had a stroke? Aunt Maddy, can you hear me? Aunt Maddy!" I tried to take her hand, but Mum stopped me.

"Don't do that! Don't touch her."

Caroline started crying.

"What's the matter with her?" asked Nick. "Is something stuck in her throat?"

"We'll have to call the doctor," I said. "Mum, do something!"

"She hasn't had a stroke, and there isn't anything in her throat. She's seeing a vision," said Mum. "It will be over soon."

"Are you sure?" Great-aunt Maddy's rigid glance

frightened me. Her pupils were hugely dilated, and she wasn't blinking at all.

"It's so cold in here all of a sudden," whispered Nick. "Don't you feel it too?"

Caroline was whimpering quietly to herself. "Make it stop."

"Lucy!" someone cried. We jumped in alarm and then realized that it was Great-aunt Maddy's voice. The temperature really had dropped. I looked around, but there were no ghosts in the room. "Lucy, oh, the dear child! She's leading me to a tree. A tree covered with red berries. Oh, where's she gone? I can't see her anymore. There's something lying between the roots of the tree. A huge jewel, a sapphire cut in the shape of an egg. A sapphire egg. It's so beautiful! And valuable. But now it's cracking—oh, it will break—but there's something inside it . . . a little chick hatching. A raven chick. Hopping over to the tree." Great-aunt Maddy laughed, but her eyes were still fixed. Her shaky hands grappled for the arms of the chair.

"The wind's rising." Great-aunt Maddy's laughter died away. "A stormy wind. Everything's going around and around. I'm flying. Flying to the stars with the raven. A tower. A huge clock high up on the tower. There's someone sitting up there on the clock dangling her legs. Come down at once, you silly girl!" Suddenly there was fear in her voice. She began to scream. "The wind will blow her down. She's gone much too high. What's she doing there? A shadow! A big bird circling in the sky! There! It's swooping down on her. Gwyneth! Gwyneth!"

I couldn't stand this any longer. I pushed Mum aside, took Great-aunt Maddy's shoulder, and shook her gently. "I'm here, Aunt Maddy! Please! Look at me!"

Great-aunt Maddy turned her head. She did look at me. Gradually some color came back into her face. "My little angel!" she said. "How silly of you to climb so high!"

"Are you okay?" I looked at Mum. "Are you sure it wasn't anything wrong with her?"

"It was a vision," said Mum. "She's all right."

"No, I'm not. It was a horrible vision," said Great-aunt Maddy. "Although the beginning was nice."

Caroline had stopped crying. She and Nick were staring at Great-aunt Maddy, looking upset.

"That was eerie," said Nick. "Did you notice how cold it got?"

"You were imagining things," I said.

"No, I wasn't!"

"It *was* eerie," said Caroline. "I had goose bumps."

Great-aunt Maddy reached for Mum's hand. "I met your niece Lucy, Grace. She still looked the same as ever. That sweet smile . . ."

Mum looked as if she was going to burst into tears.

"And I just didn't understand the rest of it," Great-aunt Maddy went on. "A sapphire egg, a raven, Gwyneth on the clock tower, and then that horrible bird. Can you make anything of all that?"

Mum sighed. "Of course not, Aunt Maddy. *You're* the one who has these visions." She sat down on one of the dining chairs beside Great-aunt Maddy.

"Yes, but that doesn't mean I understand them," said Great-aunt Maddy. "Did you write it all down so that we can tell your mother about it later?"

"No, Auntie, I didn't."

Maddy leaned forward. "Then we'd better write it down at once. Right, first there was Lucy, then the tree. Red berries . . . could it have been a mountain ash? The sapphire egg was lying there. . . . Oh, my word, I'm so hungry! I hope you didn't finish the apple cake. I deserve at least two slices today. Or three."

"THAT REALLY *was* very, very eerie," I said. Caroline and Nick had gone to sleep, and I was sitting with Mum on the edge of her bed, trying to find a good way to tell her about my problem. *Mum, something funny happened to me this afternoon, and I'm scared it could happen again.*

Mum was deeply engaged in her evening beauty routine. She'd finished her face already. Obviously good skin care paid off. You really wouldn't have thought my mum was over forty.

"That's the first time I've seen Great-aunt Maddy have one of her visions," I said.

"It was the first time she's ever had one during dinner," replied Mum, rubbing cream on her hands and massaging it in. She always said that age showed first on your hands and your neck.

"Do—do we take her visions seriously?"

Mum shrugged. "Hm, well. You heard all that confused stuff she was saying. And it can always be interpreted differently. She had a vision three days before your grandfather died. She saw a black panther jumping on his chest."

"And Grandfather died of a heart attack. So that makes sense."

"See what I mean? They always hold some truth. Want some hand cream, darling?"

"Do you believe in it? I mean, not the hand cream, Aunt Maddy's vision?"

"I think Aunt Maddy really sees what she says she does. But that doesn't mean her visions predict the future, not by a long shot. Or that it has to mean anything in particular."

"I don't understand!" I held out my hands, and Mum began putting cream on them.

"It's a bit like your ghosts, darling. I'm sure you do see them, just as I believe that Aunt Maddy has visions."

"Does that mean you believe I see ghosts but you don't believe they really exist?" I cried indignantly, taking my hands away.

"I don't *know* whether they really exist or not," said Mum. "What I believe has nothing to do with it."

"But if they didn't exist, that would mean I was just imagining them. And *that* would mean I was crazy."

"No," said my mum. "It would only mean that . . . oh, darling, I don't know what to say. Sometimes I get the feeling we have rather too much imagination in this family. I suppose we'd live more restful, happier lives if we stuck to believing what *normal* people believe."

"I get the message," I said. Maybe it wouldn't be such a great idea to come out with my news tonight. *Hey, Mum, we traveled back into the past this afternoon, me and my abnormal imagination.*

"Don't look so sad," said Mum. "I know, I know, there are more things in heaven and earth and all that. But maybe we make them seem far too important the more we think about them. I don't think you're crazy. Or Aunt Maddy either. But be honest: do you imagine Aunt Maddy's vision could have something to do with your own future?"

"Maybe."

"You do? Are you planning to climb a clock tower sometime soon—sit on the clock and dangle your legs?"

"Of course not. But maybe it was a symbol."

"Maybe," said Mum. "Or maybe not. Go to sleep now, darling. You've had a long day." She looked at the little clock on her bedside table. "Let's hope it's safely behind Charlotte by now. Oh, I do hope she's finally done it."

"But maybe Charlotte just has too much imagination as well," I said. I stood up and gave Mum a kiss.

I'd try again tomorrow.

Maybe.

"Good night."

"Good night, sweetie. I love you."

"Love you too, Mum."

When I'd closed my bedroom door behind me and climbed into bed, I felt guilty. I should have told my mother all about it. But what she said had made me think. Yeah, sure, I did have a big imagination, but daydreaming is one thing. Imagining you're traveling through time is quite another.

People who imagined that kind of thing got psychiatric treatment. And they should, if you asked me. Maybe I was like those weirdos who claim to have been abducted by aliens. Completely out of my mind.

I switched off my bedside lamp and snuggled down under the duvet. Which was worse? Being crazy or actually traveling back in time?

Probably the second, I thought. Maybe you could take tablets for the first.

In the dark my fears came back. Once again I was wondering how far I would fall from here to the ground floor. So I switched the bedside light on again and turned my face to the wall. Hoping to get to sleep, I tried thinking of something harmless and soothing, but I just couldn't do it. In the end I counted backward from a thousand.

I must have fallen asleep at some point, because I'd been dreaming of a big bird when I woke and sat up in bed, heart pounding.

There it was again, that horrible dizzy sensation in my stomach. I jumped out of bed in a panic and ran to Mum's room as fast as my trembling legs would carry me. I didn't care if she thought I was crazy—I just wanted it to stop. And I did *not* want to fall three floors down and land in a swamp!

I got no farther than the passage before I was swept off my feet. Convinced that my last hour had come, I squeezed my eyes shut. But I only fell on my knees with a bump, and the floor felt just like the familiar wooden floorboards. Cautiously, I opened my eyes. It was lighter now, as if the sun had risen in the last second. For a moment I hoped that nothing had happened. Then I saw that I had indeed landed in our corridor, but it looked different. The walls were painted dark olive green, and there were no ceiling lights.

I heard voices coming from Nick's room. Female voices.

I stood up quickly. If anyone saw me now . . . how was I going to explain where I'd suddenly come from? In my Hello Kitty pajamas.

"I'm so tired of getting up at the crack of dawn," one voice was saying. "Walter can sleep until nine in the morning. Not us! I should've stayed on the farm milking cows."

"Walter's on duty half the night, Clarrie. Your cap's crooked," said the second voice. "Tuck your hair neatly under it, or Mrs. Mason will be cross."

"She's always cross anyway," grumbled the first voice.

"There are much stricter housekeepers, Clarrie dear. Come on, or we'll be late. Mary went downstairs fifteen minutes ago."

"Yes, *and* she made her bed first. Always busy, always neat, just the way Mrs. Mason likes her housemaids. Mary does it on purpose. Have you felt her blanket? It's ever so soft. That's not fair!"

I had to get out of here, fast. But where could I go? Good thing I knew my way around the house.

"I've been given a horrid scratchy blanket," Clarrie's voice complained.

"You'll be glad of it in winter. Come along."

The door handle was pressed down. I raced over to the built-in cupboard, flung the door open, and shut it again after me, just as the door of Nick's room opened.

"I don't see why I have to have a scratchy blanket and Mary gets a nice soft one," Clarrie's voice went on. "It's so unfair. Betty can go out into the country with Lady Montrose, and we have to spend all summer in the stuffy city air."

"You really should try not to complain so much, Clarrie."

I agreed with the other woman. This girl Clarrie was a real Moaning Minnie.

I heard the two of them go downstairs and breathed a sigh of relief. That was a close one! But now what? Should I just wait in the cupboard until I traveled back again? That was probably the safest thing to do. Sighing, I crossed my arms.

Behind me in the darkness, someone grunted.

I froze with horror. What, for heaven's sake, was that?

"Is that you, Clarrie?" asked a voice from the shelf where the clean sheets were stacked. It was a male voice. "Did I oversleep?"

Heavens above! Someone actually *slept* in this cupboard! What a way to treat a person!

"Clarrie? Mary? Who's that?" asked the voice. Its owner sounded more awake now. There were noises in the cupboard. A hand reached out and touched my back. I wasn't hanging about, waiting for it to grab hold of me—I opened the cupboard door and ran for it.

"Stop! Stay where you are!"

I looked back over my shoulder. A young man in a long white shirt emerged from the cupboard to catch me.

I ran downstairs. Where on earth was I going to hide now? The footsteps of the man from the cupboard came closer, and he was shouting, "Stop, thief!"

Thief? I couldn't believe my ears. What was I supposed to have stolen? His nightcap or something?

Luckily I could have run down these stairs even in my sleep. I was already familiar with every single step. I raced down two flights of stairs at the speed of light, and then past Great-great-great-great-great-uncle Hugh's portrait—leaving it behind on my left with some regret, because the secret door behind it would have been a great way to get out of this stupid situation. But the doorknob always jammed slightly, and in the time I'd have needed to get the door open, the man in the nightshirt would have caught up with me. No, I needed a better place to hide.

On the first floor I almost collided with a housemaid carrying a big jug. She squealed as I raced past, then dropped the jug, just like in a scene from a film. Water splashed to the floor, along with broken china.

I hoped my pursuer would slip and fall on it—like in a

farce. He wouldn't get past the water and broken china too quickly, anyway. I made use of my start on him to run down the steps to the musicians' gallery, open the door to the little storage space under it, and crouch inside. It was dusty and untidy in here, the same as in my own time, and full of cobwebs. A little light fell in through the gaps between the steps, enough for me to see that at least there wasn't anyone sleeping in *this* cupboard. It was crammed with old junk, just like in the twenty-first century.

Above me, I heard loud voices. The man in the nightshirt was talking to the poor housemaid who had dropped the jug.

"The girl must be a thief! I never saw her here in the house before."

Other voices joined in.

"She ran on down. Maybe there's a whole pack of them here."

"Please, Mrs. Mason, I couldn't help it. The thief just ran into me. I expect they're after her ladyship's jewels."

"I didn't meet anyone on the stairs, so she must still be here somewhere. Make sure the front door is locked and search the house," ordered an energetic female voice. "As for you, Walter, go upstairs at once and put something on to cover your hairy legs. Not a nice sight first thing in the morning."

I could hear my heart pounding in my ears. I'd hidden in here about a million times when I was little, but I'd never been so scared of being found. Cautiously, so as not to make any noise that might give me away, I squeezed farther in among the junk. A spider ran over my arm, such a big one that I almost screeched with fright.

"Lester, Mr. Jenkins, and Tott, you search the ground floor and the cellars. Mary and I will search the first floor. Clarrie, guard the back door, and, Helen, you watch the front door."

"Suppose she tries getting out through the kitchen?"

"She'd have to get past Mrs. Craine and her iron pans first. Look in the cupboards under the stairs and behind all the curtains."

I was finished.

Oh, dammit. This was all just so—so surreal!

Here I was sitting in my pajamas in a cupboard, surrounded by fat spiders, dusty furniture, and—oh, my God, was that by any chance a stuffed crocodile?—and waiting to be arrested for theft. And all because Sir Isaac Newton had gotten his stupid sums wrong.

I felt so angry and helpless that I started crying. Maybe these people would feel sorry for me when they found me. The crocodile's glass eyes sparkled mockingly in the dim light. There were footsteps to be heard all over the house now. Dust from the steps was falling into my eyes.

But then I felt that tugging sensation in my stomach again. I'd never been so glad of it. The crocodile blurred before my eyes, everything spun wildly, and all was quiet again. And pitch-dark.

I heaved a huge sigh. Don't panic, I thought. Presumably I'd traveled home again. And I was probably now stuck among the junk under these steps in our own time. When the place also had fat spiders in it.

Something soft touched my face. In a panic, I flailed my arms and hauled my legs out from under a chest of drawers. There was a rumbling sound, boards creaked, an old lamp fell over. That's to say, I thought it was a lamp, but I couldn't see a thing. I could wriggle out, however. Relieved, I made my way to the cupboard door and crawled out of hiding. It was still dark outside the cupboard as well, but I could just about see the outline of the banisters, the tall windows, the sparkling chandeliers.

And a figure coming toward me. The beam of a flashlight dazzled me.

I opened my mouth to scream, but no sound would come out.

"Were you looking for anything in particular in that cubbyhole, Miss Gwyneth?" asked the figure. It was Mr. Bernard. "I'll be happy to help you find it."

"I, er . . . I . . ." I still felt breathless. It was the fright I'd had affecting my lungs. "What are *you* doing down here, Mr. Bernard?"

"I heard a noise," said Mr. Bernard, with great dignity. "You seem to be a little—well, dusty."

"Yes." Dusty, scratched, and tearstained. I stealthily wiped my cheeks.

Mr. Bernard's owl eyes were examining me in the beam of the flashlight. I looked defiantly back at him. It wasn't forbidden to get into a cupboard in the middle of the night, was it? And why I should was no business of Mr. Bernard's.

Did he actually sleep in his glasses?

"It's another two hours before the alarm clocks go off," he said at last. "I suggest you spend the time in your bed. I'm going to get a little more rest myself. Good night."

"Good night, Mr. Bernard," I said.

Despite a thorough search of the house, it proved impossible to lay hands on the girl thief seen early this morning in the town house of Lord Horatio Montrose (Inner Circle) in Bourdon Place. She probably escaped by climbing out of a window into the garden. The housekeeper, Mrs. Mason, drew up a list of items found to be missing: silver cutlery and valuable jewelry, the property of Lady Montrose, including a necklace given to Lord Montrose's mother by the Duke of Wellington. Lady Montrose is at present in the country.

FROM *THE ANNALS OF THE GUARDIANS*

12 JULY 1851

REPORT: DAVID LOYDE, ADEPT 2ND DEGREE

FIVE

"YOU LOOK WORN OUT," said Lesley in the school yard at break.

"I feel terrible."

Lesley patted my arm. "All the same, those dark rings under your eyes kind of suit you," she said, trying to cheer me up. "They make your eyes look extra blue."

I smiled. Lesley was so sweet. We were sitting on the bench under the chestnut tree, and we could only talk in whispers, because Cynthia Dale was sitting behind us with a girlfriend, and right beside them Gordon Gelderman was talking about football with two other boys from our class, in a voice somewhere between a duck's quack and a bear's growl. I didn't want them to overhear us. They all thought I was weird enough anyway.

"Oh, Gwen, you really ought to have told your mother."

"You've said that at least fifty times now."

"Yes, because it's true. I can't understand why you didn't."

"Because I . . . no, to be honest, I don't understand why myself. Somehow or other, I suppose I was hoping it wouldn't happen again."

"But that adventure in the night—I mean, just think what could have happened to you! Take your great-aunt's vision—it has to mean you're in danger. The clock stands for time travel, the tall tower for danger, and the bird . . . oh, you shouldn't have woken her up! It'd probably have gotten really exciting at that point. I'm going to Google the whole thing this afternoon—raven, sapphire, tower, mountain ash tree. I've found a Web site about extrasensory phenomena—it tells you lots of stuff. And I've looked up loads of books about time travel for us. And films. *Back to the Future*, parts one to three. Maybe we can find out something from those. . . ."

I thought about what fun it had always been, sitting on the sofa in Lesley's house watching DVDs. Sometimes we used to mute the sound and synchronize our own words with the pictures.

"Are you feeling dizzy?"

I shook my head. Now I knew what it had been like for poor Charlotte these last few weeks. Being asked all the time whether I was dizzy really got on my nerves. Particularly when I was always sort of listening to myself and waiting for the dizzy feeling.

"If we only knew when it will happen again," said

Lesley. "I do think it's unfair. Charlotte has been prepared for this for ages, but you've been thrown in at the deep end."

"I've no idea what Charlotte would have done last night if she'd been chased by the man who was sleeping in our built-in cupboard," I said. "I don't think the dancing and fencing lessons would have been much use there. No horse in sight for her to ride away on, either."

I giggled, imagining Charlotte in my place, running all over the house to get away from the angry young man called Walter who slept in the cupboard. Perhaps she'd have snatched a sword off the wall in the salon and slaughtered all the poor servants.

"No, silly, of course those things wouldn't have done her any good. But they wouldn't have happened to her, because that chrono-thingy would have sent her somewhere else. Somewhere nice and peaceful. A place where nothing could harm her! But you risk your life instead of telling your family they've been teaching the wrong person."

"Maybe by now Charlotte has traveled in time as well. Then they'll have what they wanted anyway."

Lesley sighed and began going through the stack of paper on her lap. She had prepared a file of useful information for me. Well, more or less useful. For instance, she had printed out photos of vintage cars. According to them, the car I'd seen on my first journey through time dated from 1906.

"Jack the Ripper was haunting the East End in 1888. The stupid thing is, no one's ever found out who he was.

All sorts of people have been suspected, but there's never been any proof. So if you ever lose your way in the East End in 1888, any man you meet is potentially dangerous. The Great Fire of London was in 1666, and there was plague in the city practically all the time, but 1348, 1528, and 1665 were particularly bad years. Then there's the Blitz in the Second World War. The air raids began in 1940 and left almost all of London in ruins. You'd better find out if your house escaped being hit. If so, you'll be safe there. Otherwise St. Paul's Cathedral would be a good place, because it did get hit once, but almost miraculously, it stayed standing. So, you could hide there."

"It all sounds dreadfully dangerous," I said.

"Yes, I always thought of time travel as more romantic. I mean, I kind of imagined Charlotte in her own historical films. Dancing with Mr. Darcy at a ball, falling in love with some sexy Highlander. Telling Anne Boleyn it would be a really, really bad idea to marry Henry VIII. That kind of thing."

"Anne Boleyn's the one they beheaded?"

Lesley nodded. "There's a great film with Natalie Portman. I could borrow us the DVD. . . . Gwen, please promise me you'll talk to your mum today."

"I promise. I'll do it tonight."

"Where's Charlotte?" Cynthia craned her neck to look around the tree trunk. "I wanted to copy her Shakespeare essay. Er—I mean I wanted to get a few ideas from it."

"Charlotte's not well," I said.

"What's the matter with her?"

"Diarrhea," said Lesley. "Very bad. Spends all her time sitting on the loo."

"Ew, spare us the details!" said Cynthia. "Can I look at your essays, then, you two?"

"We haven't finished them yet," said Lesley. "We're going to watch *Shakespeare in Love* again first."

"You can read my essay," Gordon Gelderman said in his deepest bass voice. His head appeared on the other side of the tree trunk. "All out of Wikipedia."

"I might just as well look up Wikipedia for myself," said Cynthia.

The bell rang, and break was over.

"Double English," groaned Gordon. "For a man, that's torture. But I can see Cynthia slobbering already when she thinks of Prince Charming."

"Shut up, Gordon."

Everyone knew that Gordon never shut up. "I can't imagine why you all think Mr. Whitman is so great. I mean, he's such a poof!"

"He is not!" Cynthia said indignantly, standing up.

"He's definitely gay!" Gordon followed her to the entrance. He'd be needling Cynthia all the way up to the second floor.

Lesley rolled her eyes. "Come on," she said, and gave me her hand to pull me up from the bench. "Off we go for our date with Prince Charming Squirrel!"

We caught up with Cynthia and Gordon on the stairs up to the second floor. They were still talking about Mr. Whitman.

"You can tell from that weird signet ring he wears," said Gordon. "Only gay guys wear that sort of thing."

"My grandfather always wore a signet ring," I said, although I didn't really want to get mixed up in this.

"Then your grandfather was gay too," said Gordon.

"You're just jealous," said Cynthia.

"Jealous? Me?"

"Of course you are. Because Mr. Whitman is the best-looking, most masculine, cleverest, straightest guy ever. Next to him you look like a silly, weedy little boy."

"Thanks very much for the compliment," said Mr. Whitman. He'd appeared behind us, unnoticed, with a stack of paper under his arm and, as always, breathtakingly good-looking. (Even if he did also look a bit like a squirrel.)

Cynthia went even redder than bright scarlet in the face, if that's possible. I actually felt sorry for her.

Gordon grinned nastily.

"As for you, Gordon, maybe you ought to do a little research into signet rings and their wearers," said Mr. Whitman. "I'd like you to write a short essay on the subject by next week."

Now Gordon went red. But unlike Cynthia, he could still speak. "For English or history?" he squeaked.

"I'd welcome it if you would concentrate on the historical aspects, but I leave you an entirely free hand there. Shall we say five pages by Monday?" Mr. Whitman opened our classroom door and smiled brightly at us. "In you go."

"I hate him," muttered Gordon, sitting down.

Lesley patted him consolingly on the shoulder. "I think it's mutual."

"Please tell me that was just a bad dream," said Cynthia.

"It was only a dream," I said obligingly. "Mr. Whitman didn't really hear a word about you thinking he's the sexiest man alive."

Groaning, Cynthia sank into her chair. "Earth, kindly open and swallow me up!"

I sat down at my place next to Lesley. "Poor thing—she's still as red as a tomato."

"And I think she'll be a tomato to the end of her school days. Was that ever embarrassing!"

"Maybe Mr. Whitman will give her better marks now."

Mr. Whitman glanced at Charlotte's place and looked thoughtful.

"Mr. Whitman? Charlotte's not well," I said. "I'm not sure if my aunt called the school secretary's office—"

"She has diarrhea!" bleated Cynthia. Obviously she felt an urgent need not to be the only one with something to be embarrassed about.

"Charlotte is excused," said Mr. Whitman. "She'll probably be absent for a few days. Until everything has . . . returned to normal." He turned around and wrote THE SONNET on the board in chalk. "Can someone tell me how many sonnets Shakespeare wrote?"

"What did he mean by *returned to normal*?" I whispered to Lesley.

"I didn't get the impression he was talking about Charlotte's diarrhea," Lesley whispered back.

Neither did I.

"Have you ever taken a close look at his signet ring?" Lesley whispered.

"No, have you?"

"There's a star on it. A star with twelve points."

"So?"

"Twelve points—like on a clock."

"A clock doesn't have points."

Lesley rolled her eyes. "Doesn't that ring a bell with you? Twelve! Clock! Time! *Time travel!* I bet you . . . Gwen?"

"Oh, no!" I said. My insides were going on a roller-coaster ride again.

Lesley stared at me, horrified. "Oh, no!"

I was just as horrified. The last thing I wanted was to dissolve into thin air in front of the entire class. So I got up and staggered to the door, my hand pressed to my stomach.

"I think I'm going to throw up," I told Mr. Whitman. I didn't wait for his answer. I flung the door open and tottered out into the corridor.

"Maybe someone ought to go with her," I heard Mr. Whitman say. "Lesley, please would you . . . ?"

Lesley came racing after me, firmly closing the classroom door. "Okay, quick! Into the girls' toilets. No one will see us there. Gwen? Gwenny?"

Lesley's face blurred before my eyes. Her voice seemed to come from very far away. And then she'd disappeared entirely. I was standing on my own in a corridor papered with magnificent gold-patterned wallpaper. Instead of the school's ugly linoleum floor tiles, beautiful wooden floorboards stretched ahead of me, polished to a high sheen, with elaborate patterns in the wood. It was obviously night, or at least evening, but candleholders with lighted candles were fixed to brackets on the walls, and chandeliers hung from the painted ceiling, also with candles burning in them. Everything was bathed in soft, golden light.

My first thought was *Great, I didn't fall over this time.* My second thought was *Where can I hide around here before anyone sees me?*

Because I wasn't alone in this house. I heard music from below. Violin music. And voices.

A lot of voices.

The familiar school corridor was almost unrecognizable now. I tried to remember the way the space here was divided up. Behind me had to be my classroom door, and in the room opposite, Mrs. Counter was now teaching geography to Year Six. Next to the Year Six classroom was a stockroom for equipment. If I hid in there, at least no one would see me materializing when I came back.

On the other hand, the stockroom was usually locked, so it might not be a great idea to hide there after all. If I traveled forward again through time and landed in a locked room, then supposing I found a way to get out, I'd also have to think up some plausible explanation of how on earth I got there in the first place.

But if I hid in one of the other rooms, when I traveled to my own time again, I'd be materializing out of nowhere in front of an entire classroom, including a teacher. Explaining that would probably be a lot harder.

I thought maybe I should just stay in this corridor and hope it wouldn't last long. After all, I'd been gone for only a few minutes both times I'd traveled into the past.

I leaned against the brocade wallpaper and waited hopefully for the dizzy sensation. Confused voices and laughter drifted up from down below. I heard glasses clinking and then the violins playing again. It sounded as if a lot of people were having a good time down there. Maybe James was at the party. After all, he used to live here. I imagined him very much alive, dancing somewhere downstairs.

A pity I couldn't meet him. But he probably wouldn't have been pleased if I told him how we knew each other. I mean how we *would* know each other some day, long after he died . . . er, long after he would be dead.

If I only knew what he'd died from, maybe I could warn him. *Listen, James, on the fifteenth of July a tile will fall on your head in Park Lane, so you'd better stay at home that day.* The stupid thing was that James didn't know what he'd died of. He didn't even know he was dead. Er, was going to die. Would be dead.

The longer you thought about this time travel stuff, the more complicated it got.

I heard footsteps on the stairs. Someone was running up them. No, two someones. Dammit, couldn't you even stand around here for a couple of minutes in peace and quiet? Now where? I decided on the room opposite, the one that in my own time was the Year Six classroom. The door handle stuck. It took me a couple of seconds to realize I must push it up and not down.

When I finally managed to slip into the room, the footsteps were quite close. There were candles burning in brackets on the walls here, too. How careless to leave them alight with no one in the room! At home I'd be dead if I forgot to blow out a tea light in the sewing room in the evening.

I looked around for somewhere to hide, but there wasn't much furniture in this room. Some kind of sofa with curvy gilded legs, a desk, upholstered chairs, nothing you could hide behind if you were any larger than a mouse. So all I could do was get behind one of the floor-length golden yellow curtains—not a very original hiding place. But so far no one was looking for me.

I could hear voices out in the corridor now.

"Where do you think you're going?" asked a man's voice. It sounded rather angry.

"Anywhere! Away from you, that's all," replied another voice. It was the voice of a girl, a girl in floods of tears, to be precise. To my alarm, she came right into the room. And the man came after her. Through the curtain I could see their shadows moving.

Of course, what did I expect? Of all the rooms up here, they had to choose the one where I was hiding.

"Leave me alone," said the girl's voice.

"I *can't* leave you alone," said the man. "Whenever I leave you alone, you do something rash without thinking first."

"Go away!" said the girl again.

"No, I won't. Listen, I'm sorry that happened. I ought not to have allowed it."

"But you did! Because you had eyes only for *her*!"

The man laughed a little. "You're jealous!"

"You'd like that, wouldn't you?"

Oh, great! A couple in the middle of a lovers' tiff. This could go on forever. I'd be kicking my heels behind this curtain until I traveled back and suddenly materialized in front of the windows in Mrs. Counter's geography lesson. Maybe I could tell her I'd been doing a physics experiment. Or I'd been there all the time and she just hadn't noticed me.

"The count will wonder where we are," said the man's voice.

"Then he can just send his Transylvanian friend looking for us, that's what your count can do. He's not even really a count. His title's as much of a fake as the rosy cheeks of that . . . what was her name again?" The girl gave an angry little snort through her nose as she spoke.

Somehow or other, I knew that sound. I knew it very well. I cautiously peered out from behind the curtain. The two of them were standing right in front of the door, with their profiles turned to me. The girl really was only a girl, wearing a fantastic dress, midnight blue silk and embroidered brocade, with a skirt so wide she'd probably have trouble getting through a normal doorway in it. She had snow-white hair piled up into a strange sort of mountain on top of her head, with ringlets falling to her shoulders. It had to be a wig. The man had white hair too, held together with a ribbon at the nape of his neck. In spite of having hair like senior citizens, they both looked very young and very attractive, especially the man. He was more of a boy, really, maybe eighteen or nineteen years old. But staggeringly good-looking. A perfect masculine profile. I couldn't take my eyes off him. I leaned much farther out of my hiding place than I really meant to.

"I've forgotten her name already," said the boy, still laughing.

"Liar!"

"The count's not responsible for Rakoczy's behavior," said the boy, serious again now. "He'll certainly be reprimanded for that. You don't have to like the count, you only have to respect him."

The girl snorted scornfully again, and again it sounded strangely familiar. "I don't *have* to do anything," she said, abruptly turning toward the window. That meant turning to me. I wanted to disappear right behind the curtain, but I froze mid-movement.

This was impossible!

The girl had *my* face. I was looking into my own startled eyes!

She seemed as surprised as I was, but she got over her shock faster. She made a movement with her hand.

Hide! her gesture clearly said. *Disappear!*

Breathing hard, I put my head back behind the curtain. Who was she? There just couldn't be such a likeness between us. I simply *had* to look again.

"What was that?" I heard the boy saying.

"Nothing!" said the girl. Was that by any chance also *my* voice?

"At the window."

"Nothing, I said."

"There could be someone standing behind the curtain listening to . . ." Whatever he was saying was cut short by his sound of surprise. Suddenly there was silence. Now what had happened?

Without thinking, I pushed the curtain aside. The girl who looked like me had planted her lips right on the boy's mouth. He took it passively at first, then he put his arms around her waist and pulled her closer. The girl shut her eyes.

Suddenly there were butterflies dancing in my stomach. It was odd, watching yourself kiss someone. I thought I did it pretty well. I realized that the girl was kissing the boy only to take his mind off me. Nice of her, but why was she doing it? And how was I going to get past them unnoticed?

The butterflies in my stomach turned to a flock of birds in flight, and the picture of the couple kissing blurred before my eyes. And then, suddenly, I was in the Year Six classroom with my nerves in shreds.

All was still.

I'd expected an outcry from all the students when I suddenly appeared, and someone—maybe Mrs. Counter—falling down in a faint with the shock of it.

But the classroom was empty. I groaned with relief. At

least I'd been lucky this time. I dropped into a chair and put my head down on the desk in front of it. What had just happened was more than I could take in for the moment. The girl, the gorgeous guy, the kiss. . . .

The girl hadn't just looked like me.

The girl *was* me.

There was no possible mistake. I'd recognized myself, beyond any shadow of doubt, by the little birthmark in the shape of a half-moon on my temple, the one Aunt Glenda always called Gwenny's funny little banana.

There couldn't be two different people who looked so much alike.

The first pair Opal and Amber are,
Agate sings in B flat, the wolf avatar,
*A duet—*solutio!*—with Aquamarine.*
Mighty Emerald next, with the lovely Citrine.
The Carnelian twins of the Scorpio sign,
Number Eight is digestio, *her stone is Jade fine.*
E major's the key of the Black Tourmaline,
Sapphire sings in F major, and bright is her sheen.
Then almost at once comes Diamond alone,
Whose sign of the lion as Leo is known.
Projectio! *Time flows on, both present and past.*
Ruby red is the first and is also the last.

FROM THE SECRET WRITINGS OF
COUNT SAINT-GERMAIN

SIX

NO. IT COULDN'T HAVE been me.

For one thing, I'd never kissed a boy.

Well, not really. Not like that. There was that boy Miles in the year above ours. I'd gone out with him last summer. Not so much because I was in love with him as because he was best friends with Max, Lesley's boyfriend at the time, so it seemed kind of convenient. But Miles wasn't really into kissing. What he liked was leaving love bites on my throat to distract my attention from his creeping hand. I had to go about with a scarf around my neck when the temperature was ninety degrees in the shade, and I was constantly trying to keep Miles's hands out of my shirt. (Especially in the darkness of the cinema, where he seemed to grow at least three extra.) After two weeks and a half day, our so-called relationship was terminated by mutual consent. I was "too immature" for Miles, and Miles was too . . . well, let's say affectionate for me.

Apart from him, I'd only kissed Gordon, on our class outing to the Isle of Wight, but that didn't count because it was (a) part of a game called Truth or Kiss (I'd told the truth, but Gordon had insisted it was a lie) and (b) not a real kiss. Gordon hadn't even taken his chewing gum out of his mouth first.

So except for the love-bite affair, as Lesley called it, and Gordon's pepperminty performance, I was entirely unkissed. And possibly also immature, as Miles claimed. I knew that at sixteen and a half, it was getting late, but Lesley, who had stayed with Max for a whole year, thought kissing in general was overrated. Maybe she'd just had bad luck, she said, but the boys she'd kissed so far definitely did not have the knack for it.

Kissing, said Lesley, ought really to be taught as a school subject, preferably instead of religious studies, which nobody needed.

We often discussed what the ideal kiss would be like, and there were any number of films we'd watched over and over again just because of the good kissing scenes in them.

"Ah, Miss Gwyneth. Will you condescend to speak to me today, or are you going to ignore me again?" James saw me leaving the Year Six classroom and came closer.

"What's the time?" I was looking around for Lesley.

"Do I look like a grandfather clock?" James was indignant. "You ought to know me well enough by now to be aware that time means nothing to me."

"How true." I went around the corner to take a

look at the big clock at the end of the corridor. James followed me.

"I've only been gone twenty minutes," I said.

"Gone where?"

"Oh, James! I think I was in your father's town house. It was really lovely there. Gold all over the place. And the candlelight—it was so soft and glowing."

"Yes, not dismal and tasteless like all this," said James, with a gesture that took in the mainly gray corridor. I suddenly felt very sorry for him. He wasn't all that much older than me, and his life was already over.

"James, have you ever kissed a girl?"

"What?"

"I asked if you'd ever kissed a girl."

"It's not done to talk about such things, Miss Gwyneth."

"So you've never kissed anyone?"

"I'm a man," said James.

"What kind of answer is that?" I couldn't help laughing at James's expression. "Do you know when you were born?"

"Are you trying to insult me? Of course I know my own birthday. It's on the thirty-first of March."

"What year?"

"1762." James thrust out his chin challengingly. "I was twenty-one three weeks ago. I celebrated at length with my friends in White's Club, and my father paid all my gaming debts in honor of the day and gave me a beautiful bay mare. And then I had to get that stupid fever and go to bed. Only to find everything different when I woke up, and a pert minx telling me I'm a ghost."

"I'm so sorry," I said. "You probably died of the fever."

"Nonsense! It was only a slight indisposition," said James, but there was a look of uncertainty in his eyes. "Dr. Barrow said it was not very likely that I'd have caught the smallpox at Lord Stanhope's."

"Hm," I said. I'd have to Google smallpox to find out more about it.

"*Hm*? What do you mean, *hm*?" James looked offended.

"Oh, there you are!" Lesley came running out of the girls' toilets and flung her arms around my neck. "I've been dying a thousand deaths."

"Nothing too bad happened. I did end up in Mrs. Counter's classroom when I came back, but there was no one there."

"Year Six are visiting Greenwich Observatory today," said Lesley. "My God, am I glad to see you! I told Mr. Whitman you were puking your guts up in the girls' toilets, and he said I should go back to you so I could hold your hair out of your face."

"Disgusting," said James, holding his handkerchief to his nose. "Tell your freckled friend that a lady doesn't talk about such things."

I took no notice of this. "Lesley, something kind of funny's happened . . . something that I can't explain."

"I believe you." Lesley held my mobile out to me. "Here. I took it out of your locker. Call your mother now, right away."

"Lesley, she's at work. I can't just—"

"Call her! You've gone back into the past three times

now, and I saw you do it with my own eyes the third time. All of a sudden you simply weren't there! It was really *terrible*! You must tell your mum, this minute, so that nothing else awful will happen to you. Please." Did Lesley actually have tears in her eyes?

"That freckled girl is in a dramatic mood today," commented James.

I took the mobile from Lesley and breathed deeply.

"Please," Lesley begged.

My mother worked in the administrative office of St. Bartholomew's Hospital. I dialed the number of her direct line, looking at Lesley.

She nodded and tried to smile.

"Gwyneth?" Mum had obviously recognized my mobile number on her display. She sounded worried. I'd never, ever called her from school before. "Is something the matter?"

"Mum . . . I'm not feeling too good."

"Are you sick?"

"I don't know."

"Maybe you've caught that cold that's going around at the moment. I tell you what, go home, go to bed, and I'll leave work early today. Then I'll squeeze you some fresh orange juice and make a warm compress for your throat."

"Mum, it's not a cold. It's worse. I—"

"Maybe it's the smallpox," said James.

Lesley looked at me encouragingly. "Go on!" she said under her breath. "Tell her."

"Darling?"

I took a deep breath. "Mum, I think I'm like Charlotte. I've just been . . . I've no idea when it was. And last night as well . . . in fact it really started yesterday. I was going to tell you, but then I was afraid you wouldn't believe me."

My mother did not reply.

"Mum?"

I looked at Lesley. "She doesn't believe me."

"You're not making any sense," whispered Lesley. "Go on, try again."

But I didn't have to.

"Stay right where you are," said my mother in an entirely different tone. "Wait for me at the school gates. I'm going to take a taxi. I'll be with you as soon as I can."

"But—"

Mum had already broken the connection.

"YOU'LL BE IN dead trouble with Mr. Whitman," I said.

"Who cares?" said Lesley. "I'm staying with you until your mum arrives. Don't you worry about that squirrel. I can wind him around my little finger."

"What have I done?"

"The only right thing," Lesley assured me. I'd told her as much as I could about my brief trip into the past. Lesley thought the girl who looked just like me could have been one of my ancestors.

I didn't think so. Two people couldn't be so similar. Not unless they were identical twins. Lesley thought that was a possible theory too.

"Like in *The Parent Trap,*" she said. "I'll borrow us the DVD when I get a chance."

I felt miserable. When would Lesley and I ever be able to sit comfortably together watching a movie again?

The taxi came sooner than I'd expected. It stopped outside the school gates, and Mum opened the door.

"Jump in," she said.

Lesley squeezed my hand. "Good luck. Call me when you can."

I was almost crying. "Lesley . . . *thank you!*"

"That's okay," said Lesley, who was fighting back tears herself. We always cried at the same places in films too.

I got in the taxi with Mum. I would have liked to fall into her arms, but she was looking so strange that I decided not to.

"The Temple," she told the driver. Then the glass pane between him and the back seat went up, and the taxi drove off.

"Are you angry with me?" I asked.

"No. Of course not, darling. You can't help it."

"No. I can't! It's all stupid old Newton's fault," I said, trying to make a little joke of it. But Mum was in no mood for jokes.

"You can't blame Newton either. If anyone's to blame, it's me. I'd hoped this cup would pass us by."

I looked at her, wide-eyed. "What do you mean?"

"I thought . . . hoped . . . I didn't want you to . . ." My mother never stammered. She looked tensed up, and sadder than I'd seen her since Dad died. "I didn't want to admit it. I've been hoping all this time that Charlotte would be the one."

"Well, everyone was bound to think so! No one would ever think of Sir Isaac Newton getting his sums wrong. Grandmother's going to be furious."

The taxi was threading its way through the dense traffic of Piccadilly.

"Never mind your grandmother," said Mum. "When did it first happen?"

"Yesterday! I was on my way to Selfridges."

"What time?"

"Just after three. I didn't know what to do, so I went back home to our house and rang the bell. But before anyone could open the door, I traveled forward to our own time. Then it happened again last night. I hid in the built-in cupboard, but there was someone sleeping there. A servant. Rather an angry servant. He chased me all over the house, and everyone was looking for me because they thought I was a thief. Thank goodness, I traveled back before they could find me. And the third time was just now. At school. This time I must have gone further back in time, because people were wearing wigs. . . . Mum! If this is going to happen to me every few hours now, I'll never be able to lead a normal life again! And all because silly old Newton . . ." But even I realized that I was milking the Newton joke too hard.

"You ought to have told me at once!" Mum caressed my head. "So much could have happened to you!"

"I wanted to tell you, but last night you said we have too much imagination in our family already."

"I didn't mean it that way. . . . You haven't had the slightest preparation for this. I'm so sorry."

"But it's not your fault, Mum! How could anyone have known?"

"It's my fault," said Mum. After a short, uncomfortable pause, she added, "You were born on the same day as Charlotte."

"No, I wasn't! My birthday is the eighth of October—hers is the seventh."

"You were both born on the seventh of October, Gwyneth."

I couldn't believe what she was saying. I could only stare at her.

"I lied about the date of your birth," Mum went on. "It wasn't difficult. You were born at home, and the midwife who made out the birth certificate understood what we wanted."

"But *why*?"

"It was only to protect you, darling."

I didn't understand. "Protect me? What from? It's happened now, anyway."

"We . . . I wanted you to have a normal childhood. A carefree childhood." Mum was looking intently at me. "And you might not have inherited the gene, after all."

"Even though I was born on the day worked out by Newton?"

"I'm sorry," said Mum. "And do stop going on about Sir Isaac Newton. He's only one of many who have put their minds to this matter. It's much bigger than you know. Much bigger and much older, much more powerful. And much more dangerous. I wanted to keep you out of it."

"Out of what?"

Mum sighed. "It was stupid of me. I ought to have known better. Please forgive me."

"Mum!" My voice almost broke. "I haven't the faintest idea what you're talking about." My confusion and desperation had been growing with every word she said. "All I know is that something is happening to me that shouldn't happen at all. And it's . . . it's making me a nervous wreck! I have a dizzy fit every few hours, and then I travel back into another time. I don't know how to stop it."

"That's why we're on our way to see *them*," said Mum. I could tell that my desperation hurt her. I'd never seen her look so worried before.

"And *they* are . . . ?"

"The Guardians," my mother replied. "A very old secret society, also known as the Lodge of Count Saint-Germain." She looked out the taxi window. "We're nearly there."

"Secret society! You want to take me to one of those weird sect things? Mum!"

"It's not a sect. But there's certainly something rather weird about them." Mum took a deep breath and briefly closed her eyes. "Your grandfather was a member of the Lodge," she went on. "And his father before him, and so on.

Sir Isaac Newton was a member, like Wellington; Klaproth the chemist; von Arneth the historian; Hahnemann, who thought up homeopathy; Charles of Hesse, who knew all about alchemy and astrology; and of course all the de Villiers family, with many, many more. Your grandmother claims that Churchill and Einstein were also members of the Lodge."

Most of those names meant nothing to me. "But what do they *do*?"

"That's . . . well," said Mum, "they concern themselves with ancient myths. And with time. And with people like you."

"Are there more like me, then?"

Mum shook her head. "Only twelve of you in all. And most of them died long ago."

The taxi stopped and the glass panel went down. Mum handed the driver some banknotes. "Keep the change," she said.

"But what are we doing here, of all places?" I asked as we stood on the pavement while the taxi moved off again. We'd driven down the Strand until just before Fleet Street. All around us was the noise of the city traffic. Crowds pushed and shoved their way along. The cafés and restaurants opposite were full to bursting, two red double-decker sightseeing buses stood beside the road, and the tourists on the open top decks were taking photographs of the monumental complex of buildings that was the Royal Courts of Justice.

"Among the buildings over there is the way into the Temple precincts." Mum put my hair back from my face.

I looked the way she was pointing and saw a narrow pedestrian thoroughfare. I couldn't remember ever having gone along it before.

Mum must have noticed my blank expression. "Didn't you ever get taken to the Temple from school?" she asked. "Temple Church and the gardens are well worth seeing. And Fountain Court. For my money, it's the prettiest fountain in the whole city."

I looked at her furiously. Had she suddenly mutated into a tourist guide?

"Come on, we have to cross the road," she said, taking my hand. We followed a group of Japanese tourists, all of them with large London street maps held up in front of their faces.

Behind the row of buildings, we were in an entirely different world. Gone was the hurry and bustle of the Strand and Fleet Street. Here, among the majestic, timeless buildings ranged side by side, no gaps between them, peace and quiet suddenly reigned.

I pointed to the tourists. "What are they looking for here? The prettiest fountain in the whole city?"

"They've come to see Temple Church," said my mother, ignoring my tone of annoyance. "Very old, full of myths and legends. The Japanese love all that. And Shakespeare's *Twelfth Night* was first performed in Middle Temple Hall."

We followed the Japanese for a while and then turned

left and walked along a paved path running past the buildings and turning several corners. It was almost like being in the country. Birds sang, bees hummed in the well-stocked flower beds, and even the air seemed fresh and clear.

Finally, Mum stopped. "Here we are," she said.

It was a plain building, and in spite of its immaculate façade and freshly painted window frames, it looked very old. My eyes went to the names on the brass plate, but Mum pushed me through the open door and took me up a flight of stairs to the first floor. Two young women coming down the stairs said a friendly good day.

"Where is this?" I asked.

Mum didn't reply. She pressed a bell, adjusted her blazer, and pushed her hair back from her face.

"Don't worry," she said, and I didn't know whether she meant me or herself.

The door hummed and opened, and we entered a bright room that looked like a perfectly ordinary office. Filing cabinets, desk, telephone, fax, computer . . . even the middle-aged blonde behind the desk didn't look out of the ordinary. Her glasses were a bit alarming, that was all: jet black and with such big rims that the frames hid half her face.

"How can I help you?" she asked. "Oh, it's you—Miss . . . Mrs. Montrose?"

"Shepherd," Mum corrected her. "I married. I don't use my maiden name anymore."

"Ah, of course." The woman smiled. "But you haven't

changed at all. I'd have known you anywhere by your hair." Her glance fell briefly on me. "Is this your daughter? I expect she takes after her father. How are you . . . ?"

Mum cut her short. "Mrs. Jenkins, I have to speak to my mother and Mr. de Villiers. It's urgent."

"I'm afraid your mother and Mr. de Villiers are in a meeting." Mrs. Jenkins smiled regretfully. "Do you have much—"

Mum interrupted her again. "I want to be at that meeting."

"Well . . . that . . . you know that's not possible."

"Then make it possible. Tell them I'm bringing the Ruby."

"What? But . . ." Mrs. Jenkins looked from Mum to me and back again.

"Please just do as I say." I'd never heard my mother sound so determined.

Mrs. Jenkins stood up and came around the desk. She examined me from head to foot, and I felt terrible in my ugly school uniform. I hadn't washed my hair that morning, and it was just held back in a ponytail by a rubber band. I wasn't wearing any makeup either. "Are you sure about this?"

"Of course I'm sure. Do you think I'd make some silly joke out of such a thing? Hurry, please. We may not have much time."

"Well—please wait here." Mrs. Jenkins turned and disappeared through another door between two shelves of files.

"The Ruby?" I asked.

"Yes," said Mum. "Each of the time travelers is represented by a gemstone. You're the Ruby."

"How do you know?"

"The first pair Opal and Amber are, Agate sings in B flat, the wolf avatar, A duet—solutio!—*with Aquamarine. Mighty Emerald next, with lovely Citrine. The Carnelian twins of the Scorpio sign, Number Eight is* digestio, *her stone is Jade fine. E major's the key of the Black Tourmaline, Sapphire sings in F major, and bright is her sheen. Then almost at once comes Diamond alone, whose sign of the lion as Leo is known.* Projectio! *Time flows on, both present and past, Ruby red is the first and is also the last."* Mum looked at me with a rather sad smile. "I still know it off by heart."

For some reason, her performance gave me goose bumps. It had sounded more like a magic spell than a poem, the kind of thing that wicked witches mutter in films while they stir a cauldron with green vapors rising from it.

"What's all that supposed to mean?"

"It's only a memory jingle, thought up by secretive old men to make something complicated sound even more complex," said Mum. "Twelve numbers, twelve time travelers, twelve gemstones, twelve musical keys, twelve Zodiacal ascendants, twelve steps in the alchemical process of making the philosopher's stone—"

"Philosopher's stone? What's that supposed to—?" I stopped short and sighed. I was tired of asking questions, and every answer left me more confused.

Mum didn't seem to want to answer me either. She was looking out the window. "Nothing's changed here, anyway. It's as if time has stood still."

"Did you come here a lot when you were younger?"

"My father sometimes brought me with him," said Mum. "He was a bit more outgoing about it all than my mother. About the secrets too. I liked it here as a child. And then later, when Lucy . . ." She sighed.

For a while I wondered whether to ask more questions or not, and then my curiosity won out. "Great-aunt Maddy told me Lucy is another time traveler. Is that why she ran away?"

"Yes," said Mum.

"And where did she run away to?"

"No one knows." Mum ran her fingers through her hair again. She was obviously worked up. I'd never known her to be so nervous. I'd have felt sorry for her if my own nerves hadn't been stretched to the breaking point.

We said nothing for a while. Mum looked out the window again.

"So I'm a ruby," I said. "Those are red, aren't they?"

Mum nodded.

"And what gemstone is Charlotte?"

"She isn't one," said Mum.

"Mum, do I by any chance have a twin sister you forgot to tell me about?"

Mum turned to me and smiled. "No, darling, you don't."

"Are you sure?"

"Quite sure. I was there at your birth, wasn't I?"

I heard footsteps somewhere, quickly coming closer. Mum sat up very straight, breathing deeply. Aunt Glenda came through the doorway with Mrs. Jenkins, and behind her a small, elderly man with a bald patch.

Aunt Glenda looked angry. "Grace! Mrs. Jenkins says you said—"

"It's true," said Mum. "And I don't want to waste Gwyneth's time convincing you, of all people, of the truth. I want to see Mr. de Villiers at once. Gwyneth has to be read into the chronograph."

"But that's completely ridiculous!" Aunt Glenda was almost screeching. "Charlotte has—"

"Not traveled in time yet, right?" Mum turned to the stout little man with the bald patch. "I'm sorry. I know I've met you, but I don't remember your name."

"George," he said. "Thomas George. And you are Lady Arista's younger daughter, Grace. I remember you very well."

"Mr. George," said Mum. "Of course. You came to see us in Durham when Gwyneth was born. I remember you too. This is Gwyneth. She's the Ruby you're waiting for."

"That's impossible!" said Aunt Glenda shrilly. "Utterly, totally impossible! Gwyneth was born on the wrong day. And two months premature. An underdeveloped little thing. Look at her."

Mr. George was already doing just that, scrutinizing me with a pair of friendly, pale blue eyes. I tried to look back with as much composure as possible and hide my discomfort. Underdeveloped little thing! Aunt Glenda must have lost her marbles! I was not underdeveloped. I was nearly five feet six inches tall, my bra was a size-B cup, and much to my annoyance, I was growing out of it!

"She traveled for the first time yesterday," said Mum. "I just don't want anything to happen to her. The risk grows with every uncontrolled journey back in time."

Aunt Glenda laughed sarcastically. "No one will take this seriously. It's just another pathetic attempt to make yourself the center of attention."

"Oh, do be quiet, Glenda! There's nothing I'd like more than to keep out of this whole thing, leaving your Charlotte the thankless part of laboratory guinea pig for fanatical mystery mongers and pseudoscientists obsessed with esoteric subjects! But it just so happens that Charlotte is not the one who's inherited this wretched gene—it's Gwyneth!" Mum's expression was one of rage and contempt. I was seeing an entirely new side to her.

Mr. George laughed softly. "You don't have a very high opinion of us, Mrs. Shepherd."

Mum shrugged.

"No, no, no!" Aunt Glenda dropped onto one of the office chairs. "I am not prepared to listen to this nonsense anymore. She wasn't even born on the right day. And she was premature." That bit about me being premature seemed to be especially important to her.

"Shall I bring you a cup of tea, Mrs. Montrose?" Mrs. Jenkins whispered.

"Oh, who wants your stupid tea?" spat Aunt Glenda.

"Would anyone else like some tea?"

"Not me, thank you," I said.

Meanwhile Mr. George had turned his pale blue eyes back to me. "Gwyneth. So you've already traveled in time?"

I nodded.

"Where to, if I may ask?"

"Right where I am now," I said.

Mr. George smiled. "I mean, to what period did you go back first?"

"I haven't the faintest idea," I said crossly. "There wasn't a notice up saying what year it was, and when I asked some people, they wouldn't tell me. Listen, I don't *want* this! I want it to stop. Can't you make it stop?"

Mr. George did not reply to that. "Gwyneth came into the world two months before her expected date of birth," he said to no one in particular. "On the eighth of October. I checked the birth certificate and the entry in the civil register myself. And I checked the baby, too."

I wondered what there could be to check about a baby. Whether it was real or not?

"She was born on the evening of the seventh of October," said Mum, and now her voice was trembling a little. "We bribed the midwife to move the time of birth a few hours forward on the birth certificate."

"But *why*?" Mr. George didn't seem to understand that any more than I did.

"Because . . . after all that happened to Lucy, I wanted to spare my child such stress. I wanted to protect her," said Mum. "And I'd hoped she might not have inherited the gene at all and just happened to be born on the same day as the real carrier. After all, Glenda had Charlotte, and everyone's hopes were pinned on her."

"Stop telling lies!" cried Aunt Glenda. "You did it on purpose! Your baby wasn't supposed to be born until December, but you manipulated the pregnancy and risked a premature birth just to have her born on the same day as Charlotte. It didn't work out, though! Your daughter was born a day later."

"It ought to be fairly easy to prove what you say. We must have the name and address of the midwife in our files," said Mr. George, turning to Mrs. Jenkins. "It's important to find her."

"There's no need," said Mum. "You can leave the poor woman alone. She only took a little money from us."

"We just want to ask her a few questions," said Mr. George. "Mrs. Jenkins, please find out where she lives today."

"I'm on my way," said Mrs. Jenkins, disappearing through the side door again.

"Who else knows about this?" asked Mr. George.

"Only my husband knew," said Mum, and now there was a tinge of defiance and triumph in her tone of voice. "And you can't cross-examine him, because I'm afraid he's dead."

"I know," said Mr. George. "Leukemia, wasn't it? Tragic." He began pacing up and down the room. "When did this start, did you say?"

"Yesterday," I replied.

"Three times in the last twenty hours," said Mum. "I'm afraid for her."

"Three times already!" Mr. George stopped pacing. "And when was the last?"

"About an hour ago," I said. "I think." Since these events had begun coming so thick and fast, I'd lost all sense of time.

"Then we have a little while to prepare for everything."

"You can't possibly believe this, Mr. George," said Aunt Glenda. "You know Charlotte. Now look at this girl and compare her with my Charlotte—do you seriously believe that Number Twelve is standing before you? *Ruby red, with G major, the magic of the raven, brings the Circle of Twelve home into safe haven.* Do you believe that?"

"Well, there's always the possibility," said Mr. George. "Although your motives strike me as more than mixed, Mrs. Shepherd."

"That's your problem," said Mum coolly.

"If you really wanted to protect your child, then you ought not to have left her in ignorance for so many years. Time traveling without preparation is very dangerous."

Mum bit her lip. "I just hoped it would be Charlotte who—"

"And so it is!" cried Aunt Glenda. "She's had obvious symptoms for the last two days. It could happen any time now. Perhaps it's happening at this very moment while we waste our time here listening to my jealous little sister's totally outrageous stories."

"Maybe you could switch your brain into gear for a

change, Glenda," said Mum. Suddenly she sounded tired. "Why on earth would we invent such a thing? Who but you would willingly wish something of this kind on her own daughter?"

"I insist on . . ." But Aunt Glenda left whatever she insisted on hanging in the air. "This will all turn out to be a wicked deception. There's already been sabotage, and we know where that led, Mr. George. And now that we're so close to achieving our aims, we really can't make such a terrible mistake again."

"I don't think that's for us to decide," said Mr. George. "Please follow me, Mrs. Shepherd. You too, Gwyneth." He added, with a little smile, "Don't worry, those fanatical mystery mongers and pseudoscientists obsessed with esoteric subjects don't bite."

Devouring Time, blunt thou the lion's paws,
And make the earth devour her own sweet brood;
Pluck the keen teeth from the fierce tiger's jaws,
And burn the long-lived phoenix in her blood.

William Shakespeare, Sonnet xix

SEVEN

WE WERE LED UP a staircase and down a long corridor with sharp angles at every turn, and now and then went up or down a couple of steps. The view from the few windows we passed was different every time. Sometimes we looked out into a large garden, sometimes at another building or a small dark alley. It seemed like an endless journey over wooden parquet and mosaic stone floors, past closed doors, and along lines of chairs, framed oil paintings, and glass-fronted cases full of leather-bound books and porcelain figurines, with statues and suits of armor standing just about everywhere. It was like being in a museum.

Aunt Glenda kept casting venomous glances at Mum. As for Mum, she ignored her sister as best she could. Mum was pale and looked extremely tense. I wanted to take her hand, but then Aunt Glenda would have seen how frightened I was, and that was the last thing I wanted.

We couldn't possibly still have been in the same building. I felt that we'd been through at least three more by the time Mr. George finally stopped and knocked at an enormous wooden door.

The large room we entered was paneled in dark wood, like our dining room at home. The ceiling was dark wood as well. But here everything was almost entirely covered with elaborate carvings, some of them painted. The furniture was dark and massive. The atmosphere ought to have been gloomy and sinister, but daylight was streaming into the room through the tall windows, and you looked out at a garden full of flowers. I could even see the Thames shimmering in the sunlight where the garden ended.

But it wasn't just the view and the light that brightened the place, there was something cheerful about the carvings, in spite of a few ugly grimaces and skulls. It was as if the walls were alive. Lesley would have loved feeling the real-looking rosebuds, the archaic patterns, and the amusing animal heads and searching them for secret mechanisms. There were winged lions, falcons, stars, suns and planets, dragons, unicorns, elves, fairies, trees, and ships, each carving more lifelike than the one before it.

Most impressive of all was the dragon, which seemed to be flying across the ceiling above us. He must have been at least seven yards long from the tip of his wedge-shaped tail to his large, scaly head, and I couldn't take my eyes off him. What a wonderful dragon! I was so spellbound that I almost forgot why we were there . . . or that we weren't alone. Everyone seemed completely surprised to see us.

"It looks as if there are some complications," said Mr. George.

Lady Arista, standing stiff as a board by one of the windows, said, "Grace! Oughtn't you to be at work? And Gwyneth should be at school!"

"There's nowhere we'd sooner be, Mother," said Mum.

Charlotte was sitting on a sofa right under a beautiful mermaid. Each scale in the mermaid's tail was finely carved and painted in every imaginable shade of blue and turquoise. A man in an elegant black suit, wearing black-framed glasses, was leaning against a broad mantelpiece. Even his tie was black. He was examining us with a distinctly gloomy expression, and there was a little boy of about seven clinging to his jacket.

"Grace!" A tall man rose from the desk. He had gray, wavy hair that fell to his broad shoulders like a lion's mane. His eyes were a strikingly light brown, almost the color of amber. His face was much younger than you might have expected from the gray hair that framed it. There was something fascinating about him—once seen, never forgotten, I felt sure. When the man smiled, you could see his regular white teeth. "Grace. It's been a long time." He came around the desk and offered Mum his hand. "You haven't changed at all."

To my astonishment, Mum blushed. "Thanks. I could say the same of you, Falk."

"I've gone gray." The man made a dismissive gesture.

"I'd say it suits you," said Mum.

Hello? Was she by any chance flirting with this guy?

His smile broadened a little and then his amber gaze moved from Mum to me. Once again, I felt I was being inspected uncomfortably closely.

Those eyes were really strange. They could have been the eyes of a wolf, or one of the big cats. He held out his hand. "I'm Falk de Villiers. And you must be Grace's daughter Gwyneth." His handshake was firm and warm. "The first Montrose girl I've ever known not to have red hair."

"I get my hair from my father," I said shyly.

"Could we perhaps come to the point?" asked the man in black by the mantelpiece.

Mr. de Villiers let go of my hand and looked at me with a twinkle in his eyes. "Go ahead."

"My sister's come up with an absolutely monstrous story," said Aunt Glenda. You could tell what an effort it cost her not to shout. "And Mr. George wouldn't listen to me! She claims that Gwyneth—*Gwyneth!*—has already traveled back in time. And not just once, three times already. Of course, as she knows perfectly well, she can't prove it, so she's thought up another fairy tale to explain the fact that the girl's date of birth is wrong. I'd like to remind you what happened seventeen years ago. Grace did not play a very admirable part in those events. Now that we're so close to success, I'm not surprised to see her turning up here to sabotage our plans."

Leaving her place by the window, Lady Arista had

come closer. "Is this true, Grace?" Her expression, as always, was stern and unyielding. Sometimes I wondered whether her hair, combed back so severely from her face, was the reason her features were so rigid. Maybe the muscles were simply held in one place and stuck there. At the very most, a slight widening of her eyes showed when she was upset. Like now.

"Mrs. Shepherd says she and her husband paid the midwife to enter the wrong date on the birth certificate," Mr. George interjected. "So that no one would find out that Gwyneth was a potential gene carrier."

"But why would she have done such a thing?" asked Lady Arista.

"She says she wanted to protect the child, and anyway she hoped that Charlotte had inherited the gene."

"*Hoped!* You must be joking!" cried Aunt Glenda.

"I think it sounds perfectly logical," said Mr. George.

I glanced at Charlotte, who was sitting on the sofa looking pale, her eyes moving from one to another of us. When they met mine, she quickly turned her head away

"I simply can't see any logic in it," said Lady Arista.

"We're having the story checked," said Mr. George. "Mrs. Jenkins will track down the midwife."

"Just out of interest, Grace, how much did you pay her?" asked Falk de Villiers. His eyes had narrowed more and more over the last minute, and now, as he turned to Mum, there was something very wolflike about him.

"I . . . I can't remember," said Mum.

Mr. de Villiers raised his eyebrows. "Well, it can't have been a large sum. As far as I recall, your husband's income was rather . . . modest."

"How true!" said Aunt Glenda venomously.

"If you all say so, then it can't have been much," replied Mum. The uncertainty that had suddenly come over her disappeared just as suddenly. So had the tinge of pink in her face.

"Then why did the midwife do as you wanted?" asked Mr. de Villiers. "After all, she was falsifying an official document. That's not a small offense."

Mum tilted her chin. "We told her our family belonged to a satanic cult with a pathological belief in horoscopes. We said a child born on the seventh of October would be subject to severe reprisals and we'd have to give her up to the cult for use in satanic rituals. She believed us. And as she had a soft heart, and what you might call a prejudice against Satanists, she entered the wrong birth date on the certificate."

"Satanic rituals! What impertinence!" The man by the mantelpiece hissed the words like a snake, and the little boy clung even closer to him.

Mr. de Villiers smiled appreciatively. "Not a bad story. We'll see if the midwife tells the same tale."

"I see little point in wasting our time checking such details," Lady Arista remarked.

"Quite right," said Aunt Glenda. "Charlotte could travel back in time any moment now. Then we'll know that Grace's story is a pack of lies devised to hold us up."

"Why couldn't they both have inherited the gene?" asked Mr. George. "That happened once before."

"Ah, but Timothy and Jonathan de Villiers were identical twins," pointed out Mr. de Villiers. "And they'd been foretold in the prophesies."

"Yes, the chronograph contains two carnelians for them, two pipettes of blood, duplicate compartments for the twelve elements, and two cogwheels going around," said the man by the mantelpiece. "The Ruby stands alone."

"True," said Mr. George. His round face suddenly became anxious.

"I should have thought it more important to look into the reason why my sister is telling these lies." Aunt Glenda was glaring at Mum with positive hatred. "If your idea is to get Gwyneth's blood read into the chronograph so that the device will never be of any use again, you're more naive than I thought."

"How can she expect us to believe a word of what she says anyway?" asked the man by the mantelpiece. I thought his way of acting as if Mum and I weren't even in the room was very arrogant. "I have the clearest recollections of the lies Grace told to protect Lucy and Paul at that time. It was her fault they got away from us. If it hadn't been for her, we might have been able to avert the disaster."

"Jake!" said Mr. de Villiers.

"What disaster?" I asked. And who was Paul?

"I consider that even the presence of this person in the room with us is monstrous," said the man by the mantelpiece.

"And who may you be?" Mum's voice and the look she gave him were decidedly chilly. I was impressed to see she wasn't going to be intimidated.

"That's nothing to do with the case." The man didn't even deign to look at her. The little fair-haired boy peered cautiously out from behind his back and looked at me. With the freckles on his nose, he reminded me a bit of Nick when he was younger, so I smiled at him. Poor little thing—he probably had to put up with this creep for a grandfather. His eyes widening in surprise, he returned my smile and then went back into cover behind the man's black jacket.

"This is Dr. Jacob White," said Falk de Villiers, with an unmistakable tone of amusement in his voice. "A genius in the fields of medicine and biochemistry. He's usually a bit more civil."

Jacob Gray would have suited him better. Even his face was the color of dishwater.

Mr. de Villiers looked at me and then his eyes went back to Mum. "Well, one way or another, we have to come to a decision. Are we to believe you, Grace, or do you really have some ulterior motive?"

For a few seconds Mum stared at him angrily. Then she looked down and said quietly, "I'm not here to prevent you all from carrying out your wonderful, mysterious mission. I'm here to keep my daughter out of harm's way. With the help of the chronograph, she can travel in time without danger while still leading a reasonably normal life. That's all I want."

"Oh, yes, *of course!*" said Aunt Glenda. She went over to the sofa and sat down beside Charlotte. I'd have liked to sit too. My legs were beginning to feel tired. But no one offered me a chair, so there was nothing for it but to stay on my feet.

"What I did at that time had nothing to do with your . . . *mission*," Mum went on. "To be honest, I hardly know anything about it, and I understand only about half of what I've picked up over the years."

"I can't imagine," said the gloomy Dr. White, "what gave you the audacity to interfere in such a way with matters of which you know nothing."

"I only wanted to help Lucy," said Mum. "She was my darling little niece. I'd looked after her since she was a baby, and she asked for my help. What would you have done in my place? For goodness' sake, the pair of them were so young, so much in love, and . . . I simply didn't want anything to happen to them."

"Well, a fine way you chose to go about it!"

"I loved Lucy like a sister." Mum glanced at Aunt Glenda. "*More* than a sister," she added.

Aunt Glenda took Charlotte's hand and patted it. Charlotte stared at the floor.

"We *all* loved Lucy dearly," said Lady Arista. "That made it all the more important to keep her away from that boy and his outlandish opinions, rather than encouraging her to indulge her feelings."

"Outlandish opinions, indeed! It was that red-haired

little wretch who put those silly conspiracy theories into Paul's head!" said Dr. White. "She persuaded him to commit the theft!"

"That's not true!" protested Lady Arista. "Lucy would never have done such a thing. It was Paul who took advantage of her youthful naivety and led her astray."

"Naivety! You must be joking!" snapped Dr. White.

Falk de Villiers raised his hand. "We've had this discussion often enough already, and it never gets us anywhere. I think we all know one another's views." He looked at the time. "Gideon will be back any moment now, and before that we ought to decide what to do next. Charlotte, how are you feeling?"

"I still have a headache," said Charlotte, without looking up from the floor.

"There, you see?" Aunt Glenda gave a venomous smile.

"I have a headache too," said Mum. "But that doesn't mean I'm about to start traveling in time."

"You're . . . you're just so horrible!" said Aunt Glenda.

"I think we should simply assume that Mrs. Shepherd and Gwyneth are telling the truth," said Mr. George, mopping his bald patch with a handkerchief. "Otherwise we'll be losing yet more valuable time."

"You can't be serious, Thomas!" Dr. White struck the mantelpiece with his fist so hard that the silver cup standing on it fell over.

Mr. George jumped, but he went on calmly. "According to what they say, the last time Gwyneth traveled back in time was an hour and a half to two hours ago. We could prepare her for her next journey and record it as closely as possible."

"My own opinion exactly," said Falk de Villiers. "Any objections?"

"I might as well be talking to a brick wall," said Dr. White.

"How true," Aunt Glenda agreed.

"I'd suggest the documents room," said Mr. George. "Gwyneth would be safe there, and then on her return, we could read her straight into the chronograph."

"I wouldn't let her anywhere near the chronograph!" said Dr. White.

"Good heavens, Jake, that's enough," said Mr. de Villiers. "She's only a young girl! Do you think she has a bomb hidden under her school uniform?"

"Her predecessor was only a young girl," said Dr. White in tones of contempt.

Mr. de Villiers nodded to Mr. George. "We'll do as you suggest. Will you see to the arrangements?"

"Come along, Gwyneth," said Mr. George.

I didn't move. "Mum?"

"It's all right, darling. I'll wait here for you." Mum managed a smile.

I glanced at Charlotte, who was still looking at the floor. Aunt Glenda had closed her eyes and was leaning back, resigned. She looked as if she, too, suddenly had a bad headache. My grandmother, on the other hand, was staring at me as if she was seeing me for the first time. And possibly she was.

The little boy, wide-eyed, peeped out again from behind Dr. White's jacket. Poor little thing. That nasty man hadn't once spoken to him. He acted as if he were transparent.

"See you later, darling," said Mum.

Mr. George took my arm and smiled at me encouragingly. I smiled hesitantly back. Somehow I liked him. At any rate, he was easily the friendliest of all these people, and the only one who seemed to believe us.

All the same, I didn't feel good about leaving my mum alone. When the door closed behind us and we were in the corridor, I almost started howling *I want to stay with my mummy!* But I pulled myself together.

Mr. George let go of my arm and walked ahead, first going back the way we had come, then through a door into another corridor, up some stairs, through another door into yet another corridor—it was a labyrinth. Torches made of pitch would have been more in keeping, but the corridors had modern lighting, which was nearly as bright as daylight.

"It seems confusing at first, but after a while you get to know your way around here," said Mr. George.

He went down more stairs, this time a broad stone spiral staircase that seemed to wind its way forever down into the ground. "The Knights Templars erected this building in the twelfth century. The Romans had tried building here before them, and before the Romans, the Celts. It was a sacred place to them all, and nothing has ever been changed to this day. One can feel how special it is, don't you agree? As if some great power came from this plot of ground."

I couldn't feel anything of the kind. All I felt was tired and weak. I needed more sleep to make up for last night.

When we reached the end of the staircase, we took a sharp right turn and suddenly found ourselves facing a young man. I nearly smacked my head right into his chest.

"Oops!" said Mr. George.

"Mr. George." The young guy had dark, curly hair that fell almost to his shoulders, and such bright green eyes that I thought he must be wearing colored lenses. Although I had never seen him before, I recognized him immediately. I'd have known his voice anywhere. This was the guy I'd seen on my last journey back in time.

Or more precisely, the one who'd kissed my doppelganger while I was hiding behind the curtain in disbelief.

Again, I couldn't stop staring at him. From the front, and without the wig, he looked even better—a thousand times better. I completely forgot that Lesley and I normally didn't like boys with long hair. Lesley thought they let it grow just to hide their jug ears.

He looked back with a touch of irritation, examined me briefly from head to foot, and then looked inquiringly at Mr. George.

"Gideon, this is Gwyneth Shepherd," said Mr. George, with a little sigh. "Gwyneth, this is Gideon de Villiers."

Gideon de Villiers. The polo player. The other time traveler.

"Hello," he said politely.

"Hello." Why was my voice hoarse all of a sudden?

"I think you two will be getting to know each other better." Mr. George laughed nervously. "It's possible that Gwyneth is our new Charlotte."

"What?" His green eyes scrutinized me again, this time only my face. All I could do was stare back at him stupidly.

"It's a very complicated story," said Mr. George. "You'd better go up to the Dragon Hall and let your uncle explain."

Gideon nodded. "I was on my way up in any case. See you, Mr. George. Good-bye for now, Winnie."

Who was Winnie?

"Gwyneth," Mr. George corrected him, but Gideon had already turned the corner. The sound of his footsteps died away on the stairs.

"I'M SURE YOU MUST have a great many questions," said Mr. George. "I'll answer them as well as I can."

I was glad to be able to sit down at last. I stretched my legs out in front of me. The documents room had turned out to be really comfortable, even if it had no windows and was deep down in a vaulted cellar. A fire was burning on a hearth, and there were bookshelves and bookcases all around, as well as wing chairs that looked inviting and the broad sofa on which I was now sitting. When we had come in, someone had risen from a chair at the desk, nodded to Mr. George, and left the room without a word.

"Was that man mute?" I asked. It was the first thing to come into my head.

"No," said Mr. George. "But he's taken a vow of silence. He isn't going to speak for the next four weeks."

"What good will that do him?"

"It's a ritual. The adepts have to pass a whole series of tests before being accepted into our Outer Circle. It's particularly important for them to prove that they are discreet." Mr. George smiled. "You must think us really odd. Here, take this flashlight and hang it around your neck."

"What's going to happen to me now?"

"We're waiting for your next journey back in time."

"When will that be?"

"Oh, no one can tell exactly. It's said that your distant ancestress Elaine Burghley, the second of the Circle of Twelve to be born, traveled only five times in her entire life. But then she died in childbirth at the age of eighteen. The count himself used to travel every few hours as a young man, two to seven times a day. You can imagine what a dangerous life he lived until he finally understood how to use the chronograph." Mr. George pointed to the oil painting over the hearth. "That's him, by the way. Count Saint-Germain."

"Seven times a day!" That would be terrible. I'd never get a proper night's sleep or be able to go to school.

"Don't worry. When it happens, you'll land in this room—at what period we don't know—and you'll be safe here anyway. Then just wait until you travel back. You mustn't move from the room. If by any chance you meet anyone, show this ring." Mr. George took his signet ring off his finger and handed it to me. I turned it in my hand and looked at the engraving. It was a twelve-pointed star with intertwined letters in the middle. My clever friend Lesley had been right again.

"Our English and history teacher, Mr. Whitman, has one of these too."

"Is that a question?" The fire on the hearth was reflected on Mr. George's bald patch. It was kind of a cozy sight.

I shook my head. I didn't need an answer. It was obvious: Mr. Whitman was one of these people.

"Isn't there anything else you want to know?"

"Yes, I want to know who Paul is and what happened to Lucy. And what this theft they committed was. And what my mum did back then to make everyone so cross with her." It all came bursting out of me.

"Oh." Mr. George scratched his head, looking embarrassed. "I'm afraid I can't tell you that."

"Figures," I sighed.

"Gwyneth. If you really are our Number Twelve, then we'll explain it all to you in detail, I promise. But we have to be sure first. However, I'll be happy to answer other questions."

I sat in silence.

Mr. George sighed. "Oh, very well. Paul is the younger brother of Falk de Villiers. He was Number Nine in the Circle of Twelve, the last of the de Villiers line to travel in time before Gideon. That will have to do for now. If you have anything to ask of a less inflammatory nature . . ."

"Is there a loo down here?"

"Oh. Yes, of course, just around the corner. I'll show you the way."

"I can find it for myself."

"Of course," Mr. George replied, but he followed me to the door like a small, stout shadow anyway. There, like a soldier on guard in front of Buckingham Palace, stood the man who had taken the vow of silence.

"The next door along." Mr. George pointed to the left. "I'll wait here."

In the ladies' room—a small place smelling of disinfectant with a loo and a washbasin—I took my mobile out of my pocket. No reception, of course. I'd have loved to tell Lesley about all this. At least the time display was working, and I was surprised to see that it was only noon. I felt as if I'd been here for days. I did actually need the loo.

When I came out again, Mr. George smiled at me in relief. He'd obviously been afraid I might have disappeared while I was in there.

In the documents room, I sat down on the sofa again, and Mr. George sat opposite me in an armchair.

"Well, let's go on with our question and answer game," he said. "But taking turns this time. I ask a question, you ask the next."

"Okay," I said. "You first."

"Are you thirsty?"

"Yes, I'd like some water, if there is any. Or tea."

Sure enough, there was water down here, and fruit juice and wine, as well as a kettle for tea. Mr. George made us a pot of Earl Grey.

"Your turn now," he said, sitting down again.

"If this time-travel business depends on a gene, how come a person's date of birth is so important? Why didn't they take some blood from Charlotte ages ago and test it for the gene? And why can't the chronograph send her back to some safe time in the past before she travels of her own accord and maybe gets into danger?"

"Well, first, we only *think* it depends on a gene—we don't know for certain. All we're sure of is that it's something in the blood making the carriers different from normal people. But we haven't found Factor X—as we call the time travel gene—although we've been working on research for many years, and you'll find many of the best scientists in the world in our ranks. Believe me, it would make things much easier if we could prove the existence of the gene or whatever it is in the blood. As it is, we have to rely on calculations and observations made by generations of people before us."

"If the chronograph had been tanked up with Charlotte's blood, what would have happened?"

"In the worst case it wouldn't have worked anymore," said Mr. George. "But, Gwyneth, we're talking about a tiny drop of blood—it's not like filling up a car! My turn now. If you could choose a time, when would you most like to travel back to?"

I thought about it. "Not very far back. Only ten years. Then I could see my father again and talk to him."

Mr. George looked at me sympathetically. "A very understandable wish, but I'm afraid it won't do. You can't travel back within your own lifetime. The closest you can come to that is the time just before your birth."

"Oh." That was a pity. I'd imagined traveling back to when I was at nursery school and a boy named Gregory Forbes called me an ugly toad in the school yard and kicked my shin four times. I'd have walked in like Superwoman, and Gregory Forbes would never have kicked little girls again, that was for sure.

"Your turn again," said Mr. George.

"I was supposed to draw a chalk circle at the place where Charlotte disappeared. What would the point of that have been?"

Mr. George waved the question away. "Forget all that nonsense. Your aunt Glenda insisted on it so that we could have the place guarded. Then we'd have sent Gideon back to the past to describe the position, so that the Guardians would be waiting for Charlotte and could protect her until she traveled back."

"Yes, but you couldn't have known what time she'd gone back to. So the Guardians might have been watching that place all around the clock for years on end."

"Right," sighed Mr. George. "Exactly! Now my turn again. Can you remember your grandfather?"

"Of course. I was ten when he died. He wasn't at all

like Lady Arista—he was funny and far from strict. He always used to tell my brother and me horror stories. Did you know him yourself?"

"Oh, yes. He was my mentor and my best friend." Mr. George looked thoughtfully at the fire for a while.

"Who was the little boy?" I asked.

"What little boy?"

"That little boy just now clinging to Dr. White's jacket."

"What?" Mr. George turned away from the fire and looked at me, bewildered.

Oh, really! I could hardly have put it more plainly. "That fair-haired little boy, about seven years old. He was standing beside Dr. White," I said, speaking deliberately slowly.

"But there was no little boy there," said Mr. George. "Are you making fun of me?"

"No," I said. All at once I knew what I'd seen, and I was annoyed with myself for not realizing immediately.

"A fair-haired little boy of about seven, you say?"

"It was nothing." I pretended to take a burning interest in the books on the shelf behind me.

Mr. George said no more about it, but I could feel his inquiring glance resting on me.

"My turn again," he said at last.

"This is a silly game. Couldn't we play chess instead?" There was a chess set on the table. But Mr. George wasn't going to be put off.

"Do you sometimes see things that other people don't?"

"Little boys are not *things*," I said, "but yes, I do sometimes see things when other people don't." Even I didn't know why I told him that.

For some reason or other, he seemed pleased by my admission. "Remarkable, really remarkable. How long have you had this gift?"

"Always."

"Fascinating." Mr. George looked around. "Do please tell me who else is sitting here, listening in on us."

"We're alone." I couldn't help laughing a little at Mr. George's disappointed expression.

"Oh, dear, I could have sworn this building was teeming with ghosts. This room in particular." He sipped tea from his cup. "Would you like some Jaffa Cakes?"

"That sounds great." And then—I didn't know if it was because he'd mentioned food—I suddenly had that queasy sensation in my stomach again. I held my breath.

Mr. George got to his feet and searched a cupboard. The dizzy sensation was growing stronger. Mr. George was going to get a surprise when he turned around to see that I'd simply disappeared. Maybe I ought to give him advance warning. For all I knew, he had a weak heart.

"Mr. George?"

"And it's your turn again, Gwyneth." He was arranging the cookies carefully on a plate, almost the way Mr. Bernard did. "And I think I know the answer to your next question."

I paid attention to what was going on inside me. The dizziness was dying down a bit.

Okay, false alarm.

"Right, so suppose I traveled to a time when this building didn't exist yet. Would I land underground and be suffocated?"

"Oh, I thought you were going to ask about the little fair-haired boy. Very well. According to our present state of knowledge, no one has ever traveled farther back than five hundred years. And on the chronograph we can set the date of time travel for the Ruby, meaning you, only as far back as AD 1560, the year when the first time traveler in the Circle, Lancelot de Villiers, was born. We have often regretted these restrictions. One misses out on so many very interesting years. . . . Here, have a cookie. These are my favorite."

I reached for the plate, although it was suddenly going all blurred before my eyes and I felt as if someone was going to pull the sofa away from under me.

MALE LINE OF DESCENT

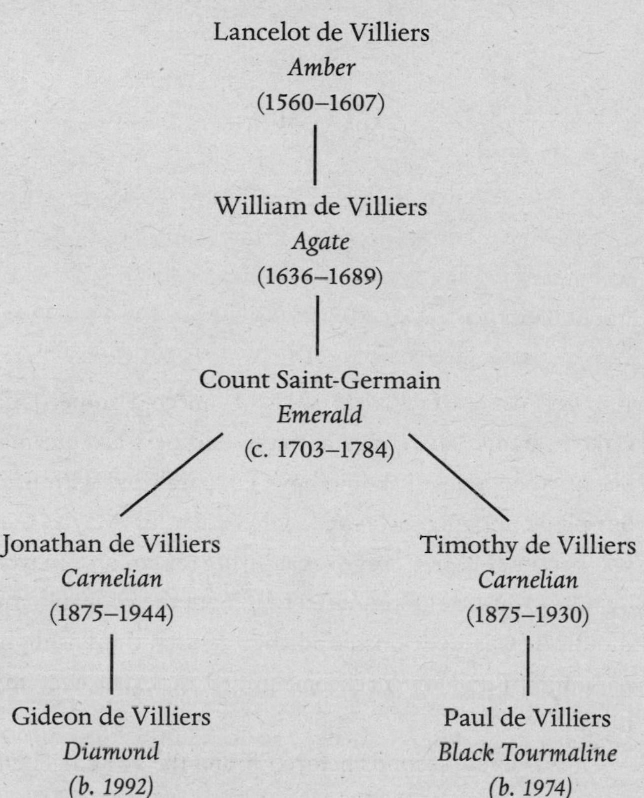

FROM *THE CHRONICLES OF THE GUARDIANS,*
VOLUME 4: *THE CIRCLE OF TWELVE*

EIGHT

I LANDED BOTTOM FIRST on cold stone, Jaffa Cake in hand. There was absolute darkness around me, blacker than black. I should have felt paralyzed with fear, but oddly enough, I wasn't frightened at all. Maybe that was because of Mr. George's reassuring remarks, or maybe by now I was just getting used to it. I put the cookie in my mouth (it was delicious!) and then felt for the flashlight hanging around my neck and pulled the cord over my head.

It was a few seconds before I found the switch. Then, in the beam of the flashlight, I saw the bookshelves and recognized the fireplace (cold and without a fire in it, unfortunately). The oil painting over it was the one I'd seen already, the portrait of the time traveler with his curled white wig, Count Thingummy. All the place really needed was a few armchairs and little tables and—of course—the comfortable sofa where I'd been sitting just now.

Mr. George had said I was simply to wait until I traveled back. And I might have done just that if the sofa had still been here. But it couldn't hurt to peek outside the door.

I cautiously made my way over to it. The door was locked. Oh, well, at least I didn't need the loo anymore.

I searched the room by the beam of the flashlight. Maybe I'd find something to tell me what year I'd landed in. There might be a calendar on the wall or lying on the desk.

The desk was covered with rolled-up papers, books, opened letters, and little boxes. The beam of my light fell on an inkwell and some quill pens. I picked up a sheet of paper. It had a rough, heavy texture, and the handwriting was so full of ornate flourishes that it was difficult to decipher.

"My dear and highly respected Doctor," it said. *"Your letter reached me today, having been on its way for a mere nine weeks. Considering what a long journey your entertaining account of the present situation in the colonies has made, one can only marvel at such speed."*

That made me smile. Nine weeks for a letter to arrive! Okay, so I seemed to be in a period when letters were still delivered by carrier pigeon. Or maybe snail mail—using actual snails.

I sat on the chair at the desk and read a couple of other letters. Rather boring stuff, and the names meant nothing to me either. Then I investigated the little boxes. The first one I opened was full of seals with elaborate designs on them, for sealing letters. I looked for a twelve-pointed star, but there were only crowns, intertwined letters, and organic patterns. Very pretty. And I found sticks of sealing wax in every color, even gold and silver.

The next little box was locked. Maybe there was a key in one of the desk drawers. I was beginning to enjoy my treasure hunt. If I liked what I found in the box, I'd take it back with me. As a kind of test. The cookie had traveled without a problem. I'd bring Lesley back a little souvenir. Surely that was allowed, since the box was neither human nor animal.

I found more quill pens and bottles of ink in the desk drawers. Letters, carefully folded and tied up, bound notebooks, a kind of dagger, a little crescent-shaped knife—and keys.

Lots and lots of keys, of all shapes and sizes. Lesley would have loved this. Probably there was a lock in this room for every one of these keys, and a little secret behind the lock. Or a treasure.

I tried some of the keys that looked small enough for the lock of the little box, but I couldn't find the right one. What a shame. There was probably valuable jewelry in it. Maybe I should just take the whole box. But it was a rather awkward shape for that, and much too big to fit neatly in the inside pocket of my jacket.

There was a pipe in the next box. A pretty one, elaborately carved, probably made of ivory, but that wasn't right for Lesley either. Maybe I should take her one of the seals? Or the pretty dagger? Or a book?

Of course I knew I shouldn't steal, but this was an exceptional situation, and I thought I had a right to some compensation. Also I had to see whether I could take objects from the past back to the present with me. I didn't have any guilty conscience, which surprised me, since I was usually disapproving when Lesley nibbled more than one of the free samples in the Harrods delicatessen department or—like only the other day—picked a flower in the park.

I couldn't decide. The dagger looked like it was probably the most valuable thing. If the stones in the handle were real, then it must be worth a fortune. But what would Lesley do with a dagger? I felt sure that she'd like a seal better. Which one, though?

The decision was taken out of my hands, because the dizzy feeling came back. When the desk blurred in front of my eyes, I grabbed the first thing within reach.

I made a soft landing on my feet. Bright light dazzled me. I quickly dropped the key I had snatched up at the last minute into my pocket along with my mobile, and looked around the room. It was just like before, when I was having a cup of tea with Mr. George, and the flickering fire in the hearth made the room nice and warm.

But Mr. George wasn't on his own anymore. He was standing in the middle of the room with Falk de Villiers and grumpy gray-faced Dr. White (along with the little fair-haired ghost boy), and they were talking quietly. Gideon de Villiers was leaning back casually against one of the bookcases. He was the first person to notice me.

"Hi, Winnie," he said.

"Gwyneth," I replied. Surely it wasn't that difficult to remember? I didn't go calling him Gilbert or anything.

The other three men turned and stared at me, Dr. White with his eyes narrowed suspiciously, Mr. George obviously delighted.

"That was almost fifteen minutes," he said. "How was it, Gwyneth? Are you feeling all right?"

I nodded.

"Did anyone see you?"

"There wasn't anyone there. I didn't move from the spot, just like you said." I handed Mr. George the flashlight and his signet ring. "Where's my mum?"

"Upstairs with the others," said Mr. de Villiers briefly.

"I want to talk to her."

"Don't worry, you can. Later," said Mr. George. "First . . . oh, I really don't know where to begin." But he was beaming all over his face. What was he so pleased about?

"You've already met my nephew Gideon," said Mr. de Villiers. "He went through the experiences that you are now having two years ago. Although he was better prepared than you've been. It's going to be difficult to make up all the ground you've lost these last few years."

"Difficult? Impossible is how I'd put it," said Dr. White.

"Anyway, there's no need," said Gideon. "I can do it all far better on my own."

"We'll see," said Mr. de Villiers.

"I think you're underestimating the girl," said Mr. George. Then he said, in a solemn, almost unctuous tone of voice, "Gwyneth Shepherd, you are now part of an ancient mystery. And it's high time you heard more about that mystery. In the first place, you should know that—"

"We mustn't go too fast," Dr. White interrupted him. "She may have the gene, but that doesn't mean she can be trusted."

"Or that she has any idea what it's all about," added Gideon.

He obviously thought I was dim.

Stuck-up idiot.

"Who knows what instructions her mother has given her?" said Dr. White. "And who knows who, in turn, gave her mother those instructions? We have only the one chronograph. We can't afford another bad mistake. I'm just suggesting you bear that in mind."

Mr. George looked as if he'd been slapped in the face. "It's possible to make things unnecessarily complicated," he murmured.

"I'll take you to my consulting room now," said Dr. White. "No offense, Thomas, but there'll be time for explanations later."

I felt a cold shudder run down my spine at his words. Going into a room alone with Dr. Frankenstein was the last thing I wanted. "I'd like to see my mum," I said, taking the risk that the rest of them might think I sounded like a toddler.

Gideon scornfully clicked his tongue.

"There's nothing to be afraid of, Gwyneth," Mr. George assured me. "We just need a little of your blood, and Dr.

White will also be responsible for your immunizations and general health. I'm afraid there are all kinds of dangerous infections around in the past, things that the human organism never encounters these days. It will all be over soon."

Did he have any idea how awful that sounded? *We only need a little of your blood,* and *it will all be over soon.*

"But I . . . I don't want to be alone with Dr. Franken . . . Dr. White," I said. I didn't care whether the man thought I was being rude or not. He had no manners himself. As for Gideon—he could think whatever he liked about me!

"Dr. White isn't as . . . as heartless as he may seem to you," said Mr. George. "You really don't have to—"

"Oh, yes, she does!" growled Dr. White.

I was beginning to lose my temper. Who did this pompous guy think he was? Why didn't he go and buy a suit in a nice color instead of tormenting me?

"Do I, though? What will you do if I refuse?" I hissed, noticing at the same time that his eyes were red and inflamed behind those black-rimmed glasses.

Much to my relief, before Dr. White could think what he would do to me if I refused (and my imagination was coming up with some unappetizing ideas at the speed of light), Mr. de Villiers interrupted us. "I'll ask Mrs. Jenkins to go with you," he said. "And Mr. George will stay with you until she arrives."

I cast the doctor a triumphant glance, the kind that's like sticking out your tongue, but he ignored me.

"We'll meet in the Dragon Hall in half an hour's time," Mr. de Villiers went on.

I didn't mean to, but as I was on my way out I turned back once, quickly, to see if my triumph over Dr. White had impressed Gideon. Obviously not, because he was looking at my legs. Probably comparing them with Charlotte's.

Hers were longer and thinner, dammit! And she certainly didn't have scratches all over her calves from clambering about last night among a lot of old junk and a stuffed crocodile.

DR. WHITE'S CONSULTING ROOM looked like any other doctor's. And when he put a white coat on over his suit and washed his hands thoroughly for a long time, Dr. White looked like any other doctor I'd ever seen. Only the little fair-haired ghost boy beside him was rather unusual.

"Jacket off, sleeves up," said Dr. White.

Mr. George translated for him. "Would you please be kind enough to take your jacket off and roll your sleeves up?"

The little ghost was watching, interested. When I smiled at him, he hastily hid behind Dr. White, only to peer out again a second later. "Can you by any chance see me?" he asked.

I nodded.

"Don't look," grunted Dr. White, tying a bandage around one arm.

"I don't mind the sight of blood," I said. "Even when it's my own."

"The others can't see me," said the little ghost.

"I know," I said. "My name's Gwyneth. What's yours?"

"Dr. White to you," said Dr. White.

"I'm Robert," said the ghost.

"That's a very nice name," I said.

"Thank you," said Dr. White. "I'll return the compliment by saying you have very nice veins." I'd hardly felt the needle prick me. Dr. White carefully filled a little tube with my blood. Then he exchanged the full tube for an empty one and filled that too.

"She isn't talking to *you*, Jake," said Mr. George.

"She isn't? Who is she talking to, then?"

"Robert," I said.

Dr. White's head jerked up. He looked straight at me for the first time. "What did you say?"

"Oh, never mind," I said.

Dr. White muttered something to himself that I couldn't make out. Mr. George gave me a conspiratorial smile.

There was a knock on the door, and Mrs. Jenkins, the secretary with the big glasses, came in.

"Ah, there you are at last," said Dr. White. "You can clear out now, Thomas, and Mrs. Jenkins will see to the proprieties. You can sit over there," he told her. "But keep your mouth shut."

"Charming as ever," said Mrs. Jenkins, but she obediently sat down on the chair he pointed out.

"See you soon," said Mr. George to me. He held up one of the little tubes with my blood in it. "I'll just go and put this in the tank," he added with a grin.

"Where's the chronograph kept? And what does it look like?" I asked as the door closed behind Mr. George. "Can you sit in it?"

"The last person to question me about the chronograph stole it nearly two years later." Dr. White took the needle out of my arm and pressed a piece of gauze on my skin to stop the bleeding. "So I'm sure you'll understand that I'm reluctant to answer such questions."

"The chronograph was stolen?"

Robert, the little ghost boy, nodded vigorously.

"By your delightful cousin Lucy herself," said Dr. White. "I remember the first time she sat here. Apparently just as innocent and naive as you seem now."

"Lucy's nice," said Robert. "I like her." Being a ghost, he probably felt as if he'd last seen Lucy only yesterday.

"Lucy stole the chronograph? But why?"

"How would I know? Schizoid personality disturbance, probably," growled Dr. White. "Obviously runs in the family. Hysterical females, all these Montrose women. And Lucy had a great deal of criminal spirit in her."

"Dr. White!" said Mrs. Jenkins. "That's not true!"

"Didn't I tell you to keep your mouth shut?" said Dr. White.

"But if Lucy stole the chronograph, how can it still be here?" I asked.

"How, indeed?" Dr. White undid the strap around my

arm. "There's a second one, of course, you clever child. When was your last tetanus jab?"

"No idea. So there are several chronographs?"

"No, only those two," said Dr. White. "You obviously haven't been vaccinated against variola major." He tapped my upper arm as he examined it. "Any chronic sicknesses? Allergies?"

"No. I haven't been inoculated against the plague either. Or cholera. Or smallpox." I thought of James. "Can you inoculate people against smallpox? I've an idea that a friend of mine died of it."

"I sincerely doubt that," said Dr. White. "Smallpox is just another name for variola major, and no one's died of it for a very long time."

"Well, my friend has been dead for a very long time."

"I thought variola was another name for measles," said Mrs. Jenkins.

"And I thought we'd agreed that you'd keep your mouth shut, Mrs. Jenkins."

Mrs. Jenkins said no more.

"Why are you so unfriendly to everyone?" I asked. "Ouch!"

"That was only a little prick," said Dr. White.

"What was it for, then?"

"Believe me, you really don't want to know."

I sighed. The little ghost called Robert sighed as well. "Is he always like this?" I asked him.

"Mostly," replied Robert.

"He doesn't really mean it." said Mrs. Jenkins.

"Mrs. Jenkins!"

"Oh, very well."

"Well, I'm through with you for now. By next time I'll have your blood group, and maybe your charming mother will be so good as to come up with your inoculation record and any records of illness."

"I've never been ill. Am I inoculated against the plague now?"

"No. Not really worth it. The jab lasts only six months, and the side effects are nasty. And if I have it my way, you'll never travel to a plague year at all. You can put your things back on, and Mrs. Jenkins will take you back up to the others."

Mrs. Jenkins rose from her chair. "Come along, Gwyneth. I'm sure you're hungry, and supper will soon be ready. Mrs. Mallory has roast veal with asparagus on the menu today, delicious."

I certainly was hungry. Even for roast veal with asparagus, and I wasn't normally a big fan of eating baby cows.

"The doctor has a kind heart, really, you know," said Mrs. Jenkins on our way up. "He just finds it rather difficult to be friendly."

"So I notice."

"He used to be quite different. Cheerful, always good-tempered. He did wear those dreadful black suits, even then, but at least with colored ties. That was before his son died—such a tragedy. He's been a different man ever since."

"Robert."

"Yes, the little boy was called Robert," said Mrs. Jenkins. "Has Mr. George been telling you about him?"

"No."

"A dear child. He drowned in a pool at a birthday party. Imagine that." Mrs. Jenkins counted years on her fingers as we walked along. "It was eighteen years ago now. Poor Dr. White."

Poor Robert. But at least he didn't look like a drowned body. Some ghosts thought it was fun to go around looking the way they did when they'd just died. Luckily I'd never yet met one with a hatchet in his head. Or without a head at all.

Mrs. Jenkins knocked at a door. "We'll just look in and say hello to Madame Rossini. She'll want to measure you."

"Measure me? What for?" But the room Mrs. Jenkins let me into gave me the answer. It was a sewing room, and in among the fabrics, clothes, sewing machines, tailor's dummies, scissors, and rolls of thread, a plump lady with a lot of sandy hair stood smiling at me.

"'Allo," she said. She had a slight French accent. "You must be Gwyneth. I am Madame Rossini, and I look after your wardrobe." She held up a tape measure. "We can't have you traveling in time in zat dreadful school uniform, *n'est-ce pas?*"

I nodded. My school uniform really was dreadful, today or any other time.

"There'd probably be a riot if you went out in the street like zat," she added, wringing her hands, tape measure and all, at the sight of it.

"I'm afraid we have to hurry. They're waiting for us upstairs," said Mrs. Jenkins.

"I'll be quick. Can you take that jacket off, pliss?" Madame Rossini put the tape measure around my waist. "Wonderful. Now the 'ips. Ah, like a young colt! I think we can use most of what I made for the other one, with maybe some leetle alterations 'ere and there."

By "the other one" she must mean Charlotte. I looked at a pale yellow dress with white lace trim hanging on a coat stand and looking like one of the costumes for *Pride and Prejudice*. Charlotte would have looked lovely in that.

"Charlotte's taller than me," I said. "And slimmer."

"Yes, a little bit," said Madame Rossini. "Like a coat 'anger." I couldn't help giggling. "But that is no problem." She measured my neck and my head as well. "For the 'ats and the wigs," she said, smiling at me. "Ah, how nice to make dresses for a brunette for once. You must choose colors so carefully for red'eads. I've had this lovely taffeta for years, a color like sunset. You could be the first that color suits—"

"Madame Rossini, *please*!" Mrs. Jenkins pointed to her watch.

"*Mais oui*, nearly finished!" said Madame Rossini, scurrying around me with the tape measure and even measuring my ankles. "Men, always in such a 'urry! But with fashion you cannot 'urry." Finally she gave me a friendly pat and said, "We will meet again soon, my little swan-necked beauty!"

She herself had no neck at all, I noticed. Her head seemed to be set directly on her shoulders. But she was really nice.

"See you soon, Madame Rossini."

Once we were out of the room again, Mrs. Jenkins walked faster, and I found it quite difficult to keep up, even though she was wearing high heels and I had my comfortable dark blue school shoes on.

"Nearly there." Yet another long, long corridor lay ahead of us. It was a mystery to me how anyone could ever find her way around this maze. "Do you live here?"

"No, I live in Islington," said Mrs. Jenkins. "I leave work at five and go home to my husband."

"What does your husband think about you working for a secret lodge with a time machine in its basement?"

Mrs. Jenkins laughed. "Oh, he has no idea of any of that. I had to sign a secrecy clause when I took the job. I can't tell my husband or anyone else what goes on here."

"Suppose you did?"

"I'd be fired, plain and simple," said Mrs. Jenkins, sounding as if she didn't like that idea at all. "Anyway, no one would believe me," she added cheerfully. "Least of all my husband. He has no imagination at all, bless him. He thinks I work on boring files in an ordinary set of legal chambers all day— Oh, my word! The file I had out—I just left it where it was. Dr. White will murder me." She looked undecided. "Can you find your way without me from here? It's only a few yards. Left around the corner, then the second door on the right."

"Left around the corner, second door on the right. No problem."

"You're a darling." Mrs. Jenkins was on her way, at top speed. How she did it in those high heels I couldn't think. Well, now I could take my time over the last "few yards." At last I could look at the paintings on the walls properly, tap a suit of armor (rusty), and run my forefinger cautiously around a picture frame (dusty). As I turned the corner, I heard voices.

"Wait, Charlotte . . ."

I quickly retreated back around the corner and leaned against the wall. Charlotte had come out of the Dragon Hall, with Gideon behind her. I'd just had time to see that he was holding her arm. I hoped they hadn't noticed me.

"This is all so embarrassing and humiliating," said Charlotte.

"No, it isn't. It's not your fault." How gentle and friendly his voice could sound!

He's in love with her, I thought, and for some silly reason, that made me feel a slight pang. I pressed even closer to the wall, although I'd have liked to see what the two of them were doing. Holding hands?

Charlotte seemed inconsolable. "Phantom symptoms! I could sink into the ground. I really did think it was going to happen any moment—"

"That's exactly what I'd have thought myself in your place," said Gideon. "Your aunt must be crazy to have kept quiet about it all these years. And I really do feel sorry for your cousin."

"Oh, you do, do you?"

"Well, think about it! How on earth is she going to manage? She hasn't the faintest idea. . . . How will she ever catch up with all the things you and I have been learning for the last ten years?"

"Yes, poor Gwyneth," said Charlotte. Somehow she didn't sound really sorry for me. "But she does have her strong points."

Oh. Well, that was nice of her.

"Giggling with her girlfriend, sending text messages, rattling off the entire cast list of films—she's really good at that sort of thing."

Not so nice after all.

I cautiously peeped around the corner.

"I thought as much when I first saw her earlier today," said Gideon. "Hey, I'm really going to miss you."

Charlotte sighed. "We had fun, didn't we?"

"Yes, but think of all the new opportunities open to you, Charlotte! I envy you that! You're free now. You can do anything you like."

"I never wanted anything but this!"

"That was because you had no choice," said Gideon. "But now the whole world's before you. You can study abroad, you can go on long journeys, while I can't be away from that damn . . . from the chronograph for more than a day, and I spend my nights in the safety of the year 1953. Believe me, I'd happily change places with you!"

The door of the Dragon Hall opened again, and Lady

Arista and Aunt Glenda came out into the corridor. I quickly withdrew my head again.

"They'll regret this yet," Aunt Glenda was saying.

"Glenda, please! We're a family, after all," said Lady Arista. "We must stick together."

"You'd better tell that to Grace," said Aunt Glenda. "She's the one who got us all into this mess. *Protect her!* Ha! No one in possession of their senses would believe a word she says! Not after all that's happened. Still, it's not our problem anymore. Come along, Charlotte."

"I'll see you to the car," said Gideon.

I waited until the sound of their footsteps had died away, and then I ventured to leave my listening post. Lady Arista was still standing there, rubbing her forehead wearily with one finger. She suddenly looked as old as the hills, not her usual self at all. The ramrod-straight, ballet-teacher look seemed to have deserted her, and even her features weren't as composed as usual. I felt sorry for her.

"Hello," I said quietly. "Are you all right?"

My grandmother straightened up at once. Everything about her seemed to slip back into place and stay there.

"Ah, there you are," she said, inspecting me. Her critical gaze went to my blouse. "Is that a dirty mark? Child, you really must learn to take a little more pride in your appearance."

The intervals between episodes of time travel differ from one gene carrier to another, unless they are controlled by the chronograph. While the observations of Count Saint-Germain led him to conclude that female gene carriers travel back considerably less often, and for shorter periods, than their male counterparts, our experience to date does not allow us to confirm his findings.

The duration of uncontrolled time travel episodes has been shown, since observations were first made, to vary from eight minutes, twelve seconds (the initiation journey of Timothy de Villiers, 5 May 1892), to two hours, four minutes (Margaret Tilney, second journey, 22 March 1894).

The window of time provided by the chronograph for travel is a minimum of thirty minutes, a maximum of four hours.

It is not known whether uncontrolled visits to periods within a gene carrier's own lifetime have ever occurred. In his writings, Count Saint-Germain assumes that it is impossible because of the continuum (see Volume 3: Laws of the Continuum*).*

Moreover, the chronograph cannot be set to take gene carriers back to periods within their own lifetimes.

FROM *THE CHRONICLES OF THE GUARDIANS,*
VOLUME 2: *GENERAL LAWS OF TIME TRAVEL*

NINE

MY MUM HUGGED ME as if I'd been away for years. I had to assure her over and over again that I was perfectly all right before she finally stopped asking.

"Are you okay too, Mum?"

"Yes, darling, I'm fine."

"So everyone's fine," said Mr. de Villiers ironically. "I'm glad we've cleared that up." He came so close to Mum and me that I could smell his cologne. (Kind of spicy and fruity with a touch of cinnamon. I felt hungrier than ever.)

"Now, what are we going to do about you, Grace?" Those wolflike eyes were firmly fixed on Mum.

"I told you the truth."

"Yes, at least so far as identifying Gwyneth's gene is concerned," said Mr. de Villiers. "But we have yet to find out why the midwife who so obligingly falsified her birth certificate sixteen years ago suddenly chose to go away in a hurry today, of all days."

Mum shrugged. "I wouldn't assume that every little coincidence is so important, Falk."

"I also think it's strange that if your baby looked like arriving two months early, you chose to have her at home. Any sensible woman would go to a hospital the moment the labor pains started."

"It simply happened too fast," said Mum, without batting an eyelash. "I was just glad the midwife could come right away."

"Hm. Even so, surely you should have gone to hospital directly after the birth to have the baby examined."

"We did."

"But not until the next day," said Mr. de Villiers. "The hospital records say that they did give the child a thorough examination, but her mother refused to have one. Why was that, Grace?"

Mum laughed. "I think you'd understand me better if you'd ever had a baby yourself. I was fine, I just wanted to be sure the baby was all right. What surprises *me* is how you got hold of a report from the hospital so quickly. I thought such details were strictly confidential."

"You're welcome to take the hospital to court for contravening the Data Protection Act," said Mr. de Villiers. "Meanwhile we'll go on looking for the midwife. I'm beginning to feel a burning interest in whatever that lady may have to tell us."

The door opened, and Mr. George and Dr. White came in, along with Mrs. Jenkins, who was carrying a whole lot of files.

Gideon strolled into the room after them. This time I took the opportunity to look at the rest of him, not just his pretty face. I was hoping to see something I didn't like about him, so I wouldn't feel quite so imperfect by comparison. Unfortunately I couldn't find a thing. He didn't have bowlegs from playing polo, or long gorilla arms, or ears too close to the sides of his head (which Lesley claimed was a sign of a miserly man). He looked annoyingly cool leaning back against the desk, crossing his arms.

What a waste of good looks. It was a shame!

"Everything's ready," said Mr. George, eyes twinkling at me. "The time machine is ready to start."

Robert, the ghost boy, waved to me shyly. I waved back.

"Well, we're all present and correct, then," said Mr. de Villiers. "That is to say, I'm afraid Glenda and Charlotte have had to leave us. They send warm good wishes to everyone."

"I bet they do," said Dr. White.

"Poor girl! Phantom symptoms for two whole days—it can't have been much fun for her," said Mr. George, with a sympathetic expression on his round face.

"And add a mother like that into the bargain," muttered Dr. White, leafing through the file folders that Mrs. Jenkins had brought with her. "What a tough time the poor child's had."

"Mrs. Jenkins, how's Madame Rossini getting on with Gwyneth's wardrobe?"

"She's just . . . wait, I'll go and ask." Mrs. Jenkins hurried out the doorway again.

Mr. George rubbed his hands, ready for action. "Then we can go!"

"But you won't take her into danger, will you?" said Mum, turning to Mr. George. "You'll leave her out of this business?"

"We will certainly leave her out of it," said Gideon.

"We'll do all we can to protect Gwyneth," Mr. George assured Mum.

"We can't leave her out of it, Grace," said Mr. de Villiers. "She's part of *this business*, as you put it. You ought to have realized that earlier. Before you began this stupid game of hide-and-seek."

"With the result that, thanks to you, the girl is entirely unprepared and ignorant," said Dr. White. "Which of course will make our mission even more difficult. But I expect that was just what you wanted."

"What I wanted was to keep Gwyneth out of danger," said Mum.

"I've gone quite a long way on my own," said Gideon. "I can see this thing through by myself."

"*That's* just what I hoped," said Mum.

I can see this thing through by myself. Ugh! I only just managed not to giggle. It could have been a line from one of those stupid action films where a hunk with a melancholy expression saves the world by fighting, single-handed, against a combat troop of 120 ninja warriors, a fleet of enemy spaceships, or a whole village of desperadoes armed to the teeth.

"We'll see what kinds of tasks she may be suitable for," said Mr. de Villiers.

"We have her blood," said Gideon. "That's all we need from her. She can come here and elapse every day as far as I'm concerned, and then everyone will be happy."

What was that he said? *Elapse*? It sounded like one of those difficult words Mr. Whitman used to confuse us with in English lessons. *"In principle not a bad effort at elapsorating the crux, Gordon, but try for a little more elaboration next time, please."* Or had it been *elucidating the crux*? Well, anyway, neither Gordon nor I nor anyone else in the class had ever heard of it. Except, of course, for Charlotte.

Mr. George saw how baffled I was looking. "By *elapse* we mean deliberately tapping your time-travel quota by setting the chronograph to take you back into the past for a couple of hours. That prevents uncontrolled travel." He turned to the others. "I'm sure that after a little while Gwyneth will surprise us all with her potential. She is—"

"She's a *child*!" Gideon interrupted him. "She has no idea about anything."

I blushed scarlet. What a nerve he had! And the scornful way he was looking at me! That stupid, conceited . . . *polo player*!

"That's not true," I said. I was not a child! I was sixteen and a half. Exactly the same as Charlotte. At my age, Marie-Antoinette had been married for years. (So I didn't know that from history lessons, but I knew it from the film with

Kirsten Dunst.) And Joan of Arc was only fifteen when she—

"Oh, no?" Gideon's voice was heavily sarcastic. "Then what, for instance, do you know about history?"

"Enough!" I said. Hadn't I just gotten an A on a history test?

"Really? Who came to the throne after George I?"

I hadn't the faintest. "George II?" I said, guessing.

Aha! He looked disappointed. I seemed to have guessed right.

"And which royal house replaced the Stuarts in 1702 and why?"

Dammit. "Er . . . we haven't got to that yet," I said.

"So I see." Gideon turned to the others. "She doesn't know anything about history. She can't even speak appropriately. Wherever we go, she'd stick out like a sore thumb. And she has no idea what's at stake. She wouldn't just be totally useless, she'd endanger the entire mission!"

I ask you! So I couldn't even speak *appropriately*? Well, I could think of several highly appropriate names I'd have liked to call him.

"I think you've made your opinion quite clear, Gideon," said Mr. de Villiers. "At this point, it would be interesting to find out what the count thinks of these developments."

"You can't do that to her!" Mum interrupted. Her voice suddenly sounded all choked up.

"The count will be delighted to meet you, Gwyneth," said Mr. George, brushing Mum's concerns aside. "The

Ruby, the twelfth, the last in the Circle. It will be a solemn moment when the two of you come face-to-face."

"No!" said Mum.

Everyone looked at her.

"Grace!" said my grandmother. "Not again!"

"No," repeated Mum. "Please! There's no need for him to meet her. Surely it will be enough for him to know that her blood makes the Circle complete."

"*Would* have made the Circle complete," said Dr. White, who was still looking through those files. "If we hadn't had to start all over again after the theft."

"Be that as it may, I don't want Gwyneth meeting him," said Mum. "Those are my conditions. Gideon can do it by himself."

"It's not up to you to decide," said Mr. de Villiers, and Dr. White snapped, *"Conditions!* So now she's making conditions!"

"But she's right! It won't do anyone any good for us to drag the girl into this too," said Gideon. "I'll explain what happened, and I'm sure the count will agree with me."

"He's going to want to see her, anyway, to get an idea of her for himself," said Falk de Villiers. "There's no danger for her. She won't even have to leave this house."

"Mrs. Shepherd, I assure you, nothing will happen to Gwyneth," said Mr. George. "I imagine your opinion of the count is based on prejudices that we'll all be very happy to dispel."

"I'm afraid you won't be able to do that."

"I am sure, dear Grace," said Mr. de Villiers, "that you'd like to tell us on what grounds you feel such a dislike for the count—a man you've never met."

Mum pursed her lips firmly.

"We're listening!" said Mr. de Villiers.

Mum said nothing. At last she whispered, "It's just . . . just a kind of feeling."

Mr. de Villiers's lips curled in a cynical smile. "I can't help it, Grace—I do get the impression that you're keeping something from us. What are you afraid of?"

"Who is this count anyway, and why aren't I supposed to meet him?" I asked.

"Because your mother has a *kind of feeling,*" said Dr. White, straightening his jacket. "The man has been dead for over two hundred years, Mrs. Shepherd."

"And that's the way I'd like him to stay," muttered Mum.

"Count Saint-Germain is the fifth of the twelve time travelers, Gwyneth," said Mr. George. "You saw his portrait in the documents room just now. He was the one who first understood the way the chronograph works and decoded the old manuscripts. He not only found out how he could travel with its aid to any year he liked, on any day he liked, he also discovered the secret behind the secret. *The Secret of the Twelve.* With the help of the chronograph, he succeeded in tracing the four time travelers in the Circle born before him and initiating them into the mystery. The count sought and gained support from the most brilliant minds of his time, mathematicians, alchemists, magicians, philosophers—they were all fascinated by his work. Together, they deciphered the Ancient Writings and worked out the birth dates of the seven time travelers yet to be born before the Circle could be closed. In the year 1745, the count founded the Society of the Guardians here in London, the Secret Lodge of Count Saint-Germain."

"The count had scientists, philosophers, and scholars such as Raimundus Lullus, Agrippa von Nettesheim, John Colet, Simon Forman, Samuel Hartlib, Sir Kenelm Digby, and John Wallis to thank for the decoding of the Ancient Writings," said Mr. de Villiers.

None of those names rang a bell anywhere in my head.

"None of those names rings a bell anywhere in her head," said Gideon sarcastically.

Could he really read thoughts? Just in case he could, I gave him a nasty look and thought, with all my might, *You . . . stupid . . . show-off!*

He looked away.

"I THOUGHT Sir Isaac Newton was one of the Guardians?" I asked.

"Indeed he was!" Mr. George replied.

"But Newton died in 1727." I surprised myself by coming up with that fact. Lesley had told me when she phoned yesterday, and for some unfathomable reason, it had stuck in my mind. I wasn't as stupid as this Gideon said after all.

"Correct," said Mr. George, smiling. "That's one of the advantages of traveling in time. You can make friends in the past as well as the present."

"And what's the secret behind the secret?" I asked.

"The Secret of the Twelve will be revealed when the blood of all twelve time travelers has been read into the chronograph," said Mr. George solemnly. "That's why the Circle has to be closed. It is the great task that we must perform."

"But I'm the last of the Twelve, right? So this Circle should be complete with me."

"And so it would be," said Dr. White, "if your cousin Lucy hadn't taken it into her head to steal the chronograph seventeen years ago."

"*Paul* stole the chronograph," said Lady Arista. "Lucy only—"

Mr. de Villiers raised his hand. "Yes, well, let's just say they stole it together. Two children who had been led astray. They wrecked the work of five hundred years. The mission was on the point of failing, and the legacy of Count Saint-Germain would have been lost forever."

"So this legacy is the secret?"

"Luckily there was a second chronograph within these walls," said Mr. George. "It wasn't expected ever to be used. It came into the hands of the Guardians in 1757. After centuries of neglect, it was defective, and the valuable jewels had been stolen from it. But after two hundred years of laborious work, the Guardians succeeded in—"

Impatiently, Dr. White interrupted him. "To cut a long story short, it was repaired, and it really was capable of working, although we couldn't check that until the eleventh time traveler, Gideon here, reached the age of initiation. We'd lost the first chronograph and with it the blood of ten time travelers. Now we had to start all over again with the second."

"So as to—er—get at the Secret of the Twelve," I said. I'd almost said "reveal." I was beginning to feel as if I'd been brainwashed.

Dr. White and Mr. George nodded solemnly by way of an answer.

"Okay, so what sort of a secret is it?"

Mum began to laugh. It was totally out of place, but she laughed with a gurgle, like Caroline when Mr. Bean is on TV.

"Grace!" hissed Lady Arista. "Pull yourself together!"

But Mum just laughed even more. "A secret is a secret is a secret," she got out between two bursts of laughter. "That's always the way."

"Just as I said: hysterical females, the whole bunch of them!" growled Dr. White.

"I'm glad you can see a funny side to all this," said Mr. de Villiers.

Mum wiped the tears of laughter from her eyes. "I'm sorry. It just suddenly came over me. To be honest, I feel more like crying, I really do."

I realized that I wasn't going to get any closer to the nature of the secret by asking questions about it.

"What's so dangerous about this count that I'm not supposed to meet him?" I asked instead.

Mum just shook her head. She was suddenly deadly serious again. I was getting worried about her. These mood swings weren't like her at all.

"Nothing," replied Dr. White. "Your mother is simply afraid you might come into contact with intellectual ideas that don't agree with her own. But she's not the one who makes the decisions here."

"Intellectual ideas," repeated my mother, and this time it was *her* voice dripping irony.

"Why don't we leave it to Gwyneth to decide if she wants to meet the count?" suggested Mr. de Villiers.

"Just for a conversation? Back in the past?" I looked inquiringly from Mr. de Villiers to Mr. George and back again. "Will he be able to answer my question about the secret?"

"If he wants to," said Mr. George. "You'll meet him in the year 1782. The count was a very old man then, but conveniently for our purposes, he was making a visit to London. On a strictly secret mission, the nature of which is unknown to historians and his biographers. He spent the night here in this house. So it will be very easy to arrange a meeting between you. Gideon will escort you, of course."

Gideon muttered something indistinct to himself, in which I caught the words "idiots" and "babysitter." How I loathed this guy!

"Mum?"

"Say no, darling."

"But why?"

"You're not ready for it yet."

"Not ready for what yet? Why aren't I supposed to meet this count? What's so dangerous about him? Oh, come on, Mum, tell me."

"Yes, tell her, Grace," said Mr. de Villiers. "She hates all this mystery mongering. I should think it hurts her, coming from her own mother in particular."

Mum did not reply.

"As you see, it's difficult extracting any really useful information from us," said Mr. de Villiers, his amber eyes studying me seriously.

My mum still didn't say anything.

I could have shaken her. Falk de Villiers was right. All these stupid hints weren't getting me anywhere.

"Then I'll have to find out for myself," I said. "Yes, I want to meet him." I don't know what had suddenly come over me, but I no longer felt like a five-year-old who wanted to run home and hide under the bed.

Gideon groaned.

"You heard what she said, Grace," said Mr. de Villiers. "I suggest you get a taxi back to Mayfair and take a tranquilizer. We'll take Gwyneth home when we've . . . finished with her."

"I'm not leaving her alone," whispered Mum.

"Caroline and Nick will soon be home from school, Mum. It's all right for you to go. I can look after myself."

"No, you can't," Mum whispered.

"I'll come with you, Grace," said Lady Arista in a surprisingly gentle voice. "I've been here for two days without a break, and my head hurts. Things have taken a really unexpected turn. But now . . . well, it's out of our hands."

"Very wise," said Dr. White.

Mum looked as if she might burst into tears any

moment. "Very well," she said. "I'll go. I'm trusting you to make sure that no harm comes to Gwyneth."

"And that she will be at school on time tomorrow morning," said Lady Arista. "She shouldn't miss too many lessons. She's not like Charlotte."

I looked at her in surprise. I'd forgotten all about school.

"Where are my hat and coat?" asked Lady Arista. There was a kind of collective sigh of relief from the men in the room. You couldn't hear it, but you could sense it.

"Mrs. Jenkins will take care of everything, Lady Arista," said Mr. de Villiers.

"Come along, my child," Lady Arista told Mum.

"Grace." Falk de Villiers took her hand and raised it to his lips. "It's been a great pleasure to see you again after so many years."

"It hasn't been all that long," said Mum.

"Seventeen."

"Six," said Mum, sounding slightly hurt. "We saw each other at my husband's funeral, but you've probably forgotten." She looked at Mr. George. "Will you take care of her?"

"Mrs. Shepherd, I promise you that Gwyneth will be safe with us," said Mr. George. "Trust me."

"I don't seem to have any other option." Mum withdrew her hand from Mr. de Villiers's and slung her bag over her shoulder. "Can I have a word with my daughter in private?"

"Of course," said Falk de Villiers. "You'll be undisturbed in the room next door."

"I'd prefer to be outside with her," said Mum.

Mr. de Villiers raised his eyebrows. "Afraid we'll eavesdrop on you? Watch you through peepholes in the portraits?" He laughed.

"I need a little fresh air, that's all," said Mum.

THE GARDEN WASN'T open to the public at this time of day. A few tourists—you could tell they were tourists from the big cameras around their necks—watched enviously as Mum opened an ornate wrought-iron gate six feet high and bolted it again behind us.

I was captivated by all the flowers in the beds, the lush green turf, and the fragrance in the air. "This was a good idea," I said. "I was beginning to feel like a cave salamander." I turned my face to the sunlight longingly. It was remarkably strong for early April.

Mum sat down on a teak bench and rubbed her hand over her forehead in the same way as Lady Arista, except that it didn't make Mum look as old as the hills. "This is a nightmare," she said.

I sank onto the bench beside her. "Yes. I hardly know what to make of it. Yesterday morning everything was still the same as ever and then suddenly . . . I feel as if my head's splitting, having to take so much in all at once—thousands of scraps of information that won't fit together properly."

"I'm so sorry," said Mum. "I hoped to spare you all this."

"What was it you once did to make them all so cross with you?"

"I helped Lucy and Paul to get away," said Mum. She glanced around briefly as if to make sure no one was listening to us. "They hid with us in Durham for a while, but of course *they* found out. And Lucy and Paul had to go on the run."

I thought about all I'd learnt today. And suddenly I realized where my cousin was.

The black sheep of the family wasn't living among the Amazonian Indians or hidden in a convent of nuns in Ireland, as Lesley and I had always imagined when we were little.

Lucy and Paul were somewhere entirely different.

"They disappeared into the past with the chronograph?"

My mother nodded. "In the end they had no choice. But it wasn't an easy decision for them."

"Why?"

"It's forbidden to take the chronograph out of your own time. If you do that, you can never travel back home again. Anyone who takes the chronograph into the past has to stay there."

I swallowed. "But why would anyone decide to do that?" I asked quietly.

"They realized there'd be no safe hiding place for them in the present with the chronograph. Sooner or later the Guardians would have tracked them down."

"But *why* did they steal it, Mum?"

"They wanted to keep the . . . the Circle of Blood from closing."

"What will happen when the Circle of Blood closes?" Good heavens, I heard myself talking just like one of them. *Circle of Blood*. Next thing I knew, I'd start speaking in verse.

"Listen, darling, we don't have much time. Even if they say the opposite now, they're going to try to get you involved in their mission. They need you to close the Circle and reveal the secret."

"What is the secret, Mum?" I felt as if I'd asked that question a thousand times already. And inside me I was almost yelling it.

"I don't know any more than the others. I can only make some assumptions. It's powerful, and it will give great power to anyone who knows how to make use of it. But power in the wrong hands is very dangerous. So Lucy and Paul believed it would be better if the secret was never revealed. With that in mind, they made great sacrifices."

"I get that idea. I just don't understand why."

"Even if some of the men in there may be driven only by scientific curiosity, there are others whose intentions aren't so honorable. I know they won't shrink from anything to achieve their ends. You can't trust any of them. *Any* of them, Gwyneth."

I sighed. None of what she'd told me seemed the least bit useful.

From where we were in the garden, we heard the

sound of an engine, and a car drew up at the front of the house. Even though cars weren't really allowed in here at all.

"Time to go, Grace!" called Lady Arista, coming out of the house.

Mum got to her feet. "Oh, what a lovely evening lies ahead! Glenda's icy looks will freeze the food on our plates."

"Why did that midwife go away today? And why didn't you have me in a hospital?"

"I wish they'd leave the poor woman in peace," said Mum.

"Grace! Come along now!" Lady Arista was tapping the tip of her umbrella against the wrought-iron gate.

"I think they're going to put you in the naughty corner," I said.

"It breaks my heart, leaving you alone."

"I could just go home with you," I said, but even as I said it, I knew I didn't really want to. It was just like Falk de Villiers said—I was a part of *this business* now, and oddly enough, I didn't mind the idea.

"No, you can't," said Mum. "You could get hurt or even killed in uncontrolled time travel. At least you're safe from that here." She hugged me. "Don't forget what I said. Trust no one. Not even your own feelings. And go very carefully with Count Saint-Germain. It's said that he can get into people's minds. He can read your thoughts and, even worse, control your will if you let him."

I hugged her back as hard as I could. "I love you,

Mum." Over her shoulder I could see that Mr. de Villiers had come out of the front door as well now.

When Mum turned she saw him, too. "And you want to be particularly careful with *that one*," she said quietly. "He's become a dangerous man." But I sensed something that sounded like admiration in her voice, so I asked, "Mum, did you ever . . . er, have something going on with him?"

She didn't even have to answer. I could see from the look on her face that I'd hit the bull's-eye.

"I was seventeen and easily impressed," she said.

"I get the idea," I told her, grinning. "Those are amazing eyes, right?"

Mum grinned back as we sauntered deliberately slowly toward the gate. "Oh, yes. Paul's eyes were just the same. But unlike his big brother, he wasn't at all condescending. No wonder Lucy fell in love with him. . . ."

"I'd love to know what happened to them both."

"Sooner or later I'm afraid you will."

"Give me the key," said Falk de Villiers impatiently. Mum handed him the key to the door through the wrought-iron pattern, and he unlocked it. "I sent for a car for you."

"We'll meet at breakfast tomorrow morning, Gwyneth," said Lady Arista, putting a hand under my chin. "Chin up! You're a Montrose, and we stay calm and composed everywhere, always."

"I'll try, Grandmother."

"That's right. Oh, dear!" She waved her arms about as if shooing flies. "What do those people think they're doing? I'm not the Queen!" But with her elegant hat, her umbrella, and the coat, all color-matched, she obviously looked so British to the tourists that they were taking photos of her from all sides.

Mum gave me a last hug. "The secret has already cost human lives," she whispered into my ear. "Don't forget that."

I watched her and my grandmother with mixed feelings until the car had turned the corner, carrying them away.

Mr. George took my hand and held it firmly. "Don't be frightened, Gwyneth. You're not alone."

He wasn't kidding. I was surrounded by loads of people I wasn't supposed to trust. I mustn't trust any of them, my mum had said. I looked into Mr. George's friendly blue eyes and searched them for something dangerous and dishonest. But I couldn't see anything of the kind.

Trust no one.

Not even your own feelings.

"Come along, we'd better go in. You must get some food inside you."

"I hope that little conversation with your mother was illuminating," said Mr. de Villiers on the way upstairs. "Let me guess: she warned you against us. We're all unscrupulous liars, am I right?"

"You'll know more about that than I do," I said. "We were talking about how you and my mother once had something going on together."

Mr. de Villiers raised his eyebrows in surprise. "She

told you *that*?" There was actually a touch of embarrassment in his expression. "Ah, well, that's a long time ago. I was young and—"

"And easily impressed." I finished the sentence for him. "That's what my mum said too."

Mr. George roared with laughter. "Oh, yes, that's right! I'd quite forgotten. You and Grace Montrose, you made a handsome couple, Falk. If only for three weeks. Then she plastered a slice of cheesecake over your shirtfront at that charity ball in Holland House and said she never wanted to say another word to you."

"It was a strawberry tart," said Mr. de Villiers, with a twinkle in his eye. "She really meant to throw it in my face, but I was lucky and she only hit my shirt. The stain never came out. She was jealous of a girl whose name I can't even remember."

"Larissa Crofts. She was the chancellor of the exchequer's daughter," said Mr. George.

"Really?" Mr. de Villiers seemed genuinely surprised. "The chancellor now or the chancellor then?"

"Then."

"Was she pretty?"

"Reasonably pretty."

"Well, anyway, Grace broke my heart, because after that she started going out with another boy from my school. I remember *his* name all right."

"Yes, because you broke his nose and his parents nearly sued you for it," said Mr. George.

"Is that true?" I was absolutely fascinated.

"It was an accident," said Mr. de Villiers. "We were on the same rugby team."

"Such revelations, Gwyneth!" Mr. George was still chuckling happily when he opened the door of the Dragon Hall.

"You can say that again." I stopped when I saw Gideon sitting at the table in the middle of the room. He came toward us, frowning.

Mr. de Villiers gently guided me in. "It was nothing serious," he said. "Love affairs between the de Villiers and Montrose families never work out. You could say they were doomed to fail from the start."

"I'd call that an entirely superfluous warning, Uncle Falk," said Gideon, crossing his arms. "She's definitely not my type."

By *she* he meant me. It was a second or maybe two before the insult sank in. My first instinct was to say something like "Well, thank God for that! I'm not too keen on arrogant show-offs, myself." But I kept quiet.

Okay, so I wasn't his type. So what? If I wasn't, I wasn't.

As if I cared.

Received exciting news from the future today. The eleventh in the Circle of Twelve, Gideon de Villiers, will elapse to spend three hours a night with us in future. We made up a bed for him in Sir Walter's office. It is cool and quiet in there, and the boy will be protected to a great extent from curious glances and stupid questions. During his visit today, all the officers on duty looked in "quite by chance."

And quite by chance, they all had questions to ask about the future.

The boy told us it would be a good idea to buy shares in Apple, whatever that may be.

From *The Annals of the Guardians*
4 August 1953
Report: Robert Peel, Inner Circle

TEN

"CLOAK: VENETIAN VELVET, lined with silk taffeta. Gown: printed linen from Germany, trimmed with Devonshire lace, with a bodice made of embroidered silk brocade." Madame Rossini carefully spread these garments out on the table. After we'd eaten, Mrs. Jenkins had taken me back to the sewing room. I liked this little room better than the formal dining room; there were wonderful fabrics lying around everywhere, and Madame Rossini was probably the only person here whom even my mother couldn't possibly have distrusted. "The *ensemble* in mid blue with touches of cream, an elegant afternoon outfit," she went on. "And matching shoes, silk brocade. More comfortable than they look. Luckily you and the coat 'anger take the same shoe size." She placed my school uniform aside. "Oh, *mon Dieu*, the most beautiful girl in the world would look like a scarecrow in this. If they would only shorten the skirt to a fashionable length. Ah, zat ugly yellow! Whoever designed this 'ated schoolgirls. He really 'ated them!"

"Can I keep my own underwear on?"

"Only the panties," said Madame Rossini. "Wrong for the period, but no one will be looking under your skirt. Or so I 'ope. If they do, you just kick zem good and 'ard. It may not look like it, but these shoes have toes reinforced with iron. 'Ave you been to the toilet? It is more difficult with the dress on."

"Yes, I have. You've asked me that three times already, Madame Rossini."

"We must make sure of everything."

The way people fussed about me here kept surprising me, and all these little details! After dinner, Mrs. Jenkins had even handed me a brand-new toiletry bag so that I could brush my teeth and wash my face.

I'd expected the corset to cut off my air supply and squeeze the roast veal right out of me, but it was surprisingly comfortable. "I thought women fell down fainting in rows from wearing these things."

"Oh, zey did. First, because they laced them too tight. And second, you could 'ave cut the air with a knife, because nobody washed, they just put on more perfume," said Madame Rossini, shuddering at the idea. "Lice and fleas lived in their wigs, and mice even made nests in them. The most beautiful fashions, but not a good time for 'ygiene. You're not wearing a corset like those poor creatures. You 'ave a special one à la Madame Rossini, comfy like a second skin."

"I see." I was terribly excited when I climbed into the

hooped petticoat. "This feels like carrying a birdcage around with me."

"Zis is nothing," Madame Rossini assured me, as she carefully put the dress over my head. "The 'oop is tiny, not like they wore at Versailles at that time. Twelve feet in diameter! And yours is not whalebone but featherweight high-tech carbon fiber! But don't worry, no one will see zat."

Pale blue fabric patterned with cream-colored sprigs of flowers was billowing all around me. It would also have looked pretty good as a sofa cover. But I had to admit that, even with the enormous skirt and seemingly impossible length, it was very comfortable, not to mention a perfect fit.

"Enchanting," said Madame Rossini, pushing me over to the mirror.

"Oh!" I said, surprised. Who'd have thought a sofa cover could look so good? And me in it. My waist seemed so small, my eyes so blue. Wow! Although my low décolletage reminded me of an opera singer about to explode.

"We'll put a leetle lace in there," said Madame Rossini, who had followed the direction of my eyes. "After all, it is an afternoon gown. In the evening, yes. You have to show what you 'ave got. I hope to have the pleasure of making you a ball gown! And now for your 'air."

"Am I going to wear a wig?"

"No," said Madame Rossini. "You are a young girl, and it is afternoon. If you make your 'air pretty and wear a 'at, that will do. We need do nothing with your skin, it is pure alabaster. And that pretty crescent-shaped mark on your temple could be a beauty spot. *Très chic!*"

Madame Rossini used heated rollers on my hair, and then skillfully fixed the front of it to my parting with hairpins and let the rest fall in soft ringlets to my shoulders. I looked at my reflection in the mirror and admired myself.

I couldn't help thinking of that costume party that Cynthia had thrown last year. I'd gone as a bus stop, for want of any better ideas, and at the end of the evening, I felt like getting hit by a bus wouldn't be so bad, because people kept asking me annoying questions about the time table and when the next bus would come along.

Ha! If I'd only known Madame Rossini then! I'd have been the star of the evening!

I turned back to the mirror once again, fascinated, but that was all over when Madame Rossini came up behind me and put "the 'at" on my head. It was a monstrous confection of straw with feathers and blue ribbons, and I thought it spoiled the whole outfit. I tried to persuade Madame Rossini that I didn't need to wear it, but she wouldn't give way.

"No, impossible! Zis is not a beauty competition, *ma chérie*. We must have authenticity."

I looked for my mobile in the jacket of my school uniform. "Could you at least take a photo of me—without the hat?"

Madame Rossini laughed. "*Bien sûr*, my dear!"

I posed, and Madame Rossini took about thirty photos of me from all sides, some of them even with the hat on. At least Lesley would have a good laugh.

"There, now I will go up and tell them you are ready. Stay here, and don't touch that 'at! It is perfect."

"Yes, Madame Rossini," I said dutifully. As soon as she had left the room I tapped in Lesley's mobile number, fingers flying, and texted her one of those hat pictures. She called back fourteen seconds later. Thank goodness, the reception here in Madame Rossini's sewing room was good.

"I'm on the bus," Lesley shouted into my ear. "But I have my notebook and pen all ready. Only you'll have to speak up!"

Talking at top speed, I told Lesley all about what had happened, trying to explain where I was and what my mum had said. Although I was talking in rather a confused way, Lesley seemed to be following me. She was thrilled when I told her I'd brought her back a key from the past. She kept saying, in turn, "Wow, crazy!" and "Do be careful!" When I described Gideon (she wanted to hear all the details), she said, "I don't think long hair's so bad. It *can* look quite sexy. Think of *A Knight's Tale*. But don't forget to check out the ears he's hiding under there."

"They don't make any difference. He's a conceited jerk, and anyway he's in love with Charlotte. Did you get that bit about the philosopher's stone down?"

"Yes, I've made notes of it all. As soon as I'm home I'll go online. This Count Saint-Germain—why does the name seem so familiar to me? Could it be from a film? No, I'm thinking of the Count of Monte Cristo."

"Suppose he really can read thoughts?"

"Just think of something harmless. Or count backward from a thousand. In steps of eight at a time. Then you won't be able to think of anything else."

"I'll try. Oh, see if you can find out anything about a little boy called Robert White who drowned in a swimming pool eighteen years ago."

"Okay, I got that," said Lesley. "Wow, this is weird! We should have gotten you a knife or pepper spray or something. . . . I know! You can take your mobile with you."

I tripped my way over to the door in my long, full dress and peered cautiously out into the passage. "What, into the past? Do you think I'll be able to call you from there?"

"Don't be silly! But you can take photos—they'd be a help to us. Oh, and I'd just love to see one of your Gideon! With his ears showing, if possible. Ears tell you a lot about a person. Especially the earlobes."

I could hear footsteps. I quietly closed the door. "Here we go. I'll be in touch later, Lesley!"

"Just be careful," said Lesley yet again, but then I closed my phone and slipped it into my décolletage. The little space under my breasts was just the right size for a mobile. I wondered what ladies in the old days used to keep in there. Little bottles of poison? Miniature revolvers? Love letters?

The first thing that went through my head when Gideon came into the room was, why doesn't *he* have to wear a hat? The second thing was, how can anyone look good in a red moiré waistcoat, dark green trousers that cut off at the knee, and striped silk stockings? If I thought anything else, it was probably, I hope to goodness no one can guess what I'm thinking right now.

The green eyes passed swiftly over me. "Nice hat."

Damn him.

"Lovely," said Mr. George, coming into the room behind him. "Madame Rossini, you've worked wonders."

"Yes, I know," said Madame Rossini. She had stayed out in the corridor. The sewing room wasn't big enough for all of us. My skirt took up half the space on its own.

Gideon had tied his hair at the back of his neck, and I saw my chance to get my own back. "Nice velvet bow," I said with all the sarcasm I could summon up. "Mrs. Counter, our geography teacher, always wears exactly the same thing."

Instead of looking angrily at me, Gideon grinned. "Oh, the bow is nothing special. You should see me in a wig."

Strictly speaking, I already had.

"Monsieur Gideon, I 'ad put out zose lemon-yellow breeches for you, not ze dark ones." When Madame Rossini was annoyed her accent was stronger, and she forgot how to say an *h* or *th* now and then.

Gideon turned to Madame Rossini. "Yellow breeches with a red waistcoat and a brown coat with gold buttons? I thought it was just too many bright colors."

"Men of ze Rococo period *liked* colors." Madame Rossini looked at him severely. "And I am ze expert here, not you!"

"Yes, Madame Rossini," said Gideon politely. "I'll listen to you next time."

I looked at his ears. They didn't stick out at all, and there was nothing else odd about them. Of course I didn't really *care*.

"Where are ze yellow chamois leather gloves?"

"Oh, I thought if I wasn't going to wear the breeches, I'd better steer clear of the gloves as well."

"Of course!" Madame Rossini huffed. "With respect to your sense of fashion, young man, we're not talking good taste here, we're talking authenticity. And I took care to pick colors that would suit your complexion, you ungrateful boy."

Grumbling, she let us go past her.

"Thank you very, very much, Madame Rossini," I said.

"Ah, my little swan-necked beauty! It was a pleasure! At least you appreciate my work." I had to grin. I liked the idea of being swan-necked.

Mr. George's eyes twinkled at me. "If you'll follow me, please, Miss Gwyneth."

"We have to blindfold her first," said Gideon, about to take my hat off my head.

"Dear me, yes. I'm afraid Dr. White insists on it," said Mr. George, with an apologetic smile.

"But it will ruin her 'airstyle!" Madame Rossini snatched Gideon's fingers away. "*Tiens!* Do you want to pull 'er 'air off 'er 'ead? Never 'eard of a 'atpin? There!" She firmly planted the hat and hatpin in Mr. George's hands. "And carry that 'at carefully!"

Gideon tied a black scarf around my eyes. I automatically held my breath as his hand touched my cheek, and unfortunately I couldn't keep myself from blushing. But luckily he couldn't see that because he was standing behind me.

"Ow!" I said. He'd caught a few of my hairs in the knot.

"Sorry. Can you still see anything?"

"No." There was nothing but darkness before my eyes. "Why can't I see where we're going?"

"You're not allowed to know exactly where the chronograph is kept," said Gideon. He put one hand on my back and propelled me forward. It was an odd feeling, walking along unable to see my way, and Gideon's hand on my back made it worse. "An unnecessary precaution, if you ask me," he said. "This house is a labyrinth. You'd never find your way back to the room. And Mr. George thinks you're beyond any suspicion of treachery anyway."

That was nice of Mr. George, even if I didn't know exactly what it meant.

My shoulder collided with some hard object. "Ow!"

"Hold her hand, Gideon, you stupid oaf," said Mr. George, sounding rather annoyed. "She's not a supermarket trolley."

I felt a warm, dry hand closing round mine and jumped nervously.

"It's okay," said Gideon. "Only me. We go down a couple of steps now. Watch out."

For a while we went on in silence, side by side, sometimes straight ahead, then down some stairs or around a corner, and I concentrated as hard as I could on not letting my hand shake. Or sweat. I didn't want Gideon thinking he made me feel awkward. Did he notice how fast my pulse was pounding?

Then my right foot suddenly met nothing, and I stumbled and would have fallen over completely if Gideon hadn't caught me with both his hands and put me back on solid ground. Now his hands were around my waist.

"Careful, there's a step here," he said.

"Yes, thanks. I noticed when my ankle turned over," I said indignantly.

"For heaven's sake, Gideon, do be careful," said Mr. George. "Here, you carry the hat, and I'll help Gwyneth."

It was easier to walk along holding Mr. George's hand. Maybe because I could concentrate more on the steps I was taking than on not letting my hand shake. Our walk lasted half an eternity. Yet again I had a feeling we were going down into the depths of the earth. When we finally stopped, I suspected they'd taken me on a couple of long detours just to confuse me.

A door was opened and closed again, and at last Mr. George took my blindfold off.

"Here we are."

"Exquisite as a young May morning," said Dr. White. But he was talking to Gideon.

"Thanks!" Gideon made a little bow. "The latest thing

from Paris. I ought really to be wearing yellow knee breeches and yellow gloves with this outfit, but I just couldn't bring myself to do it."

"Madame Rossini is furious," said Mr. George.

"Gideon!" said Mr. de Villiers reproachfully. He had just appeared behind Dr. White.

"Well, Uncle Falk, I ask you! Yellow knee breeches?"

"It's not as if you were going to meet old school friends who might laugh at you there," said Mr. de Villiers.

"No," said Gideon, putting my hat down on a table. "More likely I'll meet guys wearing embroidered pink breeches who think they look terrific," he said, shaking his head. At first I'd had to let my eyes adjust to the light. Now I looked curiously around. The room had no windows, as I'd expected, and there was no fireplace either. I couldn't see a time machine anywhere. Only a table and a few chairs, a chest, a cupboard, and some kind of saying in Latin carved into the stone wall.

Mr. de Villiers gave me a friendly smile. "Blue suits you wonderfully, Gwyneth. And Madame Rossini has done something very elegant to your hair."

"Er . . . thank you."

"We'd better hurry up. I'm dying of heat in these clothes." Gideon undid his coat so that I could see the sword hanging from his belt.

"Come over here." Dr. White went up to the table and revealed something that had been wrapped in red velvet. At first glance it looked like a large clock, the kind you might stand on a mantelpiece. "I've adjusted all the settings. The window of time available to you two is three hours."

At a second glance, I realized it wasn't a clock. It was a strange device made of polished wood and metal with any amount of knobs, flaps, and little wheels. All the surfaces were painted with miniature pictures of the sun, moon, and stars, and inscribed with mysterious signs and patterns. It was curved like a violin case and set with sparkling jewels, great big ones that couldn't possibly be real.

"Is that the chronograph? It's so small!"

"It weighs nine pounds," said Dr. White, sounding as proud as a father telling you the weight of his newborn baby. "And before you ask, yes, the stones are all genuine. This ruby alone is six carats."

"Gideon will go first," said Mr. de Villiers. "The password?"

"*Qua redit nescitis*," said Gideon.

"Gwyneth?"

"Yes?"

"The password!"

"What do you mean, password?"

"*Qua redit nescitis*," said Mr. de Villiers. "The password of the Guardians for this twenty-fourth of September."

"But it's the sixth of April."

Gideon turned his eyes to heaven. "We *arrive* on the twenty-fourth of September inside this house. If we don't want the Guardians to chop off our heads, we have to know the password. *Qua redit nescitis*. Go on, repeat it."

"*Qua redit nescitis*," I said. I was never going to be able to remember that for longer than a second. There, now it was gone again. Maybe I could write it on a scrap of paper. "What does it mean?"

"Don't tell me you're not learning Latin at school!"

"Well, I'm not," I said. I was taking French and German at school, which was more than enough.

"In full, *Qua redit nescitis horam*. "You know not the hour of your return," said Dr. White.

"Rather a flowery translation!" said Mr. George. "One could also say, 'You don't know when—'"

"Gentlemen!" Mr. de Villiers tapped his wristwatch in a meaningful way. "We don't have forever. Ready, Gideon?"

Gideon held his hand out to Dr. White, who raised one of the flaps and put Gideon's forefinger in the opening behind it. There was a faint humming sound as if cogwheels had started moving inside the device. It was almost like a tune on a music box. One of the jewels, a huge diamond, suddenly lit up from inside and bathed Gideon's face in clear white light. At the same moment, he disappeared.

"Wow, out of this world," I whispered, impressed.

"Literally so," said Mr. George. "Your turn now. Stand exactly here."

Dr. White went on. "And remember what we've told you: do as Gideon says and, whatever happens, always keep close to him." He took my hand and placed my forefinger in the opening under the flap. Something sharp pricked my fingertip, and I flinched. "Ow!"

Dr. White held my hand firmly down inside the flap. "Don't move!"

This time a big red stone on the chronograph began shining. Red light dazzled me. The last thing I saw was my huge hat lying forgotten on the table. Then everything around me went dark.

A hand took hold of my shoulder.

Oh, no. What was that stupid password? *Qua thing-ummy thingsitis.* "Is that you, Gideon?" I whispered.

"Who else?" he whispered back, and let go of my shoulder. "Well done, you didn't fall over!" A match flared, and next moment, the room was lit by a burning torch.

"Cool. Did you bring that with you?"

"No, it was here already. Hold it for a moment."

When I took the torch, I was glad I wasn't wearing that ridiculous hat. The huge nodding feathers on it would have caught fire in no time at all, and then I'd have been a pretty, blazing torch myself.

"Hush," said Gideon, although I hadn't so much as squeaked. He had unlocked the door. (Had he brought the key with him, or had it already been in the lock? I hadn't been watching.) Then he peered cautiously out into the corridor. Everything was pitch-dark.

"This place smells kind of like something decaying," I said.

"Nonsense. Come along!" Gideon closed the door behind us, took the torch from me again, and went down the dark corridor. I followed him.

"Aren't you going to blindfold me again?" I asked, only half joking.

"It's dark, you'd never remember the way," replied Gideon. "One more reason to stick close to me. We have to be back down here in three hours' time."

One more reason for me to know my way around. How was I going to manage if anything happened to Gideon, or if we were separated? I didn't think it was such a great idea not to let me know anything. But I bit back the words on the tip of my tongue. I didn't want to pick an argument with Mr. High and Mighty just now.

It smelled musty, far worse than in our own time. What year had we traveled back to again?

The smell really was pungent, as if something was decomposing down here. For some reason, I suddenly thought of rats. In films, long, dark, torchlit corridors always had rats in them! Hideous black rats with their beady little eyes glowing in the dark. Or dead rats. Oh, yeah, and spiders. There were always spiders in this kind of place. I tried not to touch the walls and pushed the thought of fat spiders clinging to the hem of my dress and slowly crawling up my bare legs out of my mind.

Instead, I counted the footsteps to every bend in the corridor. After forty-four steps, we turned right, after fifty-five, we turned left, then left again, and we reached a spiral staircase leading up. I held my skirt up as high as I could so as to keep up with Gideon. There was a light somewhere up there, getting brighter as we climbed, until finally we were in a broad corridor with many lighted torches along its walls. There was a large door at the end of the corridor, with two suits of armor standing on either side of it. They were just as rusty as in our own time.

Luckily I didn't see any rats, but all the same I had a sinking feeling that we were being watched, and the closer to the door we came, the stronger that feeling was. I looked around, but the corridor was empty.

When one of the suits of armor suddenly moved its arm and pointed a dangerous-looking spear or whatever it was at us, I froze, gasping for air. Now I knew who'd been watching us.

The suit of armor also, and totally unnecessarily, said, "Stop!" in a tinny voice.

I felt like screaming with terror, but once again not a sound would come out of my mouth. Pretty soon I realized it wasn't the suit of armor that had moved and spoken but whoever was inside it. The other suit of armor also seemed to be inhabited.

"We have to speak to the Master," said Gideon. "On urgent business."

"Password," said the second suit of armor.

"Qua redit nescitis," said Gideon.

Oh, yes—that was it. For a moment I was genuinely impressed. He'd actually remembered it.

"You may pass," said the first suit of armor, and it even held the door open for us.

There was another corridor beyond it, also lit by torches. Gideon stuck our torch in a holder on the wall and hurried on. I followed as fast as my hooped skirt would let me. By now I was out of breath.

"This is like a horror film. My heart almost stopped. I thought those things were just for decoration! I mean, suits of armor aren't exactly modern in the eighteenth century, are they? And not much use either, if you ask me."

"It's a tradition for the men on guard to wear them," said Gideon. "They do in our time as well."

"But I haven't seen any knights in armor in our time," I said. Then it occurred to me that maybe I had seen some after all. Maybe I'd just thought they were empty suits of armor.

"Get a move on," said Gideon.

Easy for him to say. He wasn't carrying a skirt the size of a tent around with him.

"Who is 'the Master'?"

"The Order is headed by a Grand Master. At this period of course it's the count himself. The Order is still young; the count founded it only thirty-seven years ago. Even later, members of the de Villiers family often held the post of Grand Master."

Did that mean Count Saint-Germain was a de Villiers? If he was, then why was he called Saint-Germain?

"What about now? Er, I mean in our time. Who's the Grand Master today?"

"At the moment, my Uncle Falk," said Gideon. "He took over from your grandfather Lord Montrose."

"Oh." My dear, kindly grandfather, Grand Master

of the Lodge of Count Saint-Germain! And I'd always thought he was totally under my grandmother's thumb.

"So what position does Lady Arista hold in the Order?"

"Oh, none. Women can't be members of the Lodge. The immediate families of the members of the Inner Circle automatically belong to the Outer Circle of initiates, but they don't have a say in anything."

That was obvious.

Maybe his way of treating me was natural to all the de Villiers family? A kind of congenital defect leaving them capable of only a contemptuous smile for women? On the other hand, he had been very gentle with Charlotte. And I had to admit that at the moment he was at least behaving himself reasonably well.

"Why do you always call your grandmother Lady Arista, by the way?" he asked. "Why don't you say Grandma or Granny?"

"I don't know. We just do," I said. "So, why can't women be members of the Lodge?"

Gideon put out an arm and shoved me behind him. "Shut up for a moment, would you?"

"What?"

There was another staircase at the end of this corridor. Daylight fell in from above, but before we reached the stairs, two men with drawn swords stepped out of the shadows, as if they'd been waiting for us.

"Good day," said Gideon. Unlike me, he hadn't batted an eyelash. But his hand had gone to his own sword.

"Password!" demanded the first man.

"Surely you were here only yesterday," said the second man, coming a little closer to take a look at Gideon. "Or your younger brother was. The likeness is remarkable."

"Is this the boy who can appear out of nowhere?" asked the other man. Both of them stared openmouthed at Gideon. They wore clothes like his, and Madame Rossini had obviously been right: in the Rococo age men did like bright colors. These two had combined red and brown with turquoise, which was then embroidered with little mauve flowers, and one of them really was wearing a lemon-yellow coat. The sight should have been appalling, but there was just something about it. It was . . . well, colorful.

They were both wearing wigs with curls like sausages over their ears and a small extra pigtail at the back of the neck tied with a velvet ribbon.

"Let's just say I know ways about this house that are unknown to you," said Gideon with a scornful smile. "I and my companion have to speak to the Master. On urgent business."

"That's right, mention yourself first," I murmured.

"The password?"

Quark edit bisquitis. Or something along those lines.

"Qua redit nescitis," said Gideon.

Well, I'd had it almost right.

FEMALE LINE OF DESCENT

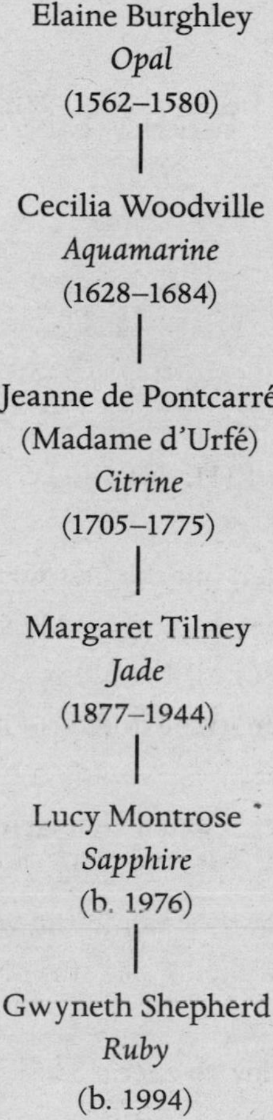

Elaine Burghley
Opal
(1562–1580)

Cecilia Woodville
Aquamarine
(1628–1684)

Jeanne de Pontcarré
(Madame d'Urfé)
Citrine
(1705–1775)

Margaret Tilney
Jade
(1877–1944)

Lucy Montrose
Sapphire
(b. 1976)

Gwyneth Shepherd
Ruby
(b. 1994)

FROM *THE CHRONICLES OF THE GUARDIANS,*
VOLUME 4: *THE CIRCLE OF TWELVE*

ELEVEN

THE MAN IN THE YELLOW coat put his sword away. "Follow me."

Curious, I looked out the first window we passed. So this was the eighteenth century! My scalp began tingling with excitement. But all I could see was an inner courtyard with a fountain in the middle of it. I'd seen it looking just the same before.

We went up more stairs. Gideon let me go first.

"You were here only yesterday?" I asked, intrigued. I whispered it so that the man in the yellow coat wouldn't hear what we were saying. He was only a couple of steps ahead of us.

"It was yesterday to them," said Gideon. "To me it's almost two years ago."

"Why were you here?"

"To introduce myself to the count, and I had to tell him that the first chronograph had been stolen."

"I don't suppose he thought much of that."

The man in yellow acted as if he wasn't trying to listen to us, but you could practically see his ears popping out from under the white sausages of hair in the effort to hear.

"He took it better than I'd expected," said Gideon. "And after the first shock, he was delighted to hear that our second chronograph really was in working order, giving us another chance to end the whole thing successfully."

"Where's the chronograph *now*?" I whispered. "I mean at this moment in this time."

"Somewhere in this building, I assume. The count won't be parted from it for long. He himself has to elapse to avoid random time traveling."

"Why can't we simply take the chronograph back with us into the future, then?"

"For a number of reasons," said Gideon. His tone of voice had changed. It wasn't quite so arrogant. More like patronizing. "The most important are obvious. One of the Guardians' golden rules for the use of the chronograph is that the continuum must never be broken. If we took the chronograph back to the future with us, the count and the time travelers born after him would have to manage without it."

"Yes, but then no one could steal it either."

Gideon shook his head. "I can see you've never thought much about the nature of time. It would be very dangerous to interrupt certain sequences of events. In the worst case scenario, you might never be born."

"I see," I said untruthfully.

Meanwhile we had reached the first floor, passing two more men armed with swords. The yellow man had a brief exchange with them in whispers. What was that password again? All I could think of was *Qua nesquick mosquitoes.* I definitely had to get myself another brain.

The two men were looking at Gideon and me with unconcealed curiosity, and as soon as we'd passed them, they went on whispering. I'd have loved to hear what they were saying.

The man in yellow knocked on a door. Another man was sitting at a desk inside the room, also wearing a wig and colorful clothes. The turquoise coat and flowered waistcoat that showed above the desk were dazzling, and below the desktop, there was a cheerful view of bright red trousers and striped stockings. I'd stopped even being surprised by this kind of thing.

"Mr. Secretary," said the man in yellow, "here's yesterday's visitor again. And he knows today's password, too."

The secretary man looked incredulously at Gideon's face. "How *can* you know the password? We announced it only two hours ago, and no one's left this house since then. And who is *she*? Women are not allowed here."

I was going to tell him my name politely, but Gideon took my arm and interrupted me. "We have to speak to the count," he said. "On urgent business. We're in a hurry."

"They came from down below," said the man in yellow.

"But the count isn't here," said the secretary. He was on his feet now, wringing his hands. "We can send a messenger—"

"No, we have to speak to the count ourselves. We don't have time to send messengers back and forth. Where is the count at the moment?"

"Visiting Lord Brompton in his new town house in Wigmore Street. A meeting to discuss something of the greatest importance. He arranged the meeting directly after your visit yesterday."

Gideon swore under his breath. "We need a coach to take us to Wigmore Street, then. At once."

"I can arrange that," said the secretary, nodding to the man in yellow. "See to it yourself, please, Wilbour."

"But—won't we be rather short of time?" I asked, thinking of the long way back through the musty cellar. "I mean, time to get to Wigmore Street in a coach." Our dentist was in Wigmore Street. The nearest Tube station was Bond Street on the Central Line, but going there from here you'd have to change several times. And like I said, that was on the Tube! I hated to think how long it would take in a horse-drawn coach. "Maybe it would be better if we came back another time?"

"No," said Gideon, suddenly smiling at me. There was something in his face that I couldn't quite interpret. A wish for adventure, maybe?

"We still have over two and a half hours," he said cheerfully. "We'll drive to Wigmore Street."

THE COACH DRIVE through London was the most exciting thing to have happened to me so far. For some reason I'd imagined the city would be very peaceful without any motor traffic—people strolling along carrying sunshades and wearing hats, a carriage now and then trotting by at a comfortable pace, no exhaust fumes, no taxis racing recklessly along and trying to run you down even when you were going over a pedestrian crossing with a green light.

In fact, it was anything but peaceful. It was raining, and even without cars and buses, the traffic was chaotic. All kinds of coaches, carriages, and carts were going along, crowding close together, spraying mud and water from the puddles all over the place. True, there were no exhaust fumes, but the street didn't smell good—there was a slight smell of decay, and then there were horse droppings and other refuse.

I'd never seen so many horses all at once before. Our coach was drawn by four of them, black and very beautiful. The man in the yellow coat was sitting on the coachman's box, guiding the horses through the turmoil at breakneck speed. The coach rocked wildly, and every time the horses went around a bend, I thought we were going to tip over. What with that and trying hard not to let the jolting make me fall against Gideon, I couldn't see much of the London that was passing by outside the coach windows. When I did look out, nothing that I saw, nothing at all, looked familiar. It was as if I'd landed in a totally different city.

"This is Kingsway," said Gideon. "You wouldn't recognize it, would you?"

Our coachman launched into a daring overtaking

maneuver to get past an oxcart and a coach like our own. This time I couldn't help it—the force of gravity flung me against Gideon.

"This guy must think he's Ben Hur," I said as I slid back into my own corner.

"Driving a coach is tremendous fun," said Gideon, and he sounded quite envious of the man on the box. "It's even better in an open carriage, of course. I'd like to drive a phaeton."

Once again the coach swayed, and I started feeling slightly nauseated. You needed a strong stomach to ride in one of these. "And I'd like to be in a Jag," I murmured.

Still, I had to admit that we arrived in Wigmore Street sooner than I'd have thought possible. I looked around as we got out in front of a very grand house, but I didn't recognize anything about this part of town from our own time, even though unfortunately, like I said, I'd had to go to the dentist more often than I wanted to. But there was a vague sense of familiarity about it all. And the rain had stopped.

The footman who opened the door claimed at first that Lord Brompton was not at home, but Gideon convincingly assured him that he knew that wasn't true and said that if the footman didn't take us both to his lordship and his lordship's visitors at once, he would lose his job that very day. He put his signet ring into the intimidated footman's hand and told him to hurry up.

"Do you have your own signet ring?" I asked as we waited in the entrance hall.

"Yes, of course," said Gideon. "Are you scared?"

"No, why? Should I be?" The coach ride had jolted me about so much that I couldn't think of anything scarier for the moment. But just as he was saying that, my heart began thudding wildly. I couldn't help thinking of what my mother had said about Count Saint-Germain. If the man really could read thoughts . . .

I felt my pinned-up hair. It was probably all untidy after that coach ride.

"It looks perfect," said Gideon with a slight smile.

What was all this about? Did he *want* to make me feel nervous?

"Our cook at home is called Brompton, too," I said, to cover up for my embarrassment. "Mrs. Brompton."

"It's a small world," said Gideon.

The footman came running downstairs, coattails flying. "The gentlemen are expecting you, sir."

We followed the man up to the first floor.

"Can he really read thoughts?" I whispered.

"Who, the footman?" Gideon whispered back. "I hope not. I was just thinking he looks like a weasel."

Was that by any chance a bit of humor? Mr. High-and-Mighty Time Traveler actually cracking a joke? I gave him a quick smile. (Well, it was worth encouraging the possibility.)

"Not the footman. The count," I said.

He nodded. "That's what people say, anyway."

"Did he read *your* thoughts?"

"If he did, I didn't notice."

With a deep bow, the footman opened a door for us. I stopped. Maybe I should simply think of nothing at all? But that was plain impossible. As soon as I tried not thinking of anything, millions of ideas flooded my brain.

"Ladies first," said Gideon, pushing me gently through the doorway.

I took a couple of steps forward and then stopped. I wasn't sure what was expected of me next. Gideon followed me in, and after another deep bow, the footman closed the door behind us.

Three men were looking at us. The first was a stout man who could only just haul himself out of his chair; the second, a younger man with a very muscular build, the only one of the three not to be wearing a wig; and the third was lean and tall, with features just like those of the portrait in the documents room.

Count Saint-Germain.

Gideon bowed, though not as deeply as the footman just now. The three men bowed back.

I didn't do anything. No one had taught me how to manage a curtsey in a hooped skirt, and curtseying didn't feel natural anyway.

"I didn't expect to see you back so soon, my young friend," said the man I took to be Count Saint-Germain. He was smiling broadly. "Lord Brompton, may I introduce my great-great-great grandson's great-great-great-grandson to you? Gideon de Villiers."

"Lord Brompton!" Another little bow. Obviously shaking hands wasn't the fashion yet.

"Visually at least, I consider that my line has turned out extremely well," said the count. "I obviously had luck in choosing the lady of my heart. The tendency to a large hooked nose has entirely died out."

"Now, now, my dear Count, there you go trying to impress me with your tall tales again," said Lord Brompton, dropping back into his chair. The chair was so tiny that I was afraid it might collapse under him there and then. His lordship wasn't just a bit plump, like Mr. George—he was really huge!

"But I have no objection," he went on, with his little piggy eyes twinkling cheerfully. "Your company is always so very entertaining. A new surprise every few seconds!"

The count laughed and turned to the younger, bare-headed man. "Lord Brompton is and always will be skeptical, my dear Miro! We must think a little harder to find some way of convincing him of our cause."

The man replied in a harsh, clipped foreign language, and the count smiled again. He turned to Gideon. "This, my dear grandson, is my good friend and companion Miro Rakoczy, better known in *The Annals of the Guardians* as the Black Leopard."

"Delighted to meet you," said Gideon.

More bows all round.

Rakoczy—why did that name seem familiar to me? And why did the sight of him make me feel so uncomfortable?

A smile curled the count's lips as his eyes slowly moved down over my figure. I automatically looked for some resemblance in him to Gideon or Falk de Villiers, but I couldn't find one. The count's eyes were very dark, and his gaze was penetrating. It immediately made me think again of what my mother had said.

Think! No, don't! But my mind had to have something to occupy it, so I sang "God Save the Queen" in my head.

The count switched to French, which I didn't understand at first (particularly as inside my head I was busy singing the national anthem at the top of my imaginary voice), but which, with some hesitation and leaving gaps on account of my poor command of French vocabulary, I translated as "And so you, pretty girl, are a [gap] of the good [gap] Jeanne d'Urfé. I was told you had red hair."

Yikes! It was probably a fact that learning vocabulary was actually essential to understanding a foreign language, like our French teacher had always said. And sadly I didn't know anyone called Jeanne d'Urfé, so I really couldn't understand what he was talking about anyway.

"She doesn't know French," said Gideon, also in French. "And she isn't the girl you were expecting."

"But how can that be?" The count shook his head. "All this is extremely [gap]."

"Unfortunately, the wrong girl was prepared for the [gap]."

Yes, *unfortunately.*

"A mistake?"

"This is Gwyneth Shepherd, a cousin of the Charlotte Montrose I mentioned to you yesterday."

"Ah, another granddaughter of Lord Montrose, the

last [gap]. And thus a cousin of the [gap]?" Count Saint-Germain's dark eyes were resting on me, and I began singing in my mind again.

Send her victorious, happy and glorious . . .

"It's the [gap, gap] that I simply do not understand."

"Our scientists say that it is perfectly possible for a genetic [gap] to—"

The count raised his hand to interrupt Gideon. "I know, I know! That may be so, according to the laws of science, but nonetheless, I do not feel happy about it."

I shared his feelings.

"No French, then?" he asked, switching to German. I was a little better at German, or at least, my mark had been a regular B for four years now, but once again there were those annoying gaps in my vocabulary. "Why has she been so poorly prepared?"

"She hasn't been prepared at all, sir. She speaks no foreign languages." Gideon was speaking German too now. "And in every other respect, she is also entirely [gap]. Charlotte and Gwyneth were born on the same day. But everyone mistakenly assumed that Gwyneth was born a day later."

"How could such a thing be overlooked?" Ah, at last I could understand every word again. They'd switched back to English, which the count spoke without a trace of foreign accent. "Why, I wonder, do I begin to feel that the Guardians of your time no longer take their work entirely seriously?"

"I think you'll find the answer in this letter." Gideon

took a sealed envelope out of the inside pocket of his coat and handed it to the count.

A piercing glance rested on me.

. . . frustrate their knavish tricks, on thee our hopes we fix, God save us all . . .

I firmly avoided his dark eyes and looked at the other two men instead. Lord Brompton seemed to have as many gaps in his French and German vocabulary as I did (his mouth was slightly open above his many double chins, and he was looking a little foolish), and the other man, Rakoczy, was inspecting his fingernails closely.

He was still quite young, maybe around thirty, and he had dark hair and a thin, long face. He could have been quite good-looking, except that his lips were twisted as if he had a very nasty taste in his mouth and his skin was pale in an unhealthy kind of way.

I was just wondering whether he'd been putting pale gray powder on his face when he suddenly raised his eyes and looked straight at me. Those eyes were pitch-black, and I couldn't see where their irises and pupils began and ended. There was an oddly dead look about them, although I couldn't have explained why.

Automatically I went back to singing "God Save the Queen" in my head. Meanwhile the count had broken the seal and unfolded the letter, and with a sigh he began to read it. Now and then he raised his head and looked at me. I still hadn't moved from the spot.

Not in this land alone, but be God's mercies known . . .

What did the letter say? Who had written it? Lord

Brompton and Rakoczy seemed to be very interested in it too. Lord Brompton was craning his fat neck to get a glimpse of the writing, while Rakoczy was concentrating more on the count's face. Obviously the disgusted twist of Rakoczy's mouth was permanent.

When he looked at me again, all the little hairs on my arms bristled. Those eyes of his were like black holes, and now I discovered why they seemed so dead. They didn't reflect light; they didn't have the bright sparkle that brings most people's eyes to life. It wasn't just peculiar, it was gruesome. I was glad there was a good five yards' distance between those eyes and me.

"Your mother, my child, appears to be an unusually obstinate woman." The count had finished reading the letter and was folding it up. "One can only speculate on her motives." He came a couple of paces closer to me, and under his penetrating gaze, I couldn't even remember the words of the national anthem anymore.

But then I saw something I hadn't noticed before. The count was old. Although his eyes were bright and full of energy, his back was straight, and the sound of his voice was lively and youthful, you couldn't miss the signs of old age. The skin on his face and hands was crumpled like parchment, blue veins showed through, and even under a layer of powder, the wrinkles on his face were obvious. His age made him look fragile. I almost felt sorry for him.

Anyway, all at once I wasn't afraid of him anymore. He was only an old man, older than my own grandfather when I knew him.

"Gwyneth knows nothing about her mother's motives or the events that have left us in this situation," said Gideon. "She has no idea at all."

"Strange, very strange," said the count as he walked once all around me. "We really have never met before."

Of course we hadn't. How could we have met before?

"But you would not be here unless you were the Ruby. *Ruby red, with G major, the magic of the raven, brings the Circle of Twelve home into safe haven.*" When he had finished circling me, he stood before me and looked straight into my eyes. "What is your magic, girl?"

. . . from shore to shore, Lord make the nations see . . .

Oh, why was I bothering with this? He was only an old man. I ought to treat him politely and respectfully and not stare at him like a terrified rabbit in the presence of a snake.

"I don't know, sir."

"What is special about you? Tell me!"

What was special about me? Apart from the fact that for the last two days I'd been able to travel back to the past? Suddenly I could hear Aunt Glenda's voice saying "Even when Charlotte was a baby, anyone could tell she was born for higher things. You can't compare her with ordinary children."

"I don't think there's anything special about me, sir."

The count clicked his tongue. "You may be right. After all, it's only a verse. A verse of doubtful origin." He suddenly seemed to lose interest in me and turned back to Gideon. "My dear boy, I read here, with admiration, what you have already done. You have tracked Lancelot de Villiers down in Flanders! William de Villiers, Cecilia Woodville—the enchanting Aquamarine—and the twins I never met: you've ticked them all off the list. And just think, Lord Brompton, this young man even visited Madame Jeanne d'Urfé, née Pontcarré, in Paris and persuaded her to donate a little of her blood."

"You mean the Madame d'Urfé to whom my father owed his friendship with Madame de Pompadour and ultimately with you as well?" asked Lord Brompton.

"The very same," said the count. "I don't know any other."

"But Madame d'Urfé has been dead these last ten years."

"Seven, to be precise," said the count. "I was at the court of Margrave Charles of Ansbach at the time. I feel greatly drawn to the German states. The interest shown there in Freemasonry and alchemy is very gratifying. And as I was told many years ago, I shall die in Germany."

"You're just changing the subject," said Lord Brompton. "How can this young man have visited Madame d'Urfé in Paris? Why, seven years ago he must still have been a child himself."

"You persist in thinking along the wrong lines, my dear sir! Ask Gideon *when* he had the pleasure of asking for a drop of Madame d'Urfé's blood."

Lord Brompton looked inquiringly at Gideon.

"May 1759," said Gideon.

His lordship uttered a shrill burst of laughter. "But

that's impossible. You can hardly be twenty years old now."

The count laughed too, but with satisfaction. "So you met her in 1759. She never told me, old mystery-monger that she was."

"You were in Paris yourself at the time, sir, but I had strict instructions not to cross your path."

"On account of the continuum, yes, I know." The count sighed. "Sometimes I am inclined to quarrel with my own rules. . . . But back to dear Jeanne. Did you have to use force? She wasn't very cooperative with me."

"So she told me," said Gideon. "As well as the way you talked her into handing over the chronograph."

"Talked her into it! She didn't even know what a marvel she'd inherited from her grandmother. The poor device was lying around unused, unrecognized, in a dusty chest in an attic. Sooner or later, it would have been entirely forgotten. I rescued it and restored it to its former glory. And thanks to the figures of genius who will enter my Lodge in the future, it is still in working order today. That is little short of a miracle."

"Madame d'Urfé also thought you were prepared to strangle her, just because she couldn't remember her great-grandmother's maiden name and date of birth."

Strangle her? Yikes! How horrible was that?

"Quite so. Such gaps in our knowledge have cost me far too much time poring over old church records, when I could have put my mind to more important matters. Jeanne is a distinctly vindictive woman. Which makes it all the more remarkable that you persuaded her to cooperate."

Gideon smiled. "It wasn't easy. But I obviously struck her as trustworthy. I also danced the gavotte with her, and I listened patiently to her complaints of you."

"How unjust. When it was I who nudged her in the direction of an exciting love affair with Casanova—and even if he was only after her money, a lot of other women envied her. What's more, I shared my chronograph with her in a truly fraternal spirit. If it hadn't been for me . . ." The count turned to me again, obviously brightening up. "An ungrateful female. I think she never really understood what was happening to her, poor old soul. Moreover, she felt insulted because her gemstone in the Circle of Twelve was only the citrine. *Why can you be Emerald and I'm only dull Citrine? No one who takes any pride in herself wears citrines these days!*" He chuckled. "She really was a very foolish creature. I wonder how often she traveled back in time in her old age. Maybe she stopped doing it entirely. She was never a greatly skilled time traveler anyway. Sometimes a whole month would pass before she disappeared. I'd say the female blood is considerably more sluggish than ours. Just as the female mind is inferior to the masculine intellect. Would you not agree with me, girl?"

Male chauvinist pig, I was thinking as I kept my eyes cast down, *stupid, pompous, boring old chatterbox.* Oh, no! Was I crazy? I wasn't supposed to be thinking of anything!

But obviously the count's mind-reading skill wasn't all it was cracked up to be, because he just chuckled again in a self-satisfied way. "Not particularly talkative, is she?" he remarked.

"She's only shy," said Gideon. "Timid."

Intimidated would have been more like it.

"There are no shy women," announced the count. "The modest way they cast their eyes down merely hides their naivety."

I was fast coming to the conclusion that there was no need to feel afraid of *him*. He was only a self-satisfied old git who hated women and liked the sound of his own voice.

"You clearly do not hold a high opinion of the fair sex," said Lord Brompton.

"Oh, I protest!" replied the count. "I adore women! Really. I just do not believe their intellect is capable of furthering the interests of mankind. That is why there is no place for women in my Lodge." He favored his lordship with a beaming smile. "And for many men, I assure you, Lord Brompton, that is the crucial argument that causes them to seek membership themselves."

"Yet the ladies love you! My father never tired of praising your success with the fair sex to the skies. We are told that women have always thrown themselves at your feet, here in London and also in Paris."

The count fell silent at once, no doubt thinking of his days as a ladies' man. Then he said, "Oh, it is not particularly difficult to beguile women and subdue them to your will, my dear sir. They're all the same. If my mind were not on higher things, I would long ago have written a manual for gentlemen, advising them on the right way to handle women."

I bet he would. I could think of a good title for it straight off. *Successful Strangulation, or How to Talk a Woman to Death*. I almost giggled. But then I realized that Rakoczy was watching me very intently, and my mood suddenly shifted.

I must be out of my mind! Those black eyes met mine for a second and then I looked down at the mosaic floor before my feet and tried to fight off the sense of panic threatening to overwhelm me. I knew for sure now that it wasn't the count I had to beware of. But that was far from meaning that I could feel safe.

"This is all most entertaining," said Lord Brompton. His double chins were quivering with delight. "You and your companions would have made good play actors, I'll be bound. As my father said, my dear Saint-Germain, you could always come up with surprising stories. But I fear you can't prove any of them. You haven't yet performed a single trick for me."

"Performed a trick!" cried the count. "Oh, my dear sir, what a doubting Thomas you are. I would long ago have lost patience with you had I not been aware of my obligations to your father, God rest his soul. Or had my interest in your money and your influence not been so great."

Lord Brompton laughed a little uncomfortably. "Well, you are honest, to be sure."

"Alchemy can't manage without its patrons." The count swung around to Rakoczy. "We must show his lordship a few of our *tricks.* He's one of those who believe only the evidence of their own eyes. But first I must have a private word with my great-grandson here and write a letter to the future Grand Master of our Lodge."

"You're welcome to make use of the study next door," said his lordship, pointing to a door behind him. "And I look forward with great excitement to a performance."

"Come along, my boy." The count took Gideon's arm. "There are some questions that I must ask you. And some things that you should know."

"We have only half an hour left," said Gideon, looking at the pocket watch fastened to his waistcoat with a gold chain. "By then, at the latest, we must set off back to the Temple."

"Half an hour will be quite sufficient," said the count. "I write fast, and I can talk at the same time."

Gideon laughed briefly. He actually seemed to think the count witty, and he had obviously forgotten that I was still there too.

I cleared my throat. Halfway to the door, he turned to look at me and raised an eyebrow inquiringly.

I answered his question just as silently, because I could hardly say it out loud. *For goodness' sake don't leave me alone with these weirdos.*

Gideon hesitated.

"She would only be in the way," said the count.

"Wait for me here," said Gideon, in an unexpectedly gentle tone of voice.

"His lordship and Miro will keep her company," said

the count. "Gentlemen, you could ask her a few questions about the future. This is a unique opportunity. She comes from the twenty-first century—ask her about the automatic trains that race along underground in London. Or the silver flying machines that rise miles up in the air with a sound like the roar of a thousand lions and can cross the sea."

Lord Brompton laughed so much that I felt seriously worried about his chair. All his rolls of fat were quivering. "Anything else?"

No way did I want to be left alone with him and Rakoczy. But Gideon just smiled, although I gave him a pleading glance.

"I'll be right back," he said.

Today Black Tourmaline, Paul de Villiers, came from the year 1992, as agreed, to elapse in the documents room here. But this time he was accompanied by a red-haired girl who gave her name as Lucy Montrose, saying that she was the granddaughter of our adept Lucas Montrose. She bore, in every respect, an unfortunate similarity to Arista Bishop (Jade line, observation number 4).

We took them both to Lucas's office. It is now clear to us all that Lucas is presumably going to propose marriage to Arista and not, as we had hoped would be the case, to Claudine Seymour. (Although it has to be admitted that Arista has better legs, and a really good backhand at tennis.)

How very strange for a man to be visited by his grandchild before he has any children of his own.

FROM *THE ANNALS OF THE GUARDIANS*

12 JUNE 1948

REPORT: KENNETH DE VILLIERS, INNER CIRCLE

TWELVE

AS THE DOOR CLOSED behind Gideon and the count, I stepped back.

"Do, pray, be seated," said Lord Brompton, indicating one of the delicate chairs. Rakoczy's lips twisted. Was that meant to be a smile? If so, he needed to give it more practice in front of the mirror.

"No, thank you. I'd rather stand." Another step back, until I almost collided with a naked stone Cupid standing on a plinth to the right of the doorway. The more distance I could put between myself and those black eyes, the safer I felt.

"And you really claim to come from the twenty-first century?"

There was no *claiming* about it. But I nodded.

Lord Brompton rubbed his hands. "Well, then—what king rules England in the twenty-first century?"

"We have a prime minister who does the actual ruling," I said, faltering slightly. "The Queen just looks after the big state occasions."

"Queen?"

"Queen Elizabeth II. She's lovely. She came to our multiethnic schools party last year. We sang the national anthem in seven different languages and Gordon Gelderman got her autograph in his English textbook and sold it for eighty pounds on eBay. But, er, of course that won't mean anything much to you. So anyway, we have a prime minister and a cabinet, and everyone eighteen and over in the country votes for members of Parliament."

Lord Brompton laughed appreciatively. "What a quaint idea, don't you think, Rakoczy? Our friend the count invents the most amusing stories. And how do matters stand with France in the twenty-first century?"

"I think they have a prime minister in France too. No king, not even for state occasions. Well, they got rid of the aristocracy in the French Revolution, you see, and the king along with him. Poor Marie-Antoinette had her head chopped off by the guillotine. Isn't that terrible?"

"Oh, yes, surely!" laughed his lordship. "Terrible folk, the French. We Englishmen can never get along with them. So now, do tell me: what country are we at war with in the twenty-first century?"

"Well, no country," I said, rather unsure of my ground here. "Not really, anyway. We just send troops here and there to help out. In the Middle East and so on. But to be honest, I don't know a lot about politics. Why not ask me something about . . . about refrigerators? Not how they work—I don't know how they work, really. I just know they *do* work, and every home in London has a fridge, and you can keep cheese and milk in it for days, and they don't go bad."

Lord Brompton did not look as if he was particularly interested in fridges either. Rakoczy stretched in his chair like a cat. I hoped he wouldn't think it was a good idea to stand up.

"Or you can ask me about telephones," I added quickly. "Not that I can explain how they work either." If I'd sized up Lord Brompton accurately, telephones were something else he wouldn't understand. To be honest, he didn't look as if he could take in even the principle of the incandescent lightbulb. I tried to think of something else that might interest him.

"And then, er . . . well, then there's this tunnel running underneath the English Channel between Dover and Calais."

This seemed to be the funniest thing Lord Brompton had ever heard. He slapped his huge thigh as he shook with laughter. "Wonderful! Wonderful!"

I was just beginning to relax a little when Rakoczy spoke—in English with a harsh accent. "And Transylvania?"

"Transylvania?" The home of Count Dracula? Did he mean it seriously? I avoided looking into those black eyes. Maybe he *was* Count Dracula. His pale complexion would suit the part, anyway.

"My native land in the beautiful Carpathians. The principality of Transylvania. What is happening in Transylvania in the twenty-first century?" His voice sounded a little hoarse, and there was definitely a note of nostalgia in it. "And what has become of the Kuruc people?"

The what people? Kuruc? I'd never heard of them.

"Er, well, things are pretty quiet in Transylvania in our time," I said cautiously. To be honest, I didn't even know where the place was. But I'm sure these Kuruc people really did live there.

"Who rules Transylvania in the twenty-first century?" Rakoczy went on. He looked very much on the alert, as if he might leap up from his chair at any moment if my answer was unsatisfactory.

Hm, yes. Who did rule Transylvania? That was a really good question. Did it belong to Bulgaria? Or Romania? Or Hungary?

"I don't know," I said truthfully. "It's so far away. I'll have to ask Mrs. Counter—she's our geography teacher."

Rakoczy looked disappointed. Maybe I'd have done better to tell a few lies. *Transylvania has been ruled by Prince Dracula for the last two hundred years. It's a nature reserve for bat species that would otherwise have died out. The Kurucs are the happiest people in Europe.* He'd probably have liked that better.

"And how are our colonies doing in the twenty-first century?" asked Lord Brompton.

To my relief, I saw that Rakoczy was leaning back

again. And he didn't crumble to dust when the sun broke through the clouds and bathed the room in bright, clear light.

For a while we talked in an almost relaxed way about America and Jamaica and some islands that I have to admit I'd never heard of. Lord Brompton seemed very upset to think that all these places now ruled themselves. (Well, I assumed they did. I wasn't absolutely certain.) Of course he didn't believe a word I said. Rakoczy took no more part in the conversation. He just looked alternately at his long, clawlike fingernails and the wallpaper, throwing an occasional glance my way.

"How sad to think that you are only an actress," sighed Lord Brompton. "Such a pity. I would like so much to believe you."

"Well, in your place I don't suppose I'd believe me either," I said understandingly. "I'm afraid I don't have any proof . . . oh, wait a minute!" I reached down into my décolletage and brought out my mobile.

"What do you have there? A cigar case?"

"No!" I opened the mobile, and it beeped because it couldn't find a network. Of course not. "This is . . . oh, never mind. I can take pictures with it."

"You mean paint them?"

I shook my head and held the mobile up so that Lord Brompton and Rakoczy appeared on the display. "Smile, please. There, that's it." There hadn't been any flash because the sunlight was so bright, which was a pity. A flash would surely have impressed the pair of them.

"What was that?" Lord Brompton had hauled his massive body out of his chair surprisingly fast, and he came over to me. I showed him the picture on the display. I'd caught him and Rakoczy very well.

"But—what is it? How is that possible?"

"It's what we call photography," I said.

Lord Brompton's fat fingers caressed the mobile. "Wonderful!" he said enthusiastically. "Rakoczy, you must see this!"

"No, thank you," said Rakoczy wearily.

"How you do it I don't know, but that's the best trick I've ever seen. Oh, what's happened now?"

Lesley was on the display. His lordship had pressed one of the keys.

"That's my friend Lesley," I said, wishing I could see her in real life. "I took the picture last week. Look, there behind her is Marylebone High Street—her sandwich came from Prêt à Manger—and there's the Aveda shop, see? It's where my mum always buys her hair spray." I suddenly felt terribly homesick. "And there's part of a taxi. A kind of coach that drives along without any horses—"

"How much would you want for this box of tricks? I'll pay you any price you ask, any!"

"Er, no, really, it's not for sale. I still need it." Shrugging regretfully, I closed my box of tricks—I mean, my mobile—and slipped it back into its hiding place inside my bodice.

Not a moment too soon, because the door opened and

the count and Gideon came back, the count smiling with satisfaction, Gideon looking rather grave. Now Rakoczy too rose from his chair.

Gideon glanced at me intently. I looked defiantly back at him. Had he expected me to make off while he was out of the room? It would have served him right. After all, he was the one who'd drummed it into me that I must stick close to him at all times, only to abandon me himself at the first opportunity.

"So, how would you like to live in the twenty-first century, Lord Brompton?" asked the count.

"I should like it very much! What fantastic ideas you do have," said his lordship, clapping his hands. "It was really most amusing."

"I knew you'd enjoy it. But you might have offered the poor child a chair."

"Oh, I most certainly did. But she preferred to stand." His lordship leaned forward and spoke in confidential tones. "I would *really* like to buy that little silver shrine, my dear count."

"Silver shrine?"

"We have to leave now, I'm afraid," said Gideon, crossing the room with a few strides and placing himself beside me.

"I understand, I understand! The twenty-first century awaits you, of course," said Lord Brompton. "I thank you most warmly for visiting me. It was wonderfully entertaining."

"I can only agree with you," said the count.

"I hope we shall have the pleasure of meeting again," said Lord Brompton.

Rakoczy said nothing. He just looked at me. And suddenly I felt as if an icy hand had been laid on my throat. I gasped for air, alarmed, and looked down at myself. Nothing to be seen. Yet I felt the fingers closing around my windpipe.

"I can press harder whenever I like."

It wasn't Rakoczy saying that—it was the count. But his lips hadn't moved.

Bewildered, I looked from his mouth to his hand. It was more than four yards away from me. How could it be around my neck at the same time? And why did I hear his voice in my head when he wasn't speaking?

"I don't know exactly what part you are playing, girl, or whether you are of any importance. But I will not have my rules broken. I am warning you. Do you understand?" The pressure of his fingers tightened.

I was paralyzed by fear. I could only stare at him, gasping for breath. Didn't anyone notice what was happening to me?

"I asked if you understood."

"Yes," I whispered.

The grip of the count's fingers slackened at once, the hand was removed. Air could stream freely into my lungs.

The count's lips curled, and he shook his wrist.

"We shall meet again," he said.

Gideon bowed. The three men bowed back. I was the only one who stood perfectly still, unable to move at all, until Gideon took my hand and led me out of the room.

EVEN WHEN we were sitting in the coach again I still felt terribly nervous—weak, exhausted, and dirty in a strange kind of way.

How had the count managed to speak to me without the others hearing? And how had he touched me when he was four yards away? My mother had been right. He *could* get into your mind and control your feelings. I'd let his conceited, erratic way of talking and his frail old appearance mislead me. I had hopelessly underestimated him.

How stupid of me.

In fact I'd underestimated this whole strange story that I'd fallen into.

The coach had started moving and was rocking just as much as it had on the outward journey. Gideon had told the Guardian in the yellow coat to hurry. As if he needed to! The Guardian had been driving like a man who was tired of life even on the way to Lord Brompton's house.

"Are you all right? You look as if you'd seen a ghost." Gideon took off his coat and put it on the seat beside him. "Quite hot for September here."

"Not a ghost," I said, unable to look him in the eye. My voice shook slightly. "Only Count Saint-Germain and one of his *tricks*."

"He wasn't particularly civil to you," Gideon admitted.

"But that was only to be expected. He obviously had other ideas of what you should be like."

When I said nothing, he went on. "In the prophesies, the twelfth time traveler is always described as rather special. *Ruby red, with G major, the magic of the raven.* Whatever that may be. Anyway, the count didn't want to believe me when I said you were just an ordinary schoolgirl."

Curiously enough, this comment immediately disposed of the weak, wretched feeling that the count's phantom touch had set off. Instead of weariness and fear, I felt a strong sense of injured pride. And fury. I bit my lip.

"Gwyneth?"

"What?"

"I didn't mean to insult you. I wasn't putting you down—I just meant you were an *average* girl, understand?"

Oh, wonderful. It got better and better.

"Perfectly," I said, glaring at him. "I couldn't care less what you think of me."

He looked at me calmly. "You can't help it."

"You don't know anything at all about me!" I said indignantly.

"Maybe not," said Gideon. "But I know lots of girls like you. They're all the same."

"Lots of girls like me? Huh!"

"I mean, girls who aren't interested in anything but hairstyles, clothes, films, and pop stars. And you're always giggling, and you go to the loo in groups. And you make snide remarks about some girl named Lisa or whatever for buying a cheap chain store T-shirt for five pounds."

Even though I was irate, I burst out laughing. "You mean to say that all these girls you know make snide remarks about someone called Lisa for buying a cheap T-shirt?"

"Well, you see what I mean."

"Yes, I do." I didn't really intend to say any more, but it just burst out of me. "You think all girls who aren't like Charlotte are stupid and superficial. Just because we had a normal childhood instead of all those fencing lessons and instruction in mysterious prophesies. The fact is, you haven't ever had time to get to know any normal girls. That's why you have all these pathetic prejudices."

"Oh, come on! I've been to school, same as you."

"Yeah, sure!" The words were just spilling out of me. "If you've been trained for your life as a time traveler only half as thoroughly as Charlotte, then you've had no time to make any friends at all, and your opinion of what you call *average* girls comes from observations you made when you were standing about the school yard alone. Or are you telling me that the other kids at your school thought your hobbies, like Latin, dancing the gavotte, and driving horse-drawn carriages, were really cool?"

Instead of being insulted, Gideon looked amused. "You left out playing the violin." He leaned back and crossed his arms.

"The violin? Really?" My anger had gone away again as fast as it had come over me. Playing the violin! Honestly!

"At least you have a bit of color back in your face. You looked as pale as Miro Rakoczy."

Definitely. Rakoczy. "How do you spell his name?"

"R-a-k-o-c-z-y," said Gideon. "Why?"

"I want to Google him."

"Oh, did you fancy him so much?"

"Fancy him? He's a vampire," I said. "He comes from Transylvania."

"He does come from Transylvania, but that doesn't make him a vampire."

"How do you know?"

"Because there are no such things as vampires, Gwyneth."

"Oh, no? If there are time machines, why wouldn't there be vampires too? Ever looked into his eyes? They're like black holes."

"That comes of drinking belladonna. He's experimenting with it," said Gideon. "A plant poison said to expand the consciousness."

"How do you know *that*?"

"It says so in *The Annals of the Guardians*. In their pages, Rakoczy is known as the Black Leopard. He saved the count from two assassination attempts. He's very strong and extremely skilled with weapons."

"Who wanted to kill the count?"

Gideon shrugged. "A man like that has many enemies."

"I can see why!" I said. "But I kind of get the impression that he can look after himself."

"Oh, he certainly can," agreed Gideon.

I wondered whether I ought to tell him what the count had done, but I decided not to. Gideon wasn't just a polite acquaintance—the way it looked to me, he and the count were bosom buddies.

Trust no one.

"You really traveled to see all those people in the past and take blood from them?" I asked instead.

Gideon nodded. "Counting you and me, eight of the twelve time travelers have now been read into the chronograph again. I'll find the other four, too."

I remembered what the count had said and asked, "How can you have traveled from London to Paris and Brussels? I thought the length of time we can spend in the past was limited to a few hours."

"Four hours, to be precise," said Gideon.

"You couldn't possibly get from London to Paris in four hours back then, let alone with spare time to dance the gavotte and collect a drop of blood from someone."

"Quite right. So we traveled to Paris with the chronograph *first*," said Gideon. "And then I went to Brussels, Milan, and Bath on separate occasions. I was able to track down the others in London."

"I see."

"Really?" Gideon's smile was ironic again. This time I ignored it.

"Yes, really, I'm beginning to get the hang of this." I looked out the window of the coach. "I'm sure we didn't drive past these meadows on the way to Lord Brompton's, did we?"

"No. We're in Hyde Park," said Gideon, suddenly wide awake and on the alert. He leaned out. "Hey, Wilbour or whatever your name is, why are we driving this way? We have to get back to the Temple by the shortest possible route."

I couldn't make out what the man on the box said in reply.

"Stop at once!" Gideon ordered. He looked pale when he turned back to me.

"What's going on?"

"I don't know," he said. "The man says his orders are to take us to a meeting place at the southern end of the park."

The horses had stopped, and Gideon opened the carriage door. "There's something wrong here. We don't have much time left before we travel back. I'll take the horses' reins and drive us to the Temple." He got out and closed the door again. "Whatever happens, stay in the coach."

At that moment, there was a loud bang. I instinctively ducked. I knew that sound only from films, but I recognized it at once as a shot being fired. I heard a soft cry, the horses whinnied, and the coach jolted forward but then came to a halt again, rocking.

"Get your head down!" shouted Gideon, and I threw myself flat on the seat.

A second shot was fired. The silence that followed the noise was more than I could stand.

"Gideon?" I sat up and looked out.

On the grass outside the window, Gideon had drawn his sword. "Keep down, I told you!"

Thank God, he was still alive. Although maybe not for much longer. Two men had appeared as if from nowhere, both dressed in black, and a third was riding a horse out of the shadow of the trees. A silvery pistol gleamed in his hand.

Gideon was fighting the other two men at the same time. They were all silent, and except for their gasping and the clash of their swords, there was nothing to hear. For a few seconds I watched, fascinated, admiring Gideon's skill with a sword. It was like something out of a film, every thrust, feint, and leap was perfect, as if stuntmen had been working on the choreography for days. But when one of the men in black cried out and fell to his knees, with a jet of blood shooting out of his throat, I came to my senses. This wasn't a film, this was for *real*. And though the swords might be deadly weapons (the man who'd been hit was now lying on the ground twitching and making horrible sounds), there didn't seem to me much they could do against pistols. Why wasn't Gideon carrying a pistol? It would have been easy to bring a useful weapon like that from home. And where was the coachman? Why wasn't he fighting beside Gideon?

By now the mounted man had come up to them and got off his horse. To my surprise, he too had drawn a sword and was attacking Gideon with it. Why didn't he use the pistol? He'd thrown it down on the grass, where it was no good to anyone.

"Who are you? What do you want?" asked Gideon.

"Only your life," said the man who had been the last to arrive.

"Well, you're not having it!"

"Oh, we shall take it, you may be sure of that!"

And as I watched it through the window, the fight went on, still like a well-rehearsed ballet. The wounded man was now lying motionless on the ground, so that the others had to fight around him.

Gideon parried every attacking thrust as if he knew in advance what his opponents were going to do, but no doubt they had also had fencing lessons since childhood. Once I saw one of the men's blades hiss toward Gideon's shoulder while he was busy parrying his other opponent's thrust. Only an agile sideways turn prevented the sword from striking home. Presumably it would have taken half Gideon's arm off. I heard wood splintering as the man's blade struck the coach instead.

This couldn't be true! Who were these characters, and why were they after us?

I quickly slid across the seat and peered through the window on the other side. Wasn't there anyone around to see what was going on here? Could you really be attacked like this in Hyde Park in broad daylight, in the middle of the afternoon? The fight seemed to last forever.

Although Gideon was holding his own against two men at once, it didn't look as if he could ever fend them off completely. His opponents were forcing him to retreat more and more, and in the end, they would surely win the fight.

I had no idea how much time had passed since I heard the first shot, or how long we still had to wait before we traveled back, but it was probably unlikely that we'd dissolve into thin air before the eyes of Gideon's attackers. I couldn't bear it any longer, sitting in this coach just watching them prepare to murder Gideon.

Maybe I could climb out the window and fetch help?

For a brief moment, I wasn't sure whether the huge hooped skirt would fit through the gap, but a second later, I was standing on the sandy carriageway trying to get my bearings.

I heard only gasping from the other side of the coach, along with curses and the pitiless ring of blade on metal blade.

"Surrender, why don't you?" gasped one of the strangers.

"Never!" Gideon replied.

Cautiously, I made my way forward to the horses. As I did so, I almost fell over something yellow. I only just managed to suppress a scream. It was the man in the yellow coat. He had fallen off the coachman's box and was lying on his back in the sand. I saw, with horror, that part of his face was missing and his clothes were drenched in blood. The eye of the undamaged part of his face was wide open, looking into nowhere.

The shot I'd heard had been aimed at him. It was a

ghastly sight; I felt my stomach churn. I'd never seen a dead person before. I'd have given anything to be sitting in the cinema now so I could close my eyes and know it wasn't real.

But this was real. This man was dead, and Gideon was out there in genuine danger of death himself.

The clash of metal roused me from my numb state. Gideon groaned, and that finally brought me back to my senses.

Before I knew what I was doing, I'd spotted the sword at the dead man's side and clutched it tightly.

It was much heavier than I'd expected, but I immediately felt better. True, I had no idea how to handle a sword, but it was certainly sharp and pointed, I knew that all right.

The fighting carried on. I risked a glance around the coach and saw that the two men had managed to force Gideon back against it on the other side. Some strands of his hair had worked free from the ribbon holding it back and fallen over his forehead. One of his sleeves was ripped wide, but to my relief I saw no blood. He was still uninjured.

I looked all around one last time, but there was no help in sight. Weighing up the sword in my hand, I stepped firmly forward. At least the sight of me would distract the two men. I might be able to give Gideon an advantage that way.

Instead, the opposite happened. The two men were fighting with their backs to me, so they didn't see me, but Gideon's eyes widened in horror when he caught sight of me.

For a fraction of a second, he hesitated, and that was long enough for one of the black-clad strangers to score another hit on him, just next to his ripped sleeve. But this time blood flowed. Gideon fought on as if nothing had happened.

"You can't last much longer!" cried the man triumphantly, attacking Gideon with more force than before. "Pray if you can, because you are about to meet your maker!"

I clasped the hilt of my sword in both hands and ran at him, ignoring Gideon's shocked expression. The men didn't hear me coming. They didn't notice me until the sword had sliced through the black coat that one of them was wearing and slid soundlessly into his flesh. For a frightful moment, I thought I must have missed—maybe I'd run the sword through the gap between the man's body and his arm. But then his breathing slowed. He let go of his weapon and dropped to the ground like a felled tree. I couldn't bring myself to release the hilt of the sword until he was lying there, nearly dead.

Oh, my God.

Gideon used the other man's momentary alarm to thrust at him so hard that he too fell to his knees.

"Are you out of your mind?" Gideon shouted at me as he kicked his opponent's sword aside with his foot and put the point of his own blade to the man's neck.

The other man collapsed entirely. "Please . . . please, let me live," he said.

My teeth were beginning to chatter.

This can't have happened. I didn't really just run a sword through a man's body—did I?

The man I'd attacked let out another gurgling breath. The other one looked as if he was about to burst into tears.

"Who are you, and what do you want from us?" asked Gideon coldly.

"I was only obeying orders. Please don't!"

"Who ordered you to do what?" A drop of blood formed on the man's throat where the point of the sword met it. Gideon's lips were tightly compressed, as if he could only just manage to keep the bladc still.

"I don't know any names. I swear I don't." And then his face, distorted by fear, began to blur in front of me. The green grass of the park spun around and around. I closed my eyes, almost relieved to fall into the whirlpool.

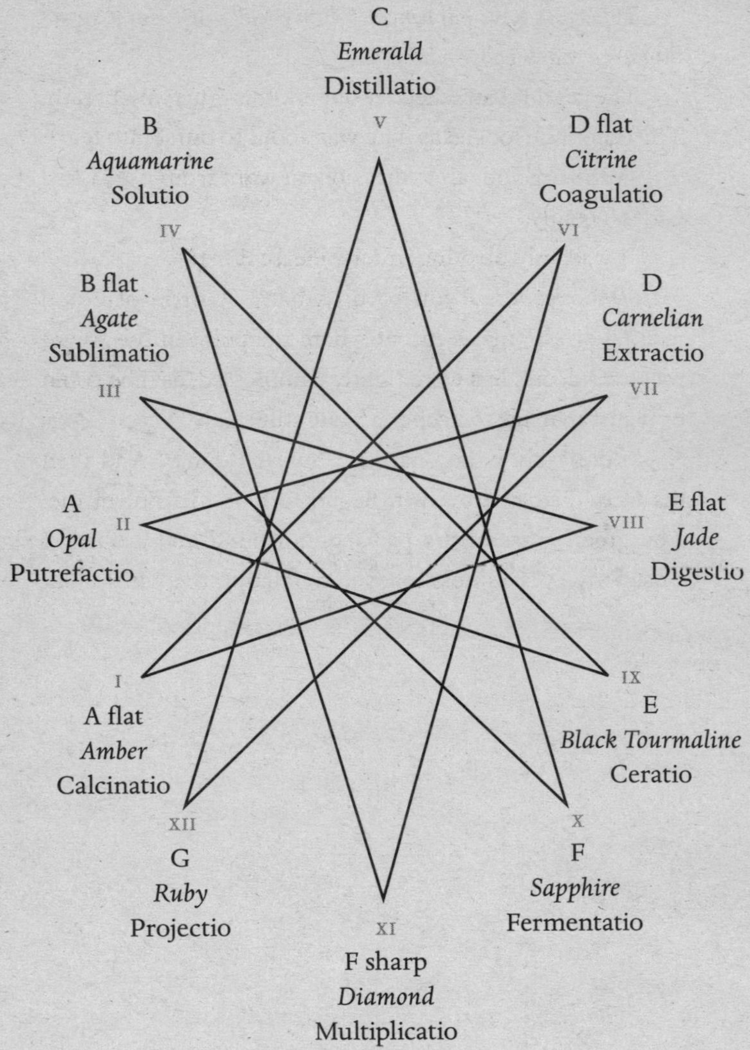

From the secret writings of Count Saint-Germain

THIRTEEN

I'D MADE A SOFT landing in the middle of my own skirts, but I was in no fit state to stand up. Every bone in my body seemed to have dissolved, I was trembling all over, and my teeth were chattering frantically.

"Get up!" Gideon held out his hand to me. He had put his sword back in his belt. I saw, with a shudder, that there was blood on it. "Come on, Gwyneth! People are already looking at us."

It was evening, and it must have been dark for some time, but we'd landed under a streetlight somewhere in the park. A jogger with headphones on glanced at us in surprise as he ran past.

"Didn't I tell you to wait in the coach?" I didn't react, so Gideon took my arm and pulled me to my feet. His face was completely drained of color. "That was incredibly reckless and . . . dreadfully dangerous and . . ." He swallowed hard and stared at me. "And, dammit all, rather brave of you."

"I thought when the blade struck a rib I'd feel it," I said, my teeth still chattering. "I didn't expect it to be like . . . like cutting up a cake. Why didn't that man have any bones?"

"I'm sure he did," said Gideon. "But you were lucky and thrust the sword somewhere in between them."

"Will he die?"

Gideon shrugged. "Not if it was a clean wound. But eighteenth-century surgery can't really be compared with an episode of *Grey's Anatomy.*"

If it was a clean wound? What did that mean? How could a wound be clean?

What had I done? I might have just killed a man!

The full realization of that almost made me sink to the ground again. But Gideon was holding me firmly. "Come on, we have to get back to the Temple. The others will be worrying."

He obviously knew exactly where we were in the park, because he led me purposefully on along the path, past two women walking their dogs who stared at us curiously.

"I'm a murderer," I whispered.

"Ever heard of self-defense? You were only defending yourself. Or rather me, come to think of it."

He gave me a crooked smile, and it occurred to me that only an hour ago, I'd have sworn he would never admit to such a thing.

And sure enough, he didn't.

"Not that it was at all necessary," he added.

"Oh, so it wasn't necessary? What about your arm? You're bleeding."

"It's nothing. Dr. White will see to it."

For a while, we went along side by side in silence. The cool evening air felt good. My pulse gradually slowed down, and my teeth stopped chattering.

"My heart missed a beat when I suddenly saw you," said Gideon at last. He had let go of my arm now. Obviously he trusted me to stay on my feet by myself.

"Why didn't you take a pistol?" I said crossly. "The other man had one!"

"In fact he had two," said Gideon.

"Then why didn't he use them?"

"He did. He killed poor Wilbour, and the shot from the second pistol only just missed me."

"But why didn't he shoot again after that?"

"Because back then each pistol fired only one shot, of course," said Gideon. "Those neat little handguns you see in the James Bond films hadn't been invented yet."

"But they *have* been invented now! Why do you take a stupid sword into the past instead of a proper pistol?"

"I'm not a professional killer," said Gideon.

"But that's just . . . I mean, otherwise what's the advantage of coming from the future? Oh! *Here* we are!" We had reached Apsley House on Hyde Park Corner. People out for an evening stroll, or jogging, or walking their dogs were giving us odd looks.

"We'll take a taxi to the Temple," said Gideon. "Got any money with you?"

"Of course not!"

"But I have my mobile," I said, fishing it out of my décolletage.

"Ah, the *silver shrine!* I might have known it was something like that. You silly—oh, give it here!"

"Hey, that's mine!"

"Yes, and do you know the number?" Gideon was already punching it in.

"'Scuse me, dear." An elderly lady was tugging my sleeve. "I just *have* to ask—are you from one of the theaters?"

"Er . . . yes," I said.

"I thought so!" The old lady was having difficulty holding on to her dachshund's leash. The dog was pulling hard as it tried to get at another dog only a few yards away. "It looks so wonderfully genuine! Only a good wardrobe mistress could have made that outfit. You know, dear, I did a lot of sewing myself in my young d—stop it, Polly! Don't pull like that!"

"They'll come and pick us up at once," said Gideon, giving me my mobile back. "We'll go on to the corner of Piccadilly."

"And where can people go to see the play you're in?" asked the old lady.

"Er, well, I'm afraid it was the last performance this evening."

"What a pity!"

"Yes, I think so too."

Gideon was pulling me on.

"Good-bye," I said to the old lady.

"I don't understand how those men could find us. Or what orders were given to that man Wilbour to get him to drive us to Hyde Park. There was no time to prepare an ambush," Gideon was muttering to himself as he walked on. Out here in the street, passersby stared at us even more than in the park.

"Are you talking to me?"

"Someone knew we'd be there. But how did he know? And how was it possible anyway?"

"Wilbour . . . one of his eyes was . . ." Suddenly I felt my stomach heave.

"What are you doing?"

I retched, but nothing would come up.

"Gwyneth, we have to get moving! Breathe deeply, and it'll pass."

I stopped dead. This was too much!

"Oh, so it'll pass?" I made myself speak very slowly and distinctly, although I really felt like screeching. "And so if I've just killed a man, will that pass, too? My entire life has been turned upside down today—will that pass? Will the fact that an arrogant, long-haired, violin-playing creep in silk stockings can't think of anything better to do than order me about, even though I've just saved his stupid life, will that disappear as well? If you ask me, it's not surprising that I feel like puking. And just in case you're wondering, you make me want to throw up too!"

Okay, so maybe my voice had risen to a bit of a screech

with that last remark, but it could have been worse. All at once I realized how good it felt to get all that off my chest. For the first time that day, I felt truly liberated, and the nausea suddenly disappeared.

Gideon was staring at me with such a blank expression that I'd have giggled if I hadn't been so angry. Aha! Just for once he seemed to be left speechless.

"And now I want to go home," I said, trying to round off my triumph with as much dignity as possible.

Unfortunately I didn't bring it off entirely, because at the thought of my family, my lip began to quiver and I felt my eyes filling with tears.

Dammit, dammit, dammit!

"It's all right," said Gideon.

His surprisingly gentle tone of voice was too much for my self-control. The tears came rolling down my cheeks before I could stop them.

"Hey, Gwyneth. I'm sorry." Gideon came right up to me, took me by the shoulder, and drew me close to him. "I'm an idiot. I was forgetting what this must be like for you," he murmured somewhere just above my ear. "And I remember perfectly well how stupid I felt the first time I traveled back. In spite of all that fencing practice. And the violin lessons. . . ."

He stroked my hair.

I just sobbed louder.

"Don't cry," he said helplessly. "It's all right."

But it wasn't all right. It was all horrible. That frantic chase around the house, only last night, when they'd thought I was a thief. Rakoczy's sinister eyes, the count with his ice-cold voice and his hand around my throat throttling me, and finally poor Wilbour and the man I'd stabbed in the back with a sword. And, most of all, the fact that I couldn't even manage to give Gideon a piece of my mind without bursting into tears and making him feel he had to comfort me!

I tore myself away.

Where was my self-respect? I felt so embarrassed. I wiped my face with the back of my hand.

"Handkerchief?" he asked, smiling, as he took a lemon-yellow square of fabric trimmed with lace out of his pocket. "No paper tissues in the Rococo age, I'm afraid, but you can have this."

I was just about to take it when a black limousine drew up beside us.

Mr. George was waiting for us inside the car, his bald patch covered with tiny beads of sweat, and at the sight of him, all the thoughts circling around and around in my head calmed down a little. I was still completely knackered, but that was all.

"We've been beside ourselves with anxiety," said Mr. George. "Oh, my God, Gideon, what happened to your arm? You're bleeding! And Gwyneth looks distraught. Is she injured?"

"Just exhausted," said Gideon briefly. "We'll take her home."

"No, not yet. We must examine you both, and your wound has to be treated immediately, Gideon."

"It stopped bleeding a long time ago. It's only a scratch, really. Gwyneth wants to go home."

"She may not have elapsed for long enough. She has to go to school tomorrow, and—"

Gideon's voice took on its familiar arrogant tone, but it wasn't meant for me this time.

"Mr. George. She's been gone for three hours. That will be enough for the next eighteen hours."

"It probably will be," said Mr. George. "But it goes against all the rules, and then we have to know whether—"

"Mr. George!"

He gave up, turned, and knocked on the window between us and the driver. The glass moved sideways with a soft swish.

"Turn right into Berkeley Street," said Mr. George. "We're making a little detour. Number 81, Bourdon Place."

I breathed a sigh of relief. I could go home. To my mum.

Mr. George was looking at me very gravely. His expression was sympathetic, as if he'd never seen a more pitiful sight. "What happened, for heaven's sake?"

"Three men attacked our coach in Hyde Park," said Gideon. "The coachman was shot."

"Oh, my God," said Mr. George. "I don't understand it, but that makes sense."

"How do you mean?"

"It's in the *Annals*—the twenty-fourth of September, 1782. A second-degree Guardian by the name of James

Wilbour was found dead in Hyde Park. Half his face was shot away. They never found out who did it."

"Well, now we know," said Gideon grimly. "That is to say, I know what his murderer looked like, but I don't know the man's name."

"And I killed him," I said in a flat voice.

"What?"

"She came up and ran Wilbour's sword into his attacker's back," said Gideon. "Well, we don't know whether she really killed him."

Mr. George's blue eyes were round. "She did *what*?"

"It was two against one," I murmured. "I couldn't just stand there watching."

"Three against one," Gideon corrected me. "But I'd already finished off one of them. I told you to stay in the coach no matter what happened."

"It didn't seem as if you were going to last much longer," I said without looking at him.

Gideon didn't answer.

Mr. George looked from one to the other of us and shook his head. "What a disaster! Your mother will murder me, Gwyneth! It was supposed to be the safest of operations. A conversation with the count in the same house, no risk at all. You wouldn't for an instant have been in danger. And instead the two of you go halfway around the city and get set upon by footpads. . . . Gideon, for heaven's sake, what on earth did you have in mind?"

"It would have been fine if someone hadn't given us

away." Gideon sounded angry now. "Someone or other must have known about our visit. Someone who was in a position to persuade this man Wilbour to drive us to a meeting place in the park."

"But why would anyone want to kill you two? And who could have known you would be visiting the count on that very day? None of it makes sense." Mr. George was chewing his lower lip. "Ah, here we are."

I looked up. Yes, we really were in front of our house, all its windows brightly lit. Somewhere inside, my mum was waiting for me. So was my bed.

"Thank you," said Gideon.

I turned and looked at him. "What for?"

"Maybe . . . maybe I really wouldn't have lasted much longer," he said. Another crooked grin flitted across his face. "I think you actually did save my stupid life."

Oh. I didn't know what to say. All I could do was look at him, noticing that my silly lower lip was beginning to quiver again.

Gideon quickly brought out his lace-edged handkerchief. This time I took it. "Better mop your face with this, or your mother might think you've been crying," he said.

He meant to make me laugh, but at this moment, that was right out of the question. At least I didn't burst into tears again.

The driver opened the car door, and Mr. George got out. "I'll take her to the door, Gideon. I won't be a minute."

"Good night," I managed to say.

"Sleep well," said Gideon, smiling. "See you tomorrow."

"GWEN! GWENNY!" Caroline was shaking me awake. "You'll be late if you don't get up now."

I pulled the covers over my head. I didn't want to wake up. Even in my dreams, I'd known there were dreadful memories waiting for me when I came out of my present blissfully drowsy state.

"Honestly, Gwenny! It's quarter past!"

I kept my eyes closed, but it was no good. Too late. The memories came rushing in at me like . . . er . . . Attila attacking the . . . er, the Vandals?

The events of the last two days were unraveling vividly before me like a film.

But I couldn't remember how I wound up in my bed, only that Mr. Bernard had opened the door to me last night.

"Good evening, Miss Gwyneth. Good evening, Mr. George, sir."

"Good evening, Mr. Bernard. I've brought Gwyneth home a little earlier than we planned. Please give my regards to Lady Arista."

"Of course, sir. Good evening, sir." Mr. Bernard was as expressionless as ever when he had closed the door behind Mr. George.

"Pretty dress, Miss Gwyneth," he had said to me. "Late eighteenth century?"

"I think so." I'd been so tired that I could have rolled up on the rug in the hall and gone to sleep on the spot. I'd never looked forward to my bed so much. I was just afraid of running into Aunt Glenda, Charlotte, and Lady Arista on my way up to the third floor. They'd all pester me with scolding and questions.

"I am afraid the family have already had dinner. But I've prepared a little snack for you in the kitchen."

"Oh, that's so kind, Mr. Bernard, but I—"

"You want to go to bed," said Mr. Bernard, and a tiny smile appeared on his face. "I suggest you go straight to your bedroom. The ladies are all in the music room. They won't hear you if you keep as quiet as a mouse. Then I will tell your mother that you are back and give her the snack to take up to you."

I'd been too tired even to feel surprised by his caution and his concern for me. I just said, "Thank you very much, Mr. Bernard," and went upstairs. I had only the vaguest memory of the snack and my conversation with Mum—I'd already been half asleep. I'm sure I couldn't have made the effort of chewing anything, but maybe it had been soup.

"Oh, how lovely!" Caroline had discovered the dress hung over the back of a chair along with its frilled petticoat. "Did you bring it back from the past?"

"No, I had it on before I went." I sat up. "Did Mum tell you about the odd thing that's happened?"

Caroline nodded. "Not that she had to *tell* us much. Aunt Glenda was shouting loud enough for all the neighbors to hear. Acting as if Mum were a thief who had stolen poor Charlotte's time-travel gene."

"How about Charlotte?"

"She went to her room and wouldn't come out, no matter how Aunt Glenda pleaded with her. Aunt Glenda shouted that Charlotte's whole life had been ruined, and it was all Mum's fault. Grandmother said Aunt Glenda had better take a tablet, or she would be obliged to call the doctor. And Aunt Maddy kept on talking about that eagle, the sapphire, the mountain ash, and the clock in the tower."

"Sounds dreadful," I said.

"It was actually exciting," said Caroline. "Nick and I think it's a good thing you have the gene instead of Charlotte, even if Aunt Glenda says you have a pea-sized brain and two left feet. She's so rude." She stroked the shining fabric of the bodice. "Can you put the dress on to show me after school today?"

"Sure," I said. "But you can try it on yourself, if you like."

Caroline giggled. "It's much too big for me, Gwenny. And now you really must get up, or you won't have time for any breakfast."

A refreshing shower finally woke me up, and as I washed my hair, my thoughts kept circling around yesterday evening or, more accurately, the half an hour (well, that's what it had felt like) that I'd spent shedding tears and snot in Gideon's arms.

I remembered how he had held me close and stroked

my hair. I'd been so upset at the time that I hadn't even thought how close we suddenly were. I felt all the more embarrassed now. Particularly because he'd really been very nice, not like his usual self at all. (Even if it was just because he felt sorry for me.) And yet I had been determined to hate him forever.

"Gwenny!" Caroline was hammering on the bathroom door. "Come on out! You can't stay in there forever."

She was right. I really couldn't stay here forever. I had to come out—into this suddenly weird new life of mine. I turned off the hot tap and let icy water trickle over me until the last of the weariness had left my body. My school uniform was still in Madame Rossini's sewing room, and two spare blouses were in the wash, so I had to put on last year's uniform, which was already a little too small for me. The blouse stretched taut over my breasts, and the skirt was slightly too short. Never mind. My dark blue school shoes were also at the Temple, so I put on my black sneakers, which wasn't really allowed. But Mr. Gilles, the principal, probably wouldn't go around all the classrooms inspecting dress code today.

There wasn't time to blow-dry my hair, so I just rubbed it as dry as I could with a towel and then combed it through. It lay wet and straight over my shoulders, not a trace left of the soft ringlets conjured up yesterday by Madame Rossini.

I looked at my face in the mirror for a moment. I didn't exactly look as if I'd had a good night's sleep, but it was better than I'd expected. I put some of Mum's antiaging cream on my cheeks and forehead. It was never too soon to start, my mother always said.

I felt like skipping breakfast, but I knew I had to face Charlotte and Aunt Glenda sooner or later. I could get it over and done with now.

I heard them talking as I came down to the first floor, long before I reached the dining room.

"The big bird is a symbol of misfortune," I heard Great-aunt Maddy saying. She was never up before ten. She loved a good sleep and thought breakfast the only unnecessary meal in the day. "I do wish someone would listen to me."

"Oh, really, Maddy! No one can make anything of this vision of yours. And we've had to listen to you going on about it at least ten times." That was Lady Arista.

"Very true," said Aunt Glenda. "If I hear another word about sapphire eggs, I shall scream."

"Good morning," I interrupted.

There was a brief silence in which they all gaped at me as if I were a little green man from Planet Zog.

"Good morning, child," said Lady Arista. "I hope you slept well."

"Fine, thank you. I was very tired."

"I'm sure it was all rather too much for you," said Aunt Glenda patronizingly.

But she was right—it had been. I sat down in my usual place opposite Charlotte, who obviously hadn't touched her toast. She looked as if the sight of me had spoilt her appetite.

Mum and Nick were smiling at me in a conspiratorial way, and Caroline pushed a bowl of cornflakes and milk over to me. At the other end of the table, Great-aunt Maddy waved to me. "My little angel! I'm so glad to see you! You'll cast some light on all this confusion. What with all the shouting yesterday evening, no one could get a clear idea of anything. Glenda was digging up ancient history from back when our Lucy ran off with that handsome de Villiers boy. I never did understand why everyone kicked up such a fuss because Grace let them stay with her for a few days. You'd think that would have been forgotten long ago. But no, no sooner has a little grass grown over it than some clumsy camel comes along and rakes it all up again."

Caroline giggled. She was probably imagining Aunt Glenda as a camel.

"This is not a TV series, Maddy," said Lady Arista sharply.

"Thank goodness, no, it isn't," said Great-aunt Maddy. "If it were, I'd have lost track of the plot ages ago."

"It's perfectly simple," said Charlotte in a chilly voice. "Everyone thought I'd have the gene, but Gwyneth has it instead." She pushed her plate away from her and stood up. "So now she'll just have to see if she can manage."

"Charlotte, wait!" But Aunt Glenda was not in time to keep Charlotte from storming out of the room. Before she followed her, she gave Mum a nasty look. "You should be ashamed of yourself, Grace!"

"She's in a dangerous mood," said Nick.

Lady Arista heaved a deep sigh.

Mum sighed as well. "I have to go to work now. Gwyneth, I agreed with Mr. George that he will pick you up from school today. You'll be sent to elapse to the year 1956, in a nice safe cellar where you can get on with your homework in peace."

"Bummer!" said Nick.

I was thinking just the same.

"And after that, you will come straight home," said Lady Arista.

"But the day will be over by then," I said. Was this going to be my routine from now on? Going to the Temple to elapse after school, sitting about in a boring cellar doing homework, then going home to dinner? What a nightmare!

Great-aunt Maddy swore under her breath because the sleeve of her dressing gown had landed in the marmalade on her toast. "This is no time of day to be up and about, that's what I always say."

"So you do," said Nick.

Mum kissed him, Caroline, and me good-bye, like every morning. Then she put a hand on my shoulder and said quietly, "If by any chance you happen to see my dad, give him a kiss from me."

Lady Arista jumped slightly at these words. She sipped her tea in silence, then looked at her watch and said, "You must hurry if you're going to be at school on time."

"I'M DEFINITELY GOING to open a detective agency someday," said Lesley. We were bunking off geography with Mrs. Counter and had squeezed into one of the cubicles in the girls' toilets. Lesley was sitting on the loo lid with a fat folder on her knees. I was leaning against the door, which was scribbled all over in ballpoint and color pen. JENNY LOVES ADAM, MALCOLM IS AN ASS, LIFE IS CRAP, and other, similar remarks.

"Investigating mysteries must be in my blood," said Lesley. "Maybe I'll study history too and specialize in old myths and ancient writings. And then I'll be like Tom Hanks in *The Da Vinci Code*. I'll look better, of course, and I'll hire a really hot guy to be my assistant."

"You do that," I said. "Sounds exciting. Whereas I'm going to spend the rest of my life hanging about in a cellar without any windows in the year 1956."

"Only for three hours a day," said Lesley. I'd brought her right up to date, and it looked as if she had a much better grasp of all these complications than I did. She'd heard it all, up to my story about the men in the park and my guilty conscience. "Better to fight back than get sliced up like a cake yourself" was her comment on that. Oddly enough, that made me feel better than any of Mr. George's or Gideon's reassurances.

Telekinesis was the word Lesley used for the count's ability to strangle me even from several yards away. Through telekinesis, she said, you could also communicate with other people without opening your mouth. She promised to find out more about it this afternoon.

She'd spent the day yesterday and half the night searching the Internet for Count Saint-Germain and all the other stuff I'd passed on to her. She dismissed my gratitude, saying it was all terrific fun.

"Anyway, this Count Saint-Germain is a rather enigmatic historical character. Even his date of birth isn't known for certain. Much mystery surrounds his origins," she said, and her face was positively glowing with enthusiasm. "Apparently he didn't age. Some people put that down to magic, others to a balanced diet."

"He *was* old," I said. "Maybe he was well preserved and looked after himself, but he was definitely old."

"Well, you've proved that bit wrong, then," said Lesley. "He must have had a fascinating personality, because he comes into a great many novels, and in some esoteric circles he was seen as a kind of guru, an Ascended Master, whatever that means. He was a member of many secret societies—the Freemasons and the Rosicrucians and several more—he was an outstanding musician, he played the violin and composed music, he spoke a dozen languages fluently, and he could apparently—listen to this!—he could apparently travel in time. Anyway, he claimed to have been present at various events when he couldn't possibly have been there."

"Except he could."

"Yes. Crazy. He was also keen on alchemy. He had an alchemist's tower of his own in Germany for doing his experiments—not sure what sort they were."

"Alchemy, that's something to do with the philosopher's stone, right?"

"Exactly. And with magic. Though the philosopher's

stone means something different to everyone. Some just tried to make gold with it, so there were all sorts of odd developments. All the old kings and princes were after people who said they were alchemists, because of course they all wanted gold. It's true that attempts to make gold led, among other things, to making porcelain, but most of the time, nothing at all happened, so the alchemists were put in prison as heretics and frauds or had their heads chopped off."

"Their own fault," I said. "They ought to have paid more attention in chemistry classes."

"But the alchemists weren't really interested in gold at all. That was just camouflage for their real experiments. The philosopher's stone is more like a synonym for immortality. The alchemists thought if they could only get the right ingredients—toad's eyes, the blood of a virgin, hairs from a black cat's tail, no, ha, ha, only joking—well, if they could get the right ingredients and mix them in the right chemical process, they'd end up with a substance that made you immortal if you drank it. The followers of Count Saint-Germain claim he had the recipe, so he was immortal. There are sources saying he died in Germany in 1784—but there are other records of people meeting him alive and well many years after that."

"Hm," I said. "I don't think he's immortal. But maybe he'd like to be? Maybe that's the secret behind the secret. It's what will happen when the Circle closes. . . ."

"Well, could be. But that's only one side of the coin, put forward by enthusiastic supporters of cryptic conspiracy theories manipulating the sources for their own purposes. Critics of such theories assume that the legends accumulating around the count are most of them pure fantasy on the part of his fans, all because of his own clever presentation of himself." As Lesley came out with all this stuff from the Internet, she reeled it off so fluently and with such enthusiasm of her own that I couldn't help laughing.

"Why not ask Mr. Whitman if you can write an essay on the subject for homework?" I suggested. "You've done so much research, I should think you could write a whole book about it."

"I don't think the squirrel would really appreciate my efforts," said Lesley. "After all, he's one of Saint-Germain's fans himself—I mean, if he's a Guardian, he has to be. As I see it he's the villain of the piece—Count Saint-Germain, I mean, not Mr. Squirrel. He threatened you and nearly strangled you, didn't he? And your mother said you were to beware of him. So she knows more than she's admitting. And I tell you what, she can only know it from this Lucy."

"I think they *all* know more than they're admitting," I sighed. "Or anyway, they all know more than me. Even you do!"

Lesley laughed. "Just consider me an external part of your own brain. The count always made a great secret of his origins. That name and title were invented, anyhow. He may have been the illegitimate son of Maria Anna von Habsburg, widow of King Charles II of Spain. Several people could have been his father. Or according to another theory, he was the son of a Transylvanian prince and was brought up in Italy at the court of the last Medici duke. One way or another, none of it can really be proved, so everyone's just groping around in the dark. But now the two of us have a new theory."

"Do we?"

Lesley rolled her eyes. "Of course we do! We now know that one of his parents must have come from the de Villiers family, anyway."

"How do we know that?"

"Oh, Gwen! You said yourself that the first time traveler was a de Villiers, so the count *must* have been a member of that family, whether or not he was born in wedlock. You understand that, don't you? Otherwise his descendants wouldn't have the same surname."

"Mm, yes," I said uncertainly. I couldn't quite sort out this theory of his descent. "But I think there's something in the Transylvanian theory too. It can't be coincidence that that man Rakoczy comes from Transylvania."

"I'll do some more research into him," Lesley promised. "Oh, watch out!" The door outside the cubicles swung, and someone came into the girls' toilets. She—at least, we assumed it was a she—went into the cubicle next to ours to use the loo. We kept perfectly still until she had gone again.

"Without washing her hands," said Lesley. "Yuck. I'm glad I don't know who that was."

"No paper towels left," I said. My legs were getting

pins and needles. "Do you think we'll be in trouble? Mrs. Counter is sure to notice we're missing. And if she doesn't, then someone will tell on us."

"All the students look the same to Mrs. Counter—she doesn't notice anything. She's called me Lilly since Year Seven, and she gets you mixed up with Cynthia, of all people. No, listen, this is more important than geography. You must be as well prepared as possible. The more you know about your enemies, the better."

"I only wish I knew who my enemies are."

"You can't trust anyone," said Lesley, just like my mother. "If we were in a film, the villain would turn out to be the least-expected person. But as we aren't in a film, I'd go for the character who tried to strangle you."

"But who set those men in black on us in Hyde Park? It can't have been the count! He needs Gideon to visit the other time travelers and get a drop of their blood so as to close the Circle."

"Yes, so he does." Lesley chewed her lower lip thoughtfully. "But maybe there are several villains in this film. I mean, Lucy and Paul could also be the baddies. Well, they stole the chronograph. And what about the man in black who stands outside number eighteen?"

I shrugged. "He was there this morning, same as usual. Why? Do you think he'll suddenly whip out a sword?"

"No, I think he's more likely to be one of the Guardians, standing there in that silly way just on principle."

Lesley turned back to her folder. "I couldn't find out anything about the Guardians themselves, by the way. They seem to be a very secret lodge indeed. But some of the names you mentioned—Churchill, Wellington, Newton—were Freemasons too. So we can assume that both secret societies had at least some connection. Oh, and I didn't find out anything on the Internet about a boy called Robert White who drowned, but you can look up all the editions of the *Times* and the *Observer* for the last forty years in the library. I'm sure I'll find something there. What else? Oh yes, mountain ash tree, sapphire, raven. . . . Well, of course you can interpret that in all sorts of different ways, but with this mysterious stuff, everything can always mean anything, which means nothing is certain. We must try to go by the facts and not all these fantastic ideas. You'll have to find out more, particularly about Lucy and Paul and why they stole the chronograph. They obviously know something that the others don't know. Or don't want to. Or that they have very different ideas about."

The door opened again. This time the footsteps were firm and energetic. And they were coming straight toward the door of our cubicle.

"Lesley Hay and Gwyneth Shepherd, come out of there at once and go back to your class!"

At first Lesley and I were stunned. Then Lesley said, "You do know these are the *girls'* toilets, don't you, Mr. Whitman?"

"I'll count to three," said Mr. Whitman. "One . . ."

We'd opened the door before he reached "three."

"I'll have to note this on your records," said Mr. Whitman, looking at us like a very stern squirrel. "I am very disappointed in you. You in particular, Gwyneth. The fact that you've taken your cousin's place doesn't mean you can do or not do exactly as you like. Charlotte never neglected her schoolwork."

"Yes, Mr. Whitman," I said. This authoritarian attitude wasn't at all like him. He was usually so charming and only ever a tiny bit sarcastic.

"Now, off you go to your class."

"How did you know where we were?" asked Lesley.

Mr. Whitman did not reply. He reached out his hand for Lesley's folder. "And for now, I'm confiscating this."

"Oh, no, you can't!" Lesley clutched the folder close to her breast.

"Give it to me, Lesley!"

"But I need it . . . for the class."

"I'll count to three. . . ."

On "two," Lesley handed him the folder, gritting her teeth. It was so embarrassing when Mr. Whitman pushed us into the classroom. Mrs. Counter obviously took it personally that we'd bunked off her class, because she ignored us until it was over.

"Were you smoking something?" Gordon asked.

"No, idiot," Lesley snapped at him. "We just wanted to talk to each other in peace."

"You cut class because you wanted to *talk*?" Gordon tapped his forehead. *"Girls!"*

"And now Mr. Whitman can look through your whole

file," I said to Lesley. "Then he'll know—I mean, the *Guardians* will know—that I've told you all about it. I'm sure I'm not allowed to."

"Yes, so am I," said Lesley. "Maybe they'll send one of those men in black to get rid of me because I know things that no one is supposed to know." She seemed to think this was an exciting prospect.

"Well, suppose that isn't such a far-out idea?"

"Then . . . well, I'm going to buy you a pepper spray this afternoon, and I'll buy myself one at the same time." Lesley patted me on the back. "Come on. We're not going to let them get the better of us?"

"No. No, we're not." I envied Lesley her unshakeable optimism. She always looked on the bright side of things. If they had a bright side.

3:00 P.M. to 6:00 P.M., Lucy and Paul came to elapse in my office. We talked about cleaning up the city and restoring the buildings on the bombed-out sites, and the extraordinary fact that, in their time, Notting Hill will be one of the most fashionable and sought-after parts of town. (They described it as "trendy.") They also gave me a list of all the Wimbledon champions from 1950 onward. I promised to put my winnings into a fund for the college education of my children and grandchildren. I am also thinking of buying one or two of the dilapidated apartment blocks in Notting Hill. You never know.

FROM *THE ANNALS OF THE GUARDIANS*
14 AUGUST 1949
REPORT: LUCAS MONTROSE, ADEPT 3RD DEGREE

FOURTEEN

CLASSES DRAGGED ON painfully slowly, lunch was disgusting, same as usual, and when we could finally go home after double chemistry in the afternoon, I felt ready for bed.

Charlotte had ignored me all day. Once, at break, I tried to speak with her, and she said, "If you were thinking of apologizing, forget it!"

"What would I want to apologize for?" I asked, feeling annoyed.

"Well, if you can't work that out for yourself—"

"Charlotte! I can't help inheriting this stupid gene instead of you."

Charlotte's eyes had sparkled with fury as she looked at me. "It's not a *stupid gene,* it's a gift. Something very special. And it's simply wasted on someone like you. But you're too childish to even understand that."

Then she had turned and marched away, leaving me standing there.

"She'll recover," said Lesley as we took our things out of our lockers. "She just has to get used to not being someone special anymore."

"But it's so unfair," I said. "After all, I haven't taken anything away from her."

"Well, basically you have." Lesley handed me her hairbrush. "Here!"

"What do you want me to do with this?"

"Brush your hair, what else?"

I obediently ran the brush through my hair. Then I asked her, "Why am I doing this?"

"I only wanted you to look pretty when you see Gideon again. Luckily you don't need any mascara. Your lashes are amazingly long and black naturally."

I'd gone bright red at the mention of Gideon's name. "Maybe I won't meet him today at all. I'm just being sent back to 1956 to do my homework in a cellar."

"Yes, but maybe you'll run into him before or after that."

"Lesley, I'm not his type."

"He didn't mean it that way," said Lesley.

"Yes, he did!"

"So what? A person can change his mind. Anyway, he's *your* type."

I opened my mouth and then closed it again. There was no point in denying it. He *was* my type, as much as I'd have liked to pretend he wasn't.

"Any girl would think he was amazing," I said. "As far as looks go, anyway. But he needles me all the time, and he orders me about, and he's just so . . . he's just so incredibly . . ."

"Great?" Lesley smiled lovingly at me. "So are you, honest! You're the greatest girl I know. Apart from me, maybe. And you can order people about yourself. Come on, I want to see this limousine that's going to fetch you."

James gave me a cool nod as we were passing his niche.

"Wait a sec," I told Lesley. "I need to ask James something."

When I stopped, the bored expression vanished from James's face, and he smiled cheerfully at me. "I've been thinking about our last conversation," he said.

"What, about kissing?"

"No, about the smallpox. It's possible I did catch it after all. Your hair is beautifully glossy today."

"Thank you. James, could you do me a favor?"

"Nothing to do with kissing, I hope."

I had to smile. "Not a bad idea," I said, "but, no, it's about manners."

"Manners?"

"Well, you're always complaining that I don't have any, and you're right. So I wanted to ask you to show me how to behave properly. In your time. How to talk, how to curtsey, how to—oh, I don't know what."

"Hold a fan? Dance? How to behave when the Prince Regent is in the room?"

"Exactly!"

"Oh, yes, I can teach you that," said James.

"Great," I said, and was turning to go. "Oh, and James? Can you fence as well? With a sword?"

"Of course," said James. "I don't wish to boast, but I am considered one of the best fencers in town by my friends at the club. Galliano himself says I have a considerable talent."

"Super!" I said. "You're a real friend."

"You want that ghost to teach you fencing?" Lesley had been following our conversation with interest. Of course she'd only been able to hear my side of it. "Can a ghost hold a sword?"

"We'll see," I said. "Anyway, he knows his way around the eighteenth century. After all, it's where he comes from."

Gordon Gelderman caught up with us on the steps. "You were talking to that niche in the wall again, Gwyneth. I saw you."

"Yes, it's my favorite bit of wall, Gordon. I'd hurt its feelings if I didn't stop and talk to it."

"You do know you're weird, right?"

"Yes, Gordon dear, I know. But at least my voice isn't breaking."

"That's a passing phase," said Gordon. "It will go away."

"It would be nice if *you* went away," said Lesley.

"I suppose you two want to talk again," said Gordon. He was always hard to shake off. "I can understand that.

After all, you've only had your heads together for five hours today. See you at the cinema later?"

"No," said Lesley.

"I can't anyway, come to think of it," said Gordon, as he followed us through the front hall like a shadow. "I have to write that stupid essay about signet rings. Did I ever tell you I can't stand Mr. Whitman?"

"Yes, but only a hundred times so far," said Lesley.

I saw the limousine waiting outside the school gate even before we came out of the building. My heart began beating a little faster. I still felt terribly embarrassed about yesterday evening.

"Wow! Look at that car, will you?" Gordon whistled softly through his teeth. "Maybe the rumors are true and Madonna's daughter really is at this school—incognito, of course."

"Of course," said Lesley, blinking at the bright sunlight. "That's why they send a limousine to fetch her. So no one will notice that she's incognito."

Several of the students were gaping at the limousine. Cynthia and her friend Sarah were standing on the steps as well, eyes popping out of their heads. But not at the sight of the limousine—at something farther to the right of it.

"And I thought that twit wouldn't have anything to do with boys," said Sarah. "Not even hot guys like that."

"Could be he's her cousin," said Cynthia. "Or her brother."

My hand was clutching Lesley's arm tightly. Sure enough, there stood Gideon in our school yard, very casual in jeans and a T-shirt. And he was talking to Charlotte.

Lesley identified him at once. "And I thought he had long hair," she said accusingly.

"He does," I said.

"Shoulder-length," said Lesley. "That's different. Very cool."

"He's gay. Bet you anything he's gay," said Gordon, leaning one arm on my shoulder so that he could see past Cynthia and me better.

"Oh, my God, he's touching her!" said Cynthia. "He's taking her hand!"

Charlotte's smile was visible all the way to where we were standing. She didn't often smile (apart from her infuriating know-it-all expression), but when she did, the look on her face was enchanting. She was even showing a dimple. Gideon was bound to notice it, and I was sure he was thinking that *she* was anything but an ordinary girl.

"He's stroking her cheek!"

Oh, my God. He was, really. The pang I felt was something I couldn't ignore. "And now he's kissing her!"

We all held our breath. It really did look as if Gideon was going to kiss Charlotte.

"But only on the cheek," said Cynthia, relieved. "So he's her cousin, after all. Gwenny, please say he's her cousin."

"No," I said. "They're not related."

"And he isn't gay either," said Lesley.

"Want to bet? I mean, look at that signet ring he's wearing."

Charlotte smiled radiantly at Gideon again and walked away with a spring in her step. Obviously her bad mood had gone away.

Gideon turned to us. I realized what a sight we were—four girls and Gordon, gaping and giggling on the steps outside school.

I know lots of girls like you.

Just as I might have expected. Oh, great!

"Gwyneth!" called Gideon. "Finally!"

Cynthia, Sarah, and Gordon collectively held their breath. To be honest, so did I. Only Lesley kept her cool. She gave me a little push. "Hurry up, will you? Your limousine is waiting."

As I went down the steps, I could feel the others' eyes on my back. Their mouths were probably open, too. Gordon's was for sure.

"Hi," I said when I had reached Gideon. It was all I could manage to say. In the sunlight his eyes were a brighter green than ever.

"Hi." He was looking at me rather too closely. "Have you grown overnight?"

"No." I tugged the jacket together over my breasts. "It's my school uniform that's shrunk."

Gideon grinned. Then he looked over my shoulder. "Friends of yours up there? I think one of them's about to faint."

Oh, my God. "That's Cynthia Dale," I said, without

turning around. "She suffers from high estrogen levels. I can introduce you if you'd like."

Gideon's smile grew wider. "Maybe I'll take you up on that some other time. Now, come on. We have a lot still to do today." He took my arm (a loud squeal could be heard from the steps) and guided me toward the limousine.

"I'm only going to do homework. In the year 1956."

"There's been a change of plan." Gideon opened the car door for me. (A synchronized screech from the steps.) "We're going to visit your great-great-grandmother. She specially asked for you to come along." He put his hand on my back to get me into the car. (Another screech from the steps.)

I let myself fall into the back seat. There was a familiar, round face already in the car, waiting for me.

"Hello, Mr. George."

"Gwyneth, my brave girl, how are you feeling today?" Mr. George was beaming as if in competition with his shiny bald patch.

Gideon sat down beside him.

"I'm . . . er, fine, thank you." I went red, because I was thinking what a picture of misery I must have been yesterday evening. At least Gideon hadn't made any cutting reference to that. He was acting as if nothing at all had happened.

"What was that about my great-great-grandmother?" I hurried to ask. "I didn't really understand."

"No, we didn't entirely understand it ourselves," said Gideon, sighing.

The limousine moved away. I resisted the temptation to look at my friends through the back window.

"Margaret Tilney, née Grand, was the grandmother of your grandmother Arista, and the last time traveler in the female line before Lucy and you. The Guardians were able to read her into the first, original chronograph without any problems after her second journey back in time. That was in 1894. For the rest of her life—she died in 1944—she elapsed regularly with the aid of the chronograph. The *Annals* describe her as very friendly and cooperative." Mr. George nervously passed his hand over his bald patch. "During the bombing of London in the Second World War, a group of Guardians went out into the country with her and the chronograph. She died there of pneumonia at the age of sixty-seven."

"How . . . how sad." I didn't understand exactly what I was supposed to make of this information.

"As you know, Gideon has already visited seven of the Circle of Twelve in the past and taken a little of their blood for the new chronograph. Six if we count the twins as one. So with your blood and his, only four of the Circle are still missing. Opal, Jade, Sapphire, and Black Tourmaline."

"Elaine Burghley, Margaret Tilney, Lucy Montrose, and Paul de Villiers," added Gideon.

"Those four have to be visited in the past and a little blood taken from each of them." I'd grasped that idea by now; I wasn't entirely clueless.

"Exactly. We didn't think there could be any complications with Margaret." Mr. George leaned back in his seat.

"With the others, yes, but there was no reason to assume that there'd be any difficulty with Margaret Tilney. The course of her life was closely recorded by the Guardians. We know where she was on every single day of it. That's why it was also easy to arrange a meeting between her and Gideon. He traveled back last night to the year 1937, to meet Margaret Tilney at our house in the Temple."

"Last night? Really? For goodness' sake, when did you get any sleep?"

"It was supposed to be a very quick visit," said Gideon. He crossed his arms over his chest. "We'd planned only an hour for the whole operation."

Mr. George said, "But contrary to our expectations, when Gideon had explained the reasons, Margaret refused to let him have any of her blood." He looked expectantly at me. Was I supposed to say something?

"Maybe . . . er . . . maybe she just didn't understand you," I said. After all, it was a very intricate story.

"She understood me perfectly." Gideon shook his head. "Because she already knew that the first chronograph had been stolen and that I'd be wanting some of her blood for the second one."

"But how could she have guessed what wouldn't happen until many years later? Could she see into the future?" No sooner had I asked than I knew the answer. Slowly, I was really getting the hang of this time travel business.

"Someone got in ahead of you and told her," I said.

Gideon nodded appreciatively. "And persuaded her not to let any of her blood be taken, whatever happened.

Even stranger was the fact that she refused to speak to me. She called the Guardians to help her and told them to keep me away from her."

"But who can it have been?" I stopped for a moment to think about it. "I suppose it can only have been Lucy and Paul. They can travel in time, they want to keep the Circle from closing."

Mr. George and Gideon exchanged a glance.

"When Gideon came back, we faced a real puzzle," said Mr. George. "We did have a vague idea of what might have happened, but no proof. So Gideon traveled back into the past again this morning for another visit to Margaret Tilney."

"You've had a busy time, haven't you?" I searched Gideon's face for signs of weariness, but I couldn't find any. Far from it—he looked wide awake. "How's your arm?"

"Fine. Listen to what Mr. George is saying. It's important."

"This time Gideon visited Margaret directly after her initiation journey in 1894," said Mr. George. "I must explain that the time travel gene, Factor X, seems to show in the blood only after that first journey. Obviously the chronograph can't recognize blood taken from travelers before that. Count Saint-Germain did some experiments on that subject in his own time, and they nearly led to the destruction of the chronograph. So there's no point in visiting a time traveler to take blood in his or her childhood. Although it would make things much easier. Do you understand?"

"Yes." Well, I said so anyway.

"So Gideon met the young Margaret this morning at the time of her second official date to elapse. She had been driven straight to the Temple after her first journey in time. And even as the preparations were being made to read her into the chronograph, she traveled for the second time. That's the longest uncontrolled journey in time so far known to us. She was gone for over two hours."

"Mr. George, you could leave out these minor details," suggested Gideon, with a trace of impatience in his voice.

"Yes, yes. Where was I? Gideon visited Margaret when she was going to elapse, and once again he explained the story of the stolen chronograph to her, and the chance of putting things right with the second one."

"Aha!" I interrupted. "So *that's* how the older Margaret knew the whole story. Gideon had told her about it himself."

"Yes, that looked like one possibility," said Mr. George. "But yet again, the young Margaret wasn't hearing the story for the first time."

"So someone else had got in ahead of Gideon. Lucy and Paul again. They traveled into the past with the stolen chronograph to tell Margaret Tilney that, sooner or later, it was very likely that someone would turn up wanting to take some of her blood."

Mr. George said nothing.

"So did she let you take her blood this time?"

"No," said Mr. George. "She refused to let him have it."

"Although at sixteen she wasn't quite as obstinate as

later, in her old age," said Gideon. "This time she let me talk to her for a while. And finally she said that she would negotiate, but only with you."

"With *me*?"

"She gave me your name. Gwyneth Shepherd."

"But . . ." I chewed my lower lip while Mr. George and Gideon watched me closely. "I thought Paul and Lucy had disappeared before I was born. How could they know my name and tell this Margaret?"

"Yes, that's the question," said Mr. George. "You see, Lucy and Paul stole the chronograph in May of the year when you were born. First they hid in the present with it. For a few months, they cleverly managed to keep eluding the detectives employed by the Guardians, laying false trails and using other tricks. They moved from city to city and traveled over half of Europe with the chronograph. But we were coming closer and closer to their hiding place, and they realized that they could escape us for good only if they took refuge in the past with the chronograph. Unfortunately they had no intention of giving up. They defended their mistaken ideals uncompromisingly." He sighed. "They were so young, so passionate. . . ." There was a slightly dreamy look in his eyes.

Gideon cleared his throat, and Mr. George stopped staring into space. He went on: "Until now we always thought they took that step here in London in September, a few weeks before your birth."

"But then they can't possibly have known my name!"

"Correct," said Mr. George. "That's why, since this morning, we have been considering the possibility that they went into the past with the chronograph only *after* your birth."

"For whatever reason," added Gideon.

"But we still have to find out how Lucy and Paul knew your name and your destiny. One way and another, Margaret Tilney refuses to cooperate with us."

I thought about it. "So how are we going to get at her blood now?" Oh, my God, surely I hadn't just said that, had I? "You won't use force, will you?" I pictured Gideon doing sinister things with ether, bonds, and a gigantic syringe—and that ruined my perfect image of him.

Mr. George shook his head. "One of the golden rules of the Guardians is that we use force only when nothing else will work. We try negotiation and amicable agreement first. So we will do as Margaret has suggested. We're going to send you to see her."

"So that I can convince her?"

"So that we can find out about her motives and her informants. She'll talk to you—she said so herself. We want to know what she has to tell you."

Gideon sighed. "There's no getting around it, but myself, I've been talking to a brick wall all morning."

"Yes, Gwyneth, and that's why at this moment Madame Rossini is making you a nice summer dress for the year 1912," said Mr. George. "You're going to meet your great-great-grandmother."

"Why 1912?"

"We picked the year at random. All the same, Gideon thinks you may be falling into a trap."

"A trap?"

Gideon said nothing, just glanced at me. And he did look worried.

"By the laws of logic, that's as good as impossible," said Mr. George.

"Why would anyone set a trap for us?"

Gideon leaned toward me. "Think about it: Lucy and Paul have the chronograph in their power, and ten of the twelve time travelers have already had their blood read into it. To close the Circle so that they can use it for themselves, they only need blood from you and me."

"But . . . Lucy and Paul wanted to stop the Circle being closed and the secret from being revealed," I said.

Once again Mr. George and Gideon exchanged a glance.

"That's what your mother thinks," said Mr. George.

And it was what I'd thought myself so far. "And you don't?"

"Look at it the other way around. Suppose Lucy and Paul want the secret all to themselves?" said Gideon. "Suppose that's why they stole the chronograph? Then all they still need to go one better than Count Saint-Germain would be our blood."

I let the words sink in. Then I said, "And since they can only meet us in the past, they have to lure us somewhere there to get at our blood?"

"They may think that they can get it only by force," said Gideon. "Just as we know, looking at it from the other angle, that they aren't going to give us their blood willingly."

I thought of the men who had attacked us yesterday in Hyde Park.

"Exactly," said Gideon, as if he had read my thoughts. "If they'd killed us, they could have had as much of our blood as they wanted. It only remains to find out how they knew we'd be there."

"I know Lucy and Paul. That's simply not their style," said Mr. George. "They grew up knowing the golden rules of the Guardians, and I'm sure they wouldn't plan to get members of their own families murdered. They would prefer discussion and negotiation—"

"You *knew* Lucy and Paul, past tense, Mr. George," said Gideon. "But can you really be sure what they are like by now?"

I looked from one to the other of them. "Well, anyway, I think it would be interesting to find out what my great-great-grandmother wants to meet me for," I said. "And how can it be a trap if we choose the time of our visit ourselves?"

"That's how I see it too," said Mr. George.

Gideon sighed, resigned. "It's all been decided now, anyway."

MADAME ROSSINI PUT an ankle-length white dress with a fine-check pattern and a kind of sailor collar over my head. It was held in around the waist by a sky-blue satin sash, and there was a ribbon bow of the same material where the collar met a buttonhole.

When I looked at myself in the mirror, I was a little disappointed. I saw the reflection of a demure, good girl. The outfit reminded me slightly of what the servers wore at Mass in St. Luke's, where we sometimes went to church on Sundays.

"The fashions of 1912 can't, of course, be compared with the extravagance of the Rococo era," said Madame Rossini as she handed me a pair of buttoned leather ankle boots. "I would say the idea was to conceal rather than reveal feminine charm."

"I'd say so too."

"And now your 'air." Madame Rossini gently pushed me down on a chair and made a long side parting in my hair. Then she put it up in strands at the back of my head.

"Isn't that a bit—well—bushy over my ears?"

"It's in period," said Madame Rossini.

"But I don't think it suits me, do you?"

"Everything suits you, my little swan-necked beauty. Anyway, this isn't a beauty contest. It's all about—"

"Authenticity. Yes, I know."

Madame Rossini laughed. "Then zat's all right."

This time Dr. White came to collect me and take me to the cellar where the chronograph was hidden. He looked very bad-tempered, as usual, but to make up for it, Robert the little ghost boy gave me a beaming smile.

I smiled back. He really was very cute with his blond curls and dimples. "Hello!"

"No need to sound so effusively pleased to see me," said Dr. White, bringing out the black blindfold.

"Oh, no! Why do I have to have that on again?"

"There's no reason to trust you," said Dr. White.

"Oh, let me do that, you clumsy fool!" Madame Rossini snatched the black blindfold from his hand. "Zis time no one is going to ruin my lovely 'airstyle!"

A pity, really. Madame Rossini herself put the blindfold on, very carefully. Not a hair was disturbed.

"Good luck, *ma petite*," she said as Dr. White led me out. I waved in what I thought was her direction by way of good-bye. Once again, it was an unpleasant feeling to be stumbling about in a void. All the same, the way was beginning to seem more familiar. And this time Robert kept warning me in advance. "Two more steps and now left through the secret doorway. Careful, mind the step. Another ten paces and then we come to the big staircase."

"Great service you give here! Thanks a lot."

"Let's leave out the sarcasm," said Dr. White.

"Why can you hear me and he can't?" asked Robert sadly.

"I'm afraid I don't know either," I said, and I felt so sorry for him it was almost too much for me. "Is there anything you'd like to tell him?"

Robert did not reply.

"Glenda Montrose was right," said Dr. White. "You really do have conversations with yourself."

I put out my hand to feel my way along the wall. "Oh, I recognize this spot. Now there's another step—yes, there it is—and after twenty-four footsteps, we turn right."

"You've been counting!"

"Only out of boredom. Why are you so suspicious, Dr. White?"

"I am not at all suspicious. I trust you implicitly. *At the moment.* At the moment, you are behaving reasonably well, or at the worst you are only somewhat infected by your mother's crazy notions. But no one knows what you'll grow into, so I would be very sorry if you knew where the chronograph was kept."

"The cellar can't be all that large," I said.

"You've no idea," said Dr. White. "We've already lost people there."

"Really?"

"Yes." There was a touch of laughter in his voice, so I knew he was only joking. "Others have wandered around the passages for days before they found a way out."

"I'd like to tell him I'm sorry," said Robert. Obviously it had taken him a long time to work out what he wanted me to say.

The poor little boy. I'd have liked to stop and give him a big hug. "But it wasn't your fault."

"Are you so sure?" Dr. White must still be thinking of the people lost in the cellar.

Robert was sniffling. "We had a quarrel in the morning. I told him I hated him and I wished I had a different father."

"But he wouldn't have taken it seriously. I'm sure he didn't."

"Yes, he did. And now he thinks I didn't love him, and I can't tell him I do." That high little voice, audibly trembling now, almost broke my heart.

"Is that why you're still here?" I asked.

"I don't want to leave him on his own. I know he can't see me or hear me, but maybe he somehow senses that I'm here."

"Oh, *darling!*" I really couldn't bear it. I had to stop. "I'm sure he knows you love him. All fathers know that children sometimes say things they don't really mean."

"Right you are," said Dr. White, his voice suddenly sounding husky. "If you tell children they can't watch TV for two days just because they left a bicycle out in the rain, I suppose it's not surprising if they shout at you and say things they don't mean."

He pushed me on.

"I'm so glad to hear you say that, Dr. White."

"Me too!" said Robert.

For the rest of the way, Robert and I were very cheerful. A heavy door was pushed open and latched again behind us.

The first thing I saw when I took the blindfold off was Gideon, with a top hat on his head. I burst out laughing. Aha! This time he was the one in the silly hat!

"She's in an exceptionally good mood today," said Dr. White. "Thanks to long conversations with herself." But his voice didn't sound quite as cutting as usual.

Mr. de Villiers joined in my laughter. "I'd call it comical myself," he said. "Makes him look like a circus ringmaster."

"How nice that you two are so amused," said Gideon.

Except for the top hat, he looked good. Long dark trousers, dark coat, white shirt—a bit as if he were going to a wedding. He looked me up and down, and I held my breath, waiting in suspense for him to take revenge. In his place, I could have thought up at least ten insulting remarks about my appearance right away.

He didn't say anything. He just smiled.

Mr. George was busy with the chronograph. "Has Gwyneth had all her instructions?"

"I think so," said Mr. de Villiers. He had talked to me about Operation Jade for half an hour while Madame Rossini was finishing my dress. Operation Jade! I felt rather like secret service agent Emma Peel. Lesley and I loved Uma Thurman in *The Avengers*.

I still couldn't follow Gideon's firmly held theory that we could be lured into a trap. Margaret Tilney had expressly wanted to talk to me, yes, but she hadn't specified a time. Even if she did want to trap me, she couldn't know what day and time in her life we would turn up.

And it was really very unlikely that Lucy and Paul would be waiting for us at exactly the moment in time we chose. June 1912 was the date that had been picked. Margaret Tilney was thirty-five then, living with her husband and her three children in a house in Belgravia. And that was where we were going to call on her.

I looked up and saw Gideon's glance resting on me. Or more precisely on my neckline. This was too much!

"Are you by any chance staring at my breasts?" I asked indignantly.

He grinned. "Not directly," he whispered back.

Suddenly I knew what he meant. In the Rococo era it was a lot simpler to hide things behind lace trimming, I thought.

Unfortunately we had also attracted Mr. George's attention.

He leaned forward. "You don't have a mobile in there, do you?" he asked. "You're not allowed to take things from our own time into the past."

"Why not? It could be very useful!" (And that photo of Rakoczy and Lord Brompton had been brilliant!) "It would have been a lot easier if Gideon had had a proper pistol with him last time."

Gideon rolled his eyes.

"Suppose you lost your mobile in the past," said Mr. de Villiers. "Whoever found it wouldn't be able to make out what kind of thing it was. But then again, maybe he would. And then your mobile could even change the future. So could a pistol. And I hate to think what might happen if mankind thought up the idea of sophisticated weapons any sooner than they did."

"Such items would also be proof of your and our existence," said Dr. White. "One little mistake could change everything and then the continuum would be in danger."

I bit my lower lip as I wondered if losing a pepper

spray in another time might change the future of mankind. Maybe any change would be only for the good if the right person found it. . . . Maybe I should tell Lesley to call off the plan to buy pepper spray, though, just to be safe.

Mr. George put out his hand. "I'll look after that for you."

Sighing, I put my hand down inside my collar and gave him my mobile. "But I want it back at once afterward!"

"Are we finally ready?" asked Dr. White. "The chronograph is prepared."

I was ready. I had a slight tingling inside me, and I had to admit that I liked it much better here than having to sit in a cellar in some boring year to do my homework.

Gideon looked inquiringly at me. Maybe he was wondering what else I might have hidden away. "Ready, Gwyneth?" he asked.

I smiled at him. "Ready when you are."

The time is out of joint; O cursed spite
That ever I was born to set it right!

William Shakespeare, *Hamlet*

FIFTEEN

ONE OF THE GUARDIANS' cabs, a horse-drawn hackney carriage, took us from the Temple to Belgravia, driving along the banks of the Thames, and this time I could recognize a fair amount of the London I knew outside the window. The sun shone on Big Ben and Westminster Abbey, and I was pleased to see people strolling down the broad avenues with hats, sunshades, and pastel-colored dresses just like mine. The parks were full of green spring foliage; the streets were well paved and not at all mucky.

"This is like the set of a musical," I said. "I'd love one of those sunshades."

"We've picked a good day," said Gideon. "And a good year." He had left his top hat in the cellar, and since I'd have done exactly the same in his place, I didn't blame him.

"Why don't we simply wait for Margaret in the Temple when she goes there to elapse?"

"I've tried that twice already. It wasn't easy to convince the Guardians of those days of my good intentions, in spite of having the password and the signet ring and so on. It's always tricky assessing the reaction of Guardians in the past. If they're in any doubt, they're more likely to back the time traveler they know and are duty bound to protect than a visitor from the future, someone they know either not at all or only very slightly. Like last night and this morning. We may be more successful if we visit her at home. And it's bound to be more of a surprise."

"But couldn't she be guarded day and night by someone just waiting for us to turn up? We know she's expecting that. She's been expecting it for years, right?"

"*The Annals of the Guardians* don't say anything about additional personal protection. They just stipulate that a novice Guardian has to keep a discreet eye on the place where every time traveler lives."

"The man in black!" I cried. "A man just like that stands outside our house."

"Obviously not making himself particularly inconspicuous," said Gideon, grinning.

"Not in the least. My little sister thinks he's a wicked magician." I thought of something. "Do you have any brothers and sisters yourself?"

"A little brother," said Gideon. "Well, not all that little now. He's seventeen."

"And how old are you?"

"Nineteen," said Gideon. "Or as good as nineteen, anyway."

"So if you've left school, what do you do?"

"Officially I'm down to study at the University of London next year," he said. "But I think I can take this term off."

"What subject?"

"Inquisitive, aren't you?"

"Only making polite conversation," I said. I'd picked up that expression from James. "So what *are* you going to study?"

"Medicine." He sounded a bit embarrassed.

I bit back a surprised "oh!" and looked out the window again. Medicine. Interesting. Interesting. Interesting.

"Was that your boyfriend at school today?"

"What? Who?" I looked at him, taken aback.

"That guy behind you with his hand on your shoulder." It sounded perfectly casual, almost as if he wasn't interested.

"You mean Gordon Gelderman? God, no!"

"So if he's not your boyfriend, how come he can touch you?"

"He can't. To be honest, I hadn't noticed he was doing it." I hadn't noticed because I was fully occupied watching Gideon exchanging sweet nothings with Charlotte. The memory made me blush furiously. He'd kissed her. Or almost.

"Why are you going red? Because of this Gordon Gallahan?"

"Gelderman," I corrected him.

"Whatever. He looked like an idiot."

I couldn't help laughing. "He sounds like an idiot too," I said. "And he's useless at kissing."

"I wasn't actually asking for the precise details." Gideon bent down to retie his shoelaces. When he straightened up again, he crossed his arms and looked out the window. "Here we are, look. Belgrave Road. Excited by the idea of meeting your great-great-grandmother?"

"Yes, very." I immediately forgot what we'd just been talking about. How strange all this was. The great-great-grandmother I was about to visit was some years younger than Mum.

She'd obviously married someone rich, because when the cab stopped outside the address in Eaton Place, it was a very posh house. And the butler who opened the door to us was posh too. Even more so than Mr. Bernard. He was actually wearing white gloves!

He examined us suspiciously when Gideon handed him a card and said we were paying a surprise teatime call. He was sure, said Gideon, that his good friend Lady Tilney would be very pleased to hear that Gwyneth Shepherd had come to visit her.

"I suspect he doesn't think you're posh enough," I said as the butler disappeared with the visiting card. "No hat and no side-whiskers."

"No mustache either," said Gideon. "Lord Tilney has one from ear to ear. See that portrait of him in front of us?"

"Wow," I said. My great-great-grandmother had weird taste in men. It was the kind of mustache you'd have to put in curlers at night.

"Suppose she just gets the butler to say she's not at home?" I asked. "Maybe she doesn't want to see you again so soon."

"'So soon' is good—as far as she's concerned the last time was eighteen years ago."

"As long as that?" A tall, slim woman with her red hair piled up in a style not unlike mine was standing on the stairs. She looked like Lady Arista, but thirty years younger. I saw, to my surprise, that the upright way she walked was just like Lady Arista as well.

When she stopped in front of me, neither of us said anything, we were so absorbed in looking at each other. I could see a trace of Mum in my great-great-grandmother. I don't know what or whom Lady Tilney saw in me, but she nodded and smiled, as if satisfied with the way I looked.

Gideon waited for a while, and then he said, "Lady Tilney, I still want to make the same request as I did eighteen years ago. We need a little of your blood."

"And I still say what I said eighteen years ago. You are not having any of my blood." She turned to him. "However, I can offer you tea, although it's still a little early. But we can talk better over a cup of tea."

"Then in any case, we would be delighted to take a cup of tea with you," said Gideon, laying on the charm.

We followed my great-great-grandmother up the stairs to a room on the street side of the house. There was a small round table by the window laid for three with plates, cups, cutlery, bread, butter and jam, and in the middle a platter of scones and wafer-thin cucumber sandwiches.

"It looks almost as if you were expecting us," I said, while Gideon took a good look around the room.

She smiled again. "It does, doesn't it? One might think so. But in fact I am expecting some other guests. Do please sit down."

"No, thank you, in the circumstances we'd rather not," said Gideon, suddenly very much on the alert. "And we won't trouble you for long. We'd just like to have answers to a few questions."

"And what are they?"

"How do you know my name?" I interjected. "Who told you about me?"

"I had a visitor from the future." Her smile widened. "It happens to me quite often."

"Lady Tilney, I tried to explain, last time, that your visitor was telling you lies," said Gideon. "You're making a great mistake by trusting the wrong people."

"That's what I'm always telling her," said a male voice. A young man had appeared in the doorway. He casually sauntered closer. "Margaret, I always say, you're making a great mistake by trusting the wrong people. Oh, those look delicious. Are they for us?"

Gideon had breathed in sharply. Now he put out his hand and clasped my wrist.

"Not a step closer!" he said.

The other man raised one eyebrow. "I'm only helping myself to a sandwich, if you have no objection."

"Do please help yourselves. And if you will just excuse me for a moment . . . ," said my great-great-grandmother.

As she left the room, the butler appeared in the doorway. In spite of the white gloves, he now looked like the bouncer of some really trendy club.

Gideon swore under his breath.

"Don't worry about Stillman," said the young man. "Although apparently he did once break a man's neck. An accident, wasn't it, Stillman?"

I stared at the young man. I couldn't help it. He had the same eyes as Falk de Villiers, yellow as amber. Like a wolf's.

"Gwyneth Shepherd!" When he smiled at me, he looked even more like Falk de Villiers, except that he was at least twenty years younger and his hair was jet black and cut short. The way he was looking at me was scary. He seemed friendly, but there was something in his eyes that I couldn't interpret. Maybe anger? Or pain?

"It's a pleasure to meet you." For a moment, his voice sounded husky. He offered me his hand, but Gideon grabbed me with both arms and pulled me close.

"Don't you touch her!"

The raised eyebrow again. "What are you afraid of, young man?"

"I know exactly what you want from her!"

I could feel Gideon's heart beating against my back.

"Blood?" The man took one of the tiny, thin sandwiches and put it into his mouth. Then he held both his hands out to us, palms upward, and said, "Look, no syringe, no scalpel, nothing. Now, let go of the poor girl. You're crushing her." That strange glance again when he looked back at me. "My name is Paul. Paul de Villiers."

"That's what I thought," I said. "You're the man who persuaded my cousin Lucy to steal the chronograph. Why did you do it, Mr. de Villiers?"

Paul de Villiers's mouth twisted. "It's funny to hear you call me Mr. de Villiers."

"And I think it's funny that you know me."

"Don't talk to him," said Gideon. His grip had relaxed slightly, and now he was holding me close to him with only one arm. With the other, he opened a side door behind him and glanced into the next room. Another man in white gloves was standing there.

"That's Frank," said Paul. "And since he isn't as big and strong as Stillman, he has a pistol, did you notice?"

"I noticed," said Gideon, closing the door again.

He'd been right. We *had* fallen into a trap. But how was that possible? Margaret Tilney couldn't have been laying a tea table for us and stationing a man with a pistol in the next room every day of her life.

"How did you know we'd be here today?" I asked Paul.

"Hm. If I were to tell you I didn't know, I just happened to look in by chance, I'm sure you wouldn't believe me, would you?" He took a scone and sat down. "How are your dear parents?"

"Keep your mouth shut!" snapped Gideon.

"But I was only asking how her parents are!"

"Fine," I said. "Mum, at least. My father's dead."

Paul looked shocked. "Dead? But Nicholas is a man like an oak tree, so strong and healthy!"

"He had leukemia," I said. "He died when I was seven."

"Oh, my God. I'm so very sorry." Paul was looking at me sadly and seriously. "It must have been terrible for you, growing up without a father."

"Don't talk to him," Gideon repeated. "He's just trying to keep us here until reinforcements arrive."

"Do you still think I'm after your blood and hers?" There was a dangerous glint in the yellow eyes.

"I do indeed," said Gideon.

"And you think Stillman and I, plus Frank and a pistol, couldn't deal with you on our own?" asked Paul sarcastically.

"I certainly do," said Gideon.

"Well, I'm sure my dear brother and the other Guardians have made you into a real fighting machine," said Paul. "After all, you've had to pull the chestnuts out of the fire for them. Or should I say the chronograph? In my time, we just learnt a bit of fencing and how to play the violin, to keep the tradition going. But I bet you can do martial arts and all that stuff. You need to know those things if you're going to travel around the past getting people to shed blood."

"So far those people have given me their blood willingly."

"But only because they don't know where that will lead!"

"No. Because they don't want to see the destruction of

all that the Guardians have been studying, protecting, and working for through the centuries."

"Blah, blah, blah! Yes, they kept going on at us in that emotional way as well. But *we* know the truth about Count Saint-Germain's intentions."

"And what is the truth?" It burst out of me.

There were footsteps on the stairs.

"Here come the reinforcements," said Paul, without turning.

"The truth is that as soon as Mr. de Villiers here opens his mouth, he tells lies," said Gideon.

The butler stood aside to make way for a graceful red-haired girl coming into the room. She was a little too old to be Lady Tilney's daughter.

"I don't believe it," said the girl. She was looking at me as if she'd never seen anything more peculiar in her life.

"You can believe it all right, Princess," said Paul. His voice sounded loving and a little concerned.

The girl was standing in the doorway as if rooted to the spot.

"You're Lucy," I said. There was no mistaking the family likeness.

"Gwyneth," said Lucy. She really only breathed my name.

"Yes, it's Gwyneth," said Paul. "And the one clutching her as if she were his favorite teddy bear is my cousin, or my nephew, or whatever you like to call it. Unfortunately he's very, very anxious to leave us."

"Please don't go!" said Lucy. "We have to talk to you both."

"Another time," said Gideon smoothly. "Maybe when there aren't so many strangers around the place."

"It's important!" said Lucy.

Gideon laughed out loud. "I agree with you there!"

"You're welcome to leave, young man," said Paul. "Stillman will show you to the door. But Gwyneth will stay a little longer. I have a feeling it will be easier to talk to her. She hasn't yet been through all the brainwashing that you . . . oh, hell!"

The curse was caused by the little black pistol that had suddenly appeared from nowhere in Gideon's hand. He was aiming it calmly at Lucy.

"Gwyneth and I will now leave the house without any fuss," he said. "Lucy will accompany us to the door."

"You bastard," said Paul under his breath. He had risen to his feet and was looking undecidedly from Stillman to Lucy and us and back again, all in turn.

"Sit down," said Gideon. His voice was cold as ice, but I could feel his pulse racing. He still kept me firmly pressed to him with one arm around me. "And you, Stillman, sit down too, please. There are still plenty of cucumber sandwiches."

Paul sat down and looked at the side door.

"One word from you to Frank and I fire," said Gideon.

Lucy was staring at him, wide-eyed, but she didn't seem frightened. Unlike Paul, who appeared to think that Gideon meant it seriously.

"Do as he says," he told Stillman, and the butler left his post in the doorway and sat down at the table, giving us a nasty look.

"You've already met him, haven't you?" Lucy was looking Gideon straight in the eye. "You've met Count Saint-Germain."

"Three times," said Gideon. "And he knows exactly what you two are planning. Turn around." He put the barrel of the pistol against the back of Lucy's head. "Now move forward."

"Princess . . ."

"It's all right, Paul."

"For God's sake, they've given him a Smith & Wesson automatic. I thought that was against the golden rules."

"We'll let her go once we're out in the street," said Gideon. "But if anyone up here moves before then, she's dead. Come on, Gwyneth. They'll have to try to get at your blood some other time."

I hesitated. "Maybe they really do just want to talk," I said. I felt enormously interested in what Lucy and Paul had to say. On the other hand, if they were really as harmless as they made out, why those bodyguards posted in the rooms? With guns? I remembered the men in the park.

"I'm certain they don't just want to talk," said Gideon.

"There's no point," said Paul. "They've brainwashed him."

"It's the count," said Lucy. "He can be very convincing, as you know."

"We'll be seeing each other again," said Gideon. We had now reached the top of the stairs.

"Is that meant to be a threat?" asked Paul. "We'll be 'seeing' each other again? We most certainly will!"

Gideon kept the pistol aimed at the back of Lucy's head until we had reached the front door.

I expected Frank to race out of the other room, but nothing stirred. There was no sign of my great-great-grandmother either.

"You can't allow the Circle to be closed," said Lucy urgently. "And you must never visit the count in the past again. Gwyneth in particular must never meet him!"

"Don't listen to her!" Gideon had to let go of me to open the front door with one hand while still keeping the pistol aimed at Lucy with the other. He looked out into the street. I could hear voices on the floor above. Anxiously, I looked up the stairs. There were three men and a pistol up there, and up there was where we wanted them to stay.

"I've met him already," I told Lucy. "Yesterday—"

"Oh, no!" Lucy's face turned a shade paler. "Does he know your magic?"

"What magic?"

"The magic of the raven," said Lucy.

"The magic of the raven is just a myth." Gideon took my arm and led me down the steps and out into the street. There was no sign of our cab.

"That's not true, and the count knows it."

Gideon was still pointing the pistol at Lucy's head, but now he looked back up to the first floor. Very likely Frank was standing there with his pistol. We were still under cover of the porch roof.

"Wait," I told Gideon. I looked at Lucy. There were tears in her large blue eyes, and for some reason I found it hard not to believe her.

"What makes you so sure she's not telling the truth, Gideon?" I asked quietly.

He looked at me for a moment, taken off balance. His eyes flickered. "I just am," he whispered.

"That doesn't sound so sure," said Lucy. Her voice was gentle. "You two can trust us."

Could we really? Then why had they done the impossible and trapped us here?

I saw the shadow only out of the corner of my eye.

"Watch out!" I shouted. Stillman was already coming down. Gideon spun round at the last moment as the hefty butler swung his fist back to strike.

"No, Stillman!" That was Paul's voice from the stairs.

"Run!" shouted Gideon, and I made a split-second decision.

I ran as fast as I could in my little buttoned boots. I expected to hear a shot with every step I took.

"Talk to Grandfather!" Lucy called after me. "Ask him about the Green Rider!"

GIDEON DIDN'T CATCH UP with me until I reached the next corner. "Thanks!" he gasped, putting the pistol away again. "If you hadn't given me the heads-up, it would have been a close call. This way."

I looked round. "Are we being followed?"

"I don't think so," said Gideon. "But we'd better hurry, just in case we are."

"Where did that man Stillman come from? I had my eye on the stairs the whole time."

"There's probably another staircase in the house. I didn't think of that either."

"Where did the Guardian with the cab go? He was supposed to be waiting for us."

"No idea," said Gideon.

I was getting a stitch in my side. I wouldn't be able to keep this speed up much longer. Gideon turned into a narrower side street and finally stopped outside a church porch.

HOLY TRINITY said the notice board outside.

"What are we going to do here?" I gasped.

"Make our confession," said Gideon. He looked around before opening the heavy door, then he pushed me into the dimly lit interior and closed the door again.

We were immediately surrounded by peace and quiet, the smell of incense, and that solemn feeling you get the moment you step inside a church.

It was a pretty church, with colored stained glass windows, pale sandstone walls, and little tea lights flickering, each of them a prayer or a good wish.

Gideon led me down one of the aisles to an old-fashioned confessional, drew the curtain aside, and pointed to the seat inside the little cubbyhole.

"You can't be serious," I whispered.

"Yes, I can. I'll sit on the other side, and we'll just wait here until we travel back."

Puzzled, I dropped onto the seat. Gideon drew the curtain in front of my nose. A moment later, the little barred peephole between me and the other seat was pushed aside. "Comfortable?"

I was getting my breath back, and my eyes were adjusting to the dim light.

Gideon was looking at me with an air of great solemnity. "Well, my daughter, let us thank the Lord for the shelter of his house."

I stared at him. How could he be so casual, almost exuberant? For goodness' sake, he'd held a pistol to my cousin's head! It couldn't just have left him cold.

"How can you make jokes now?"

Suddenly he looked embarrassed. He shrugged. "Can you think of a better way to pass the time?"

"Yes! We could try making sense of what just happened! Why do Lucy and Paul say someone's brainwashed you?"

"How would I know?" He ran his fingers through his hair, and I saw that his hand was shaking slightly. Not so cool as he made out after all, then. "They're trying to make you uncertain. Me too."

"Lucy told me to ask my grandfather. She probably doesn't know he's dead." I thought of the tears in Lucy's eyes. "Poor thing. It must be terrible never to be able to see any of your family again because they're in the future."

Gideon did not reply. For a while we said nothing. I looked out through a gap in the curtain at the chancel of the church. A little gargoyle, about knee-high to a human, hopped out of the shadows and looked at us. I quickly looked away. If he noticed I could see him, he was sure to make a nuisance of himself. Gargoyle ghosts can really be pests. I knew that from experience.

"Are you sure you can trust Count Saint-Germain?" I asked as the gargoyle hopped closer.

Gideon took a deep breath. "He's a genius. He's discovered things that no one before him . . . yes, I trust him. Whatever Lucy and Paul think, they're on the wrong track." He sighed. "At least, I was still perfectly sure until a little while ago. It all seemed so logical."

Obviously the little gargoyle thought we were boring. He climbed a pillar and disappeared into the organ loft.

"And now it isn't anymore?"

"I only know that I had everything under control until you came along," said Gideon.

"Oh, are you holding me responsible because for the first time in your life, not everyone's dancing to your tune?" I raised my eyebrows, just as I'd seen him do. It felt good. I almost grinned, I was so proud of myself.

"No." He shook his head and groaned. "Gwyneth, why is everything so much more complicated with you than with Charlotte?" He leaned forward, and there was something in his eyes that I'd never seen there before.

"Was that what you were discussing with her in the school yard today?" I asked, feeling slightly jealous.

Damn. Now I'd given him an opening. A beginner's mistake!

"Jealous?" he promptly asked, with a broad grin.

"Not in the least!"

"Charlotte always did as I said. You don't. Which is a real pain. But kind of amusing too. And sweet." This time it wasn't just his look that made me feel confused.

Embarrassed, I pushed a strand of hair back from my face. My stupid hairstyle had come entirely undone during our dash. There was probably a trail of hairpins from Eaton Place to the door of this church.

"Why don't we go back to the Temple?"

"It's cozy here. If we go back to the Temple, there'll be more endless discussions. And to be honest, I can do with a change from being ordered about by Uncle Falk."

Aha! My move now. "Not a good feeling, is it?"

He shook his head. "No, not really."

I heard sounds in the nave outside. I jumped, and peered through the curtain. But it was only an old lady lighting a candle. "Suppose we travel back in the next second? I don't want to land on the lap of some child from a confirmation class. And I can't imagine that the parish priest would be thrilled."

"Don't worry." Gideon laughed quietly. "There's never anyone in this confessional in our own time. Father Jacobs calls it the lift to the underworld. He's a member of the Lodge, of course."

"How much longer until we go back, then?"

Gideon looked at his watch. "We still have a bit of time."

"Then we might as well use it sensibly." I giggled. "Weren't you going to make your confession, my son?" It just slipped out, and it took a moment for me to realize what I was doing.

I was sitting with Gideon in a church confessional about a hundred years in the past, flirting with him for all I was worth! Good heavens! Why hadn't Lesley given me a folder full of instructions for that?

"Only if you're going to tell me about your own sins too."

"I'm sure you'd like that." I quickly changed the subject. We were definitely on thin ice here. "You were right about the trap, by the way. But how could Paul and Lucy know that we'd be there today and not some other time?"

"I haven't the slightest idea," said Gideon, suddenly leaning so far toward me that our noses were only an inch or so apart. His eyes looked dark in the twilight of the church. "But maybe *you* do."

I blinked at him. That unsettled me—in two ways: first because I could make nothing of that remark, and second because he was so close. "Me?"

"You could be the one who told Lucy and Paul about our meeting."

"What?" I must be looking totally stupid. "What nonsense! When do you suppose I could have done that? I don't even know where the chronograph is kept. And I'd never let anyone—" I stopped before I could say anything else silly.

"Gwyneth, you have no idea what you may do later on."

I had to spend a moment digesting that. Then I said, "It could just as easily have been you."

"Yeah." Gideon retreated into his side of the confessional, and I saw the flash of his white teeth in the dim light. He was smiling. "I think we're going to have a rather exciting time in the near future."

That gave me a warm tingly feeling inside. Presumably the prospect of more adventures ought to have scared me, but at that moment I felt nothing but wonderful happiness.

Yes, it *would* be exciting.

We said no more for a while. Then Gideon asked me, "Back in that coach, when we were talking about the magic of the raven—do you remember?"

Of course I remembered. Every single word.

"You said I couldn't have that magic because I was only a perfectly ordinary girl. And you know lots of girls like me. Girls who go to the loo in groups and say mean things about Lisa because she—"

A finger fell on my lips. "I know what I said." Gideon had leaned toward me from his side of the cubbyhole. "And I'm sorry."

What? I sat there thunderstruck, unable to move or even breathe. His fingers gently touched my lips, stroked my chin, and felt their way up my cheek to my temple.

"You're not ordinary, Gwyneth," he whispered as

he began stroking my hair. "You're totally, absolutely extraordinary. You don't need the magic of any raven to be special to me." He leaned as close as he could get, with his head and arms through the opening of the confessional window, and when his lips touched my mouth, I shut my eyes.

Okay. So now *I* was going to faint.

Sunny day, 73 degrees in the shade.

Lady Tilney arrives punctually at nine to elapse.

Traffic in the city held up by a protest march: a group of deranged females demanding votes for women. We'll be founding colonies on the moon before they get what they want.

Otherwise, no unusual incidents.

FROM *THE ANNALS OF THE GUARDIANS*

24 JUNE 1912

REPORT: FRANK MINE, INNER CIRCLE

EPILOGUE

Hyde Park, London

24 June 1912

"THESE SUNSHADES are really useful," she said, twirling hers in a circle. "I can't understand why they went out of fashion."

"Maybe because it rains all the time here?" He smiled sideways at her. "But I agree, they're very attractive. And white lace summer dresses suit you wonderfully. I'm even getting used to the long skirts. It's always such a nice moment when you take them off."

"I don't think I'll ever get used to not wearing jeans anymore," she said sadly. "I miss them badly every day."

He knew very well it wasn't just the jeans she missed so badly, but he was careful not to say so. They walked on for a while in silence.

The park seemed so peaceful in the summer sun; the city spread out behind them looked as if it were built to last forever. But he remembered that in two years' time, the First World War would begin, and German zeppelins would be dropping bombs on London. Maybe they'd have to retreat to the country for a while.

"She looks just like you," she said suddenly.

He knew at once who she was talking about. "No, she looks like you, Princess! It's only her hair she gets from me."

"And that way of tilting her head to one side when she's thinking something over."

"She's beautiful, isn't she?"

She nodded. "Isn't this strange? Two months ago we held her in our arms as a newborn baby, and now she's sixteen, and half a head taller than me. And only two years younger!"

"Yes, crazy!"

"I'm so relieved that she's all right. But Nicholas . . . why did he have to die so early?"

"Leukemia. I'd never have expected that. Poor girl, to lose her father so young." He cleared his throat. "I hope she'll keep away from that boy, my . . . er, nephew, or whatever he is. These family trees are impossible."

"Oh, it's not all that difficult—your great-grandfather and his great-great-grandfather were twin brothers. So your great-great-grandfather is also his great-great-great-grandfather." She laughed, noticing his blank expression. "I'll draw you a family tree sometime."

"I tell you, no one can work it out. Anyway, I don't like the young man. Did you notice the way he was ordering her about? Luckily she wasn't taking it lying down."

"She's in love with him."

"No, she isn't."

"Yes, she is. She just doesn't know it yet."

"So how do you think *you* know it?"

"Oh, because he's simply irresistible. My God, did you see his eyes? Green like a tiger's. I think I felt a bit weak at the knees myself when he flashed them at me, even though he was angry."

"What? You can't mean that seriously! Since when have you liked green eyes?"

She laughed. "Don't worry. Your eyes are the best of all. For me, at least. But I think she likes green eyes best."

"She's not in love with that arrogant young man!"

"I tell you, she is. And he's just like you when you were younger."

"What? That . . . ! He's not in the least like me. *I* never ordered *you* about, never!"

She grinned. "You did, too!"

"Only when it was necessary." He tipped his hat back on his head. "I just want him to leave her alone."

"You're jealous."

"Well, yes," he admitted. "Isn't that normal? When I next see him, I'm going to tell him to keep his hands off her."

"I've an idea we'll be crossing their path quite often in the near future," she said, and now she wasn't smiling. "And I've an idea you ought to start polishing up your skill at fencing. There's something in the air, and it's coming our way."

He threw his walking stick in the air and caught it nimbly as it came down. "I'm ready. How about you, Princess?"

"Ready when you are."

THE CAST OF MAIN CHARACTERS

IN THE PRESENT

IN THE MONTROSE FAMILY:

Gwyneth Shepherd, in Year Ten at school, discovers one day that she can travel in time

Grace Shepherd, Gwyneth's mother

Nick and *Caroline Shepherd*, Gwyneth's younger brother and sister

Charlotte Montrose, Gwyneth's cousin

Glenda Montrose, Charlotte's mother, Grace's elder sister

Lady Arista Montrose, grandmother of Gwyneth and Charlotte, mother of Grace and Glenda

Madeleine (Maddy) Montrose, Gwyneth's great-aunt, sister of the late Lord Montrose

Mr. Bernard, butler in the Montrose household

AT ST. LENNOX HIGH SCHOOL:

Lesley Hay, Gwyneth's best friend

James Augustus Peregrine Pympoole-Bothame, the school ghost

Cynthia Dale, in Gwyneth's class
Gordon Gelderman, in Gwyneth's class
Mr. Whitman, teacher of English and history

AT THE HEADQUARTERS OF THE GUARDIANS IN THE TEMPLE:

Gideon de Villiers, like Gwyneth, can travel in time
Falk de Villiers, Gideon's uncle twice removed, Grand Master of the Lodge of Count Saint-Germain, to which the Guardians belong
Thomas George, member of the Inner Circle of the Lodge
Dr. Jacob White, medical doctor and member of the Inner Circle of the Lodge
Mrs. Jenkins, secretary at the headquarters of the Guardians
Madame Rossini, dress designer and wardrobe mistress at the headquarters of the Guardians

IN THE PAST

Count Saint-Germain, time traveler and founder of the Guardians
Miro Rakoczy, his close friend, also known as the Black Leopard
Lord Brompton, acquaintance and patron of the count's
Margaret Tilney, time traveler, Gwyneth's great-great-grandmother, Lady Arista's grandmother
Paul de Villiers, time traveler, younger brother of Falk de Villiers
Lucy Montrose, time traveler, niece of Grace, daughter of Grace and Glenda's elder brother, Harry

QUESTIONS FOR THE AUTHOR

© Arena Portrait

What was your inspiration for writing the books?

For quite some time, I have had the dream of writing fantasy novels. My love for books with fantasy elements is just one of the many reasons for that. I really like the combination of comedy and fantasy that can be seen in works like those of Terry Pratchett and Jonathan Stroud, for example. They are true masters of the genre. When it comes to romantic-fantasy for all ages, however, I find that there are not enough funny books. So, trying to fill that niche was the obvious thing for me to do.

What's your favorite part of the book and what character did you most enjoy writing?

There are many scenes that I really like. But, I think I enjoyed the scenes with Xemerius, the little gargoyle demon, the most. He is one of my favorite characters in the entire trilogy and I had the hardest time saying good-bye to him when I had finished writing the books. Well actually, you can't really get rid of him. Right this moment, he is sitting next to me, making stupid comments.

If you could give a character one piece of advice, what would it be?

Don't mess with time travel. You'll only get confused.

Did you identify with any of your characters?

I don't like to admit it, but there are striking similarities between Gwendolyn's Great-aunt Maddy and me. I constantly keep forgetting that I still have curlers in my hair, I have strange visions—very handy actually, they make for good ideas for stories—and I'm terribly nosy. Also, I have a soft spot for lemon drops (and all kinds of other candy for that matter). The only difference between me and Great-aunt Maddy is that I'm a bit younger and also that I have found and married my great love.

Was there a particular scene in the book that was easy or difficult for you to write?

Chasing Gwendolyn, Gideon, Leslie and the others through London, obnoxious gargoyles who jump off rooftops to follow you around, ghosts who won't realize that they have been dead for at least a few centuries—I have no difficulties with any of that. More difficult, however, is the whole business of time travel. I think it's important that a novel has a logical plot, no matter how many fantasy elements it has. This is really not that simple with time travel stories. Your brain cells start to fuse together the more you think about these things and by the end you'll have smoke coming out your ears. (You won't believe it, I bought a book on quantum physics. But that just confused me even more.)

What's your favorite part about writing for teens?

I always wanted to write books for children and teens so

that I wouldn't forget what it feels like to be fourteen. However, I have since realized that there's really no need to worry. Even my mom acts like a fourteen-year-old every now and then. And she's seventy-five!

What makes you laugh?

Sometimes it can take a while, but I can usually laugh about anything.

What do you do on a rainy day?

My favorite thing to do on a rainy day is this: sitting in the lobby of the Covent Garden Hotel in London with a nice cup of tea in my hand and watching all the umbrellas on the enchanting Monmouth Street. What I end up doing instead: getting the wet cats off the couch, yelling at my son Lennart to take his wellies and wet raincoat off the expensive rug and pleading with the universe that the sun will be out again soon.

If you were stranded on a desert island, who would you want for company?

My husband, my son, and of course, we won't forget the cats.

If you could travel in time, where would you go and what would you do?

Well, I chicken out easily. I wouldn't dare to go back very far. And in any case, I wouldn't stay long. Just the idea of not having a modern flushing toilet really gives me the creeps. But I imagine being in England during the Regency period must be very charming somehow, even with the outhouses and all that. Just like in a Jane Austen movie. And if I get dressed up for the trip by Madam Rossini, then

I wouldn't even mind going back to the 17th or 18th century—maybe even without the wig.

Do you ever get writer's block? What do you do to get back on track?

Writer's block is one thing I just can't afford to have. But if things don't go so well and if I have enough time, I'll just do something else that day. Other than that, turning up the music and dancing around the room has helped in the past.

What do you want readers to remember about your books?

Life is fun if you can manage to appreciate it with all its weirdness.

KERSTIN GIER is the bestselling author of the Ruby Red trilogy, which has been translated into seventeen languages. The next two books in the series are *Sapphire Blue* and *Emerald Green*. She lives in Germany.